KNIGHT RISING

ROBERT CHARLESTON

Published by Tactical 16 Publishing

Colorado Springs, CO

www.Tactical16.com

ISBN: 978-1-943226-88-7 (paperback)

CONTENTS

For the one who made this entire story possible.

CHAPTER 1

SATURDAY, 1 JUNE 2019

"CLEAR ON LANE TWO! Open the door!"

A slender inmate, hands cuffed and lips tight, offered no resistance as the guard, a hulking monstrosity of a man, pressed a nightstick into the prisoner's orange-clad back. The fabric showed a wide stripe of sweat brought on by the Texas heat.

"Pick up the pace, asshole. Lawyer's waitin', and that fucker can't be cheap."

The guard's sneer was borderline audible. The guy was right; that *fucker* was not cheap. At last count, the legal bill would soon pass $800,000, with no hope on the horizon and nothing ahead but years as a convicted felon, doomed to spend the remainder of life avoiding gang-rape, shivs, and other inmates out to make a name for themselves. That was how it worked here: survive, no matter what.

As they passed a particular cell, the prisoner inside threatened very specific bodily harm and spat at them.

Would killing that bitch over there add ten more years to my sentence? Thoughts of this nature had become all too common since that first night here.

"We're clear. Close the door!"

The sliding door rumbled back into place, slamming shut with

"

callous indifference to all within earshot. That was one thing about prison that few on the outside seemed to understand: the walls, bars, doors... they did not discriminate. Gangs and cliques of all flavors would fight anyone for looking at them sideways, but the edifice itself saw no color, only customers.

The duo entered the room and moved toward the center, where the hot air at least wafted, thanks to the vents in the ceiling. It wasn't much in terms of relief, but any break from the Texas summer heat and humidity, especially while locked away on the inside, made a world of difference. The gray-painted concrete walls were losing their luster, with visible chips present throughout, and the light fixtures were shielded by beat-up metal cages. It appeared as though this room had seen quite a bit of action over the years, but surely nothing of the sort would happen today, not with the behemoth guard standing nearby. Closed-circuit cameras posted at the four corners covered every square inch of the room, rendering the notion of hiding completely useless. Two-way mirrors also flanked the metal table in the middle of the room, and the chairs left everything to be desired.

"Sit down," the guard said sternly. He stowed his nightstick on his belt, looping it through the sleeve, his eyes locked on me.

Following orders was easy for a veteran, but knowing that I did not belong in a place like this made anything seem impossible, even something as simple as placing my posterior in a chair. Glancing sideways, the name tape on the guard's uniform came into view: O'MALLEY. Multiple scars zigzagging down his forearms told the story of a man who had seen far too much in one lifetime, and if that was not enough, his randomly missing teeth certainly rounded out the image.

Is he always this much of a douchebag? Or was it the job that made him like this?

Anyone who had not faced down a prison riot—or seven—could never truly understand. O'Malley opened one of the cuffs and slid the chain under the bar attached to the table before securing it again. "I'll be in the next room," he said. He leaned in and quietly added, "Normally, I'd tell you not to try anything stupid, but considerin' why you're here, I'm hopin' you'll do just that." His breath indicated either a few drinks with lunch or, perhaps, he had just brushed his teeth—both seemed plausible.

"I'll play nice."

The Mountain That Guards appeared appeased by that answer. He walked over to the other side of the room. "Inmate secure. Open the door!"

The buzz seemed louder than usual as O'Malley twisted the knob and jerked the door back. There stood a professional-looking fellow with a misplaced smile and leather briefcase, probably a Prada or maybe a Samsonite. His Armani suit and Cartier watch complimented his clean-shaven appearance nicely but could not distract from his boyish looks. Though probably at least thirty years old, he looked all of nineteen.

Shit. I'll bet his suit and that briefcase cost more than I used to make in a month.

As Eldridge Forsythe, a rising star in his firm, shuffled into the room, the size disparity between him and O'Malley became more obvious—and hilarious. It was like William "The Refrigerator" Perry standing next to the average pee-wee league football player.

"Counselor, you know the drill. Don't attempt to pass nothin' unauthorized, and don't approach that side for any reason. If you think somethin's about to happen, just back away from the table, and we'll be in here fuckin' ricky-tick." His jargon was familiar.

Marines... gotta love 'em.

Eldridge nodded to the guard, and the door closed behind him. An awkward pause ensued. Then the attorney tried to make small talk. "How have you been?" he asked, seemingly oblivious to my plight as I sat there. The sustained silence seemed to say it all, and he finally got the point. Taking a seat and popping the locks on his war chest, he continued, "Look, I'm going to level with you and be as forthcoming as I can. My firm took your case because we all believed in your innocence. The senior partners thought an acquittal was all but guaranteed, but everything the prosecution presented at trial may have upended any chance of getting you out of here. The jury started deliberations yesterday, and they're still going. That could be a good sign. But you need to prepare yourself for the prospect of staying here for the long term. Or worse."

Nothing. I sat there, "Prisoner 386497," shackled inside and out, made no overt acknowledgement, no reply to this revelation. No eye contact was made, despite Eldridge's best efforts to secure my attention.

"Your family has mortgaged the house to cover the legal fees, and even that senator withdrew her support for you." Still, I offered no response. "Has anything that I've said taken hold? Your parents are on the cusp of homelessness." He lowered his voice. "Do... do you even care?"

Of course I care, you fucking idiot! I was a police officer! Do you have any idea how much of a target that makes me? Verbalizing these thoughts would have summoned the guards.

I finally spoke. "They'll be fine. The rest of the family will band together and take care of them." The words were tinged with confidence, but something about them lacked all sincerity, and the attorney pounced.

"Is that going to matter if they lose their child? Don't forget that Texas very proudly supports the death penalty. I think it's mentioned in the welcoming packet when you cross the state line."

His attempt at humor went over about as well as could be expected.

"I'm sorry—bad joke. Your record of service in the military and after is fairly impressive, but we're in a different world now. There's an army of protesters outside that courthouse hoping you'll end up with a needle in your arm before the end of the year."

Huh. Seems I managed to draw a crowd after all.

"Cool. How many protesters are we talking about?"

Shocked at the cavalier reply, Eldridge responded, "Several dozen, maybe a hundred. They're holding signs, chanting, shouting, facing off with counter-protestors. It reminds me of some of the antiwar demonstrations from the last twenty years." With that remark, our eyes finally locked, and the attorney knew that it was in his best interest to retract that statement sooner rather than later. "Forget I said that. I'm just trying to get you to understand exactly what's at stake. You've been here for nine months, your family is hemorrhaging money, and as we speak, twelve people are deciding whether or not you will die for what happened. Now, it's not common for someone in your position to get the death penalty, but like I said, this is Texas, and elections are coming up next year. Judges who overturn convictions or don't honor the will of the people typically don't last long in the Lone Star State."

What about vets? Do we get to last long anywhere? We leave one battlefield for another back home.

"Listen," Eldridge uttered after a ragged breath, "it doesn't seem like we're getting anywhere, and I'm doing this as a personal favor to your mother because she asked me to; I'm actually off the clock."

Wow. Your generosity knows no bounds. Did you drive here in the company BMW or your personal Mercedes? Prick.

Eldridge carefully slid a form over to me and followed it with a pen so expensive that he probably had it insured. "Just sign by the X about two-thirds of the way down. All it says is that I came here today to discuss legal matters, and that I apprised you of the situation with the trial and the deliberations. There's no fine print."

With a deep breath and a few strokes of the pen, it was accomplished. "Done."

I slid the materials back, but not before taking another moment to admire the craftsmanship of the writing utensil.

Seriously, who carries an ink pen inlaid with diamonds and gold into a prison? I could score a shitload of cigarettes with this.

"Thank you," Eldridge replied.

His words were genuine, but the circumstances did not lend themselves to appreciating sincerity, not when you have witnessed your cellmate's murder in the yard for refusing to join an Aryan gang. It was hard to believe that a human body could hold that much blood, and it was even harder to believe that no one else saw it coming.

Eldridge rose from his seat, fastened the buttons on his suit, and gathered his effects.

"I don't know if this will provide you any comfort," he said, "but it really is impossible to know how long a jury will take to reach a verdict. I mean, O. J. Simpson was acquitted in less than four hours, so—"

"Well, shit, counselor. I suppose we won't beat that record, now will we?"

In an instant, the professionalism and compassion in the attorney's eyes vanished. Without even looking at me, he glanced at the mirror to his left and loudly exclaimed, "We're done here." The piercing buzz rang out like shots in a war zone, and without another word, Eldridge disappeared down a lengthy corridor, only to be replaced with the considerably less friendly O'Malley. The contempt on his face matched the intensity with which he slammed the door behind him, and when he approached the table where I sat, I saw the immense effort on his part not to flip it over.

"Hold still," the guard uttered as he opened the one cuff. He then closed it once it was free of the table. "Jesus, do you have any fuckin' clue who that guy is? There's a hundred people in here who would kill to have him as their lawyer. What the fuck is wrong with you?"

Hmm. Let's think about that. I was wrongfully accused of murder. My defense team hired a second-string quarterback to get the job done. My family is two steps away from living on the streets. I've been in jail for nearly a year, and your fucked-up grill reeks of prison food and vodka. I think that sums it up.

"I suppose the stress of waiting on the verdict is taking its toll on me. If he comes back, I won't act like that again."

This time, O'Malley appeared less than content with the answer, and were it not for the cameras in the room, his nightstick likely would have made swift contact with my knuckles.

"Get up. Back to the block." He gestured toward the door at the back of the room. His nightstick made an appearance yet again, as though he needed extra leverage against someone a third his size who was also wearing handcuffs, an orange jumpsuit, dingy white socks, and crappy shoes made in-house by the inmates themselves. The fashion statement was undeniable. It screamed "weakness."

Rising from the seat, I caught a glimpse in the two-way mirror, and gasped internally at the reflection. The pallid visage looked less human every day.

Fuckin' hell... I look like shit. Is that... gray hair?

The trek to the cellblock took longer than expected. O'Malley ordered his companion to wait near the guards' break room as he stared at the television, hoping to catch a headline announcing that a verdict had been reached.

"Don't take this personally, but we got a pool goin' 'bout how this plays out," he gleefully snickered, not once tearing his eyes from the screen. The chyron at the bottom mentioned the jury's deliberations, the courthouse protests, and how the whole country was watching Texas to see how this adventure panned out.

"Yeah," another guard said, "I got a hundred bucks on you getting death. Sanchez thinks the judge will go easy and just give you life without parole. One guard even thinks you'll get off scot-free, so somebody's gettin' some cash outta this."

How flattering. My life hangs in the balance, and these assholes are casting lots.

"Fuckin'-A," O'Malley muttered, popping the top on his afternoon Coca-Cola. He polished off the whole can in one sitting.

The accompanying belch was reminiscent of both sixth-grade recess and the infantry grunts from downrange, but it did elicit a faint smile of remembrance from me.

I never thought I'd prefer being back in the desert. How's that for irony?

"He'd fire my ass for saying this, but I think even the warden's in on it," Sanchez faintly said as she finished kitting up and headed toward the general population area. For her, "gen pop" was an assignment. For the inmates not in isolation, it was a place to gather and play cards, watch TV, talk, incite riots. The usual deal on the inside.

"Well, back to it. Let's move," O'Malley directed, and they returned to the long hallway that led toward B Block. He never saw an update on the verdict, though he *was* obviously pleased at the sight of so many protestors calling for the death of an unconvicted inmate. How was that for camaraderie? Two veterans, separated only by position, and one hoped that the other would die.

"Deliberations only last for about four or five hours a day, so it may take some time to hear anything concrete," I informed the giant.

O'Malley shot a sideways glance over at me and barked, "How the hell d'you know that?"

"I've spent a lot of time in court over the years. I wasn't always on trial for murder."

"Heh. Right." He seemed to accept that answer, and we kept moving further down the hall, passing gen pop, the cafeteria, and the most disgusting latrines this side of Andersonville's Stockade Creek.

Not sure how much more I can take. I'm probably gonna die here while these fuckwits try to make a quick buck over my corpse.

"Hold here, feet behind the red line," the guard said casually, pressing his mammoth thumb into the intercom switch. "O'Malley plus one inmate for transfer back to B Block from holdin'. Request manual open on cell 217."

A few seconds passed before a woman's voice on the other end replied, "Copy that: O'Malley plus one inmate to cell 217. Proceed." The buzz kicked in once more as the door slowly slid to the left and disappeared.

"Almost home," the Mountain said with a smile so arrogant that he should run for Congress.

This will never be my home. Somehow, I will leave this place. With a tab, or on a slab.

That damn nightstick was out again and pressed into my back with more force than before, likely just a show for the other prisoners so that they would remember who was boss. The long corridors gave way to a much smaller and cramped space, with a vastly different tone than anywhere else in the waking nightmare. O'Malley and I ascended the stairs to the second floor, made a left turn, and stopped just outside the cell, the nightstick finally getting a reprieve from duty.

"You know the drill," he snapped as he casually fished the keys from his pocket and then opened cell number 217. I walked inside, turned around, and for the first time in a long time, Prisoner 386497 did not flinch or even blink as O'Malley slammed the door shut. He removed the cuffs through the slot in the door, clipped them to his belt, and covertly fired off one last parting shot: "I'm lookin' forward to the day you get what's comin' to ya. From that judge, someone in the yard, down in gen pop, the shower—all the same to me. Have a good fuckin' night." The sound of his footsteps reverberated as he descended the stairs and disappeared down the hallway.

And here we are... back "home."

A collection of books sat perched on the desk, along with legal pads, pencils, some family photos, a dust-laden copy of a burgundy Bible. Such was the life of an inmate awaiting determination of guilt or innocence. Whenever the time came to rest or lay down, the mattress sank in with any amount of body weight; it was barely three inches thick and supported by a solid steel frame. If ever there was a time for prisons to invest in Serta, this was it. And the pillow? It was basically an extension of the mattress, all of which married nicely with linens that were not even long enough to cover the length of the bed.

Even those Army blankets were better than this shit, and they probably saw action in Korea.

I slipped off my shoes and stretched out on what barely qualified as a bed, and my mind began to wander.

How the hell did I end up here? What kind of fucked up shit did I do in a past life that justified sending me to this shithole? Still a few hours between now and dinner, and that may kill me before the jury even makes the announcement. How's that for a headline? "INMATE FORGOES LETHAL INJECTION, DIES FROM KILLER MEAL." A light chuckle followed before reality returned.

My family is going broke. My lawyer walked out. I'm surrounded by actual felons—some of whom I personally arrested—and the world's angriest guard has a hard-on for my death. Tried going back to the family faith, but where is God in this hell? With everything I've been through, how could anyone believe in anything after all that? The chaplain's polite enough, but he seems unaware that this is a prison, not some parish with a potluck after the baptisms.

Rolling over on the bed, as if trying to escape the tired conundrum, rest was still elusive.

What am I going to do? Even if they find me innocent, I'll never get a decent job. No hope for a retrial, can't escape. A mountain of evidence against me. Surrounded by enemies, some of them wearing uniforms. I didn't get stabbed last week, but who knows if they'll try again? Killing an ex-cop guarantees lifelong cred. And yet, the question remains: why am I here? How could I have known what would happen?

"No one was supposed to die."

CHAPTER 2

TUESDAY, 17 AUGUST 1999

"GET OFF THE DAMN BUS, now! Move it!"

"Grab your shit and get in formation! This day hasn't even started yet!"

The drill sergeants' collective energy could power Las Vegas for a week. Clutching his duffel bag and slinging it over his shoulders, Private Richard Knight departed the bus with as much speed as could be mustered by a man surrounded by controlled chaos. Fresh out of high school and barely eighteen years old, his platoon was herded off the bus and down a long sidewalk to a large building, where they were ordered to stand at attention in the blistering Missouri heat.

Sweat was already beading and dripping down the back of Knight's neck as the drill sergeants continued their verbal onslaught against the new recruits. "Hurry the fuck up!" one of them screamed. "You've been here all of thirty seconds, and I am not impressed!" The voice certainly did not match the noncom's frame. Knight's eyes darted to his right, and he saw by name tag and insignia just who was commanding this exercise in intimidation. Somehow standing taller than her counterparts despite her five-foot-four stature, Sergeant First Class Wilkes was going absolutely ballistic on a soldier as he struggled to secure the straps on his duffel and stand in the formation. Despite his outward signs of distress, she showed no sign of relenting. The refined image of her close-cropped black hair, flashing dark-brown eyes, and carefully arched brows was blown to smithereens by her choice curses and abusive delivery. "For fuck's sake, Cathell, what the actual fuck is wrong with you? It's just a damn duffel! How do you expect to handle a suspect if you can't even manage your luggage? Jesus, figure it out!"

Knight could not help but cringe a bit.

Holy shit. This is only the first day...

Wilkes stood so close to her target that the brims of their respective hats danced with every word that she shouted, and she clung to him like a tick, ignoring everyone else in the vicinity. Her perfectly rolled up sleeves revealed multiple tattoos, but they were impossible to discern against her dark brown skin. Knight had heard of the Army's collective ability to project immense power, but this soldier was doing it all by herself. Cathell finally figured out the mechanism and slung the bag on both shoulders, returning to attention and finally absolving himself of Wilkes' wrath.

He'll definitely be one to watch. Let's hope he doesn't go "Private Pyle" on anyone, Knight thought to himself, recalling Stanley Kubrick's Vietnam drama.

After another half hour of Wilkes and crew "welcoming" the class of 175 soldiers to their new home, they were marched into an auditorium adorned with national and state flags, and, at long last, given the chance to breathe. But that moment of respite was short-lived. The soldiers removed the duffel bags from their shoulders only to wrap their arms around them on their laps, to accommodate sitting in the venue. This became less comfortable as seconds turned into what felt like hours. A drill sergeant called the room to attention, but a few did not move quickly enough for those in charge.

"On your feet!" Wilkes screeched out the words like a banshee as the rest of the platoon sprang up and the room fell silent. Then the absence of noise was broken by the sound of heavy footsteps plodding toward the stage. A broad-shouldered colonel strode down the center aisle, followed closely by an enlisted associate; their combined presence was more than enough to intimidate these future warriors. The officer, a tall, black man with razor-sharp creases and not a speck of hair on his head, exuded an aura of invincibility, which was surpassed only by the sergeant major trailing him. The sergeant major, clearly a robust product of a near-forgotten era, took a position at the edge of the stage and waited his turn.

"At ease. Take your seats," said the colonel. His tone was forceful, yet a welcomed relief from the blitzkrieg that had occurred earlier. "Class One-Four-Nine-Nine, welcome to Fort Leonard Wood. I'm Colonel McLaughlin, commander of the 14th MP Brigade, and on behalf of myself and the sergeant major, I'd like to welcome you to One Station Unit Training. Over the next twenty weeks, we will offer you the challenge of becoming members of one of the most unappreciated, reviled, and loathed careers across the whole of the United States Army. Some of you may have been expecting me to tell you that MPs are respected by all who wear the uniform, but I prefer to keep things as real as possible. And trust me... we're not." He let this sink in, then continued. "Military police are charged with securing the installation, protecting lives and property, controlling traffic, preventing crime, responding to emergencies, and a host of other tasks. When someone at my rank is speeding on base, you, even as junior enlisted soldiers, are not only authorized, you are *required* to exercise your positional authority, and administer a ticket to that colonel. He may not like it; he may even threaten to call your commander. But that's your job." The colonel went on to outline some of the finer points of the field and the course as the recruits sat motionless, listening intently to their leader and hoping to avoid having to write a ticket to a colonel in the future.

"Having said all of that, I'm going to turn the floor over to my senior enlisted advisor. Sergeant Major, they're all yours." The colonel gestured toward the crowd, as his counterpart moved toward the center of the stage. If Knight thought that the colonel had been around the world, this guy clearly had seen his share of shenanigans, as evidenced by the Ranger Tab, Jump Wings, and Combat Infantryman Badge adorning his fatigues. Any doubts that this man's age could possibly inhibit him from taking down all of the soldiers in the auditorium were put to rest over the next few minutes.

"Everybody sit up straight and listen up!" Anyone not already stiff as a board certainly was after hearing that, including the ones who had begun to slouch in their seats. "I'm Command Sergeant Major

Hendriksen, and like the colonel said, I'm his senior advisor. As you may have guessed, I've been around the block a few times. Back in 1970, I was drafted and did my tour with the 25th Infantry in 'Nam before the Army made me an MP."

Holy shit, this guy was in Vietnam. I wonder if he has any good war stories...

"And yeah, I've got more than a few war stories, but none of them are good." At this, Knight's eyes grew wide as he marveled at the man's insight into what the new troops were thinking and what they needed to hear. "War is hell on Earth. It's an absolute nightmare that doesn't end, so you had better pray that you never end up in one." Sergeant Major Hendriksen had the entire room's attention locked on him as he ran down his expectations of the class, speaking with such authority that even the drill sergeants were rendered children at his feet.

What little hair that was visible on his head was white as cotton, and his blue eyes burned with intensity as he spoke of the profession of arms, the importance of study hall, and not marrying anyone in the class (which elicited a few laughs). He encouraged the students to always ask questions if anything was unclear. "Your time here will not be easy, but nothing worth having is. You'll spend the next few days getting processed into the barracks and schoolhouse, issuing some equipment, and preparing you for what lies ahead. Training officially begins tomorrow, but it wouldn't surprise me if things were to kick off early. Am I correct, Drill Sergeant Wilkes?" He looked toward the back of the room.

"Yes, Sergeant Major!" A brief reply, but those three words said it all. Knight wondered just how intense things would become between now and then.

"Then I suppose we're done here. Sir, do you have anything more to add?" the sergeant major asked of his only superior in the room. Colonel McLaughlin simply shook his head. How could he possibly follow that speech? "Alright, then. Sergeant Wilkes, you know what to do."

She did.

As though they had just sat on thumbtacks, the soldiers leapt from their seats at her direction and stood completely still as the command team departed the room, their footsteps fading along with the soldiers' hope of a reprieve from what was to come. The drill sergeants, four in total, took positions in the front and back of the auditorium, and immediately began barking out orders to move toward the side doors. Their voices echoed throughout the room as the group struggled to make it outside. The easy part of the day was over.

MONDAY, 15 NOVEMBER 1999

Knight stood at parade rest opposite his instructor, anxiously awaiting the discussion that he had been dreading for three days, and wondering just how bad the news would be.

Seated at his desk, Drill Sergeant Shrieves leafed through some papers in a manila folder, the evidence of a student in need of guidance. The thirty-year-old Montana native, sporting a flattop and a perfectly trimmed mustache, placed the folder on the desk and began expressing his concern.

"I'm not gonna sugarcoat things, Knight. Your academic performance recently has been mediocre at best. You've done well at the physical aspects of the course, which is good; ours can be a physically demanding field. But the last thing we need is MPs out there on the line who can't remember the procedure for making an arrest, or who don't execute things to the letter when a suspect is getting out of hand. Things like that can cost a conviction in military courts, and no self-respecting law enforcement professional wants that on their conscience. Do you understand what I'm saying?" Shrieves looked up at his student with moderate concern in his eyes, laying out the issues he saw in Knight's performance and hoping that he had not rattled his cage too much. The kid was not failing the course by any stretch of the imagination, but his grades had dropped noticeably when the class began the most recent block of instruction.

"Yes, Drill Sergeant," Knight said with as much confidence as he could summon. "I study for hours every night and weekend, but I'm really not getting this new block. It's a lot tougher than the last one."

"This is the part where we begin weeding out soldiers who thought the job was just arresting people and waving their arms at the gate. It is *supposed* to be difficult. The law is one of the few things separating us from the animals, and if those charged with enforcing it don't know what they're doing, then the world turns to shit." Shrieves took on a more serious tone as he continued to apprise Knight of his status in the course.

The realization that his future might be in jeopardy hit him quite hard. "Drill Sergeant, I will study whatever I have to and do whatever is needed to pass this course. When I commit to something, I go all in. And I am committed to becoming an MP."

The private delivered this statement to his instructor with such bravado that Shrieves sat back in his chair, raised his eyebrows and said, "Okay. Don't tell me—show me. We're in Missouri, after all."

It took Knight a moment to catch the reference, but he did, and simply responded, "Yes, Drill Sergeant." Shrieves dismissed him, and he headed toward the cafeteria to join the rest of his platoon.

Lunch was cut short due to the verbal counseling from his instructor, but Knight still had enough time to grab a bite from the short-order line and make it back to the barracks before class. The talk with Shrieves resonated deeply within him, and it caused him to take inventory of how things had gone since he arrived.

Three months down, two months to go.

Knight contemplated the implications of another sixty days in Missouri, though the location did not seem to bother him as it did the others in his class. Being from Georgia, Missouri was hardly the culture shock that it was to soldiers like Evans, whose upbringing in the Bronx rendered him nearly incapable of handling the summer and early fall temperatures of the Midwest. Knight was on hand when his classmate collapsed from heat exhaustion during physical training, and he was then tasked with making sure that Evans drank enough water to float the Titanic. Through his close observation, Evans had not passed out since that fateful day.

Twelve students had already been dropped from the course for academic reasons and another five for discipline. Knight wondered how he would fare in the weeks to come. When it came to the fitness tests, marksmanship drills, self-defense classes, and basic scenarios, his performance was solid, as Shrieves had said. He would never be accused of having the highest overall scores, but nothing indicated a soldier in need of remedial training… until this latest block of instruction. The spike in difficulty was something Knight was not prepared for, and he dreaded the prospect of the next written exam, which was a mere two weeks away. Every day after the physical training formation, barracks preparations, class, and lunch, he had run through all the details in his head, sometimes out loud. He redoubled his efforts today, after talking with Shrieves.

"Form 4137 deals with evidence and property, Form 2713 is a prisoner observation report. Field Manual 3-39 governs all MP operations…"

He had not noticed, but he nearly walked right into another student who was standing near the barracks doorway.

"Knight! Ya gotta snap out of it, man. You're gonna do fine!" The words from Evans, whom Knight jokingly, and privately, viewed as the "lanky Yankee," offered little in the way of reassurance—especially for someone who very nearly did not graduate from high school a mere six months ago. His abilities in math and science, and the drive to care about such trivial subjects, had all been lacking to an alarming degree. But now, at Fort Leonard Wood, there were real-world applications to what he was learning, and that made all the difference… until more abstract concepts began to appear in the course materials.

Evans reiterated his encouragement, but it still rang hollow.

"Thanks," Knight managed to say. "How many is that so far?" he asked, pointing to the canteen in Evans' hand. His colleague briefly shook the canteen to determine how much remained.

"Five, and I just had lunch." He clutched his stomach as the idea of eating food with that much water in his system was making him ill.

Knight tried to mentally crunch some numbers. *Thirty-two ounces per canteen, five canteens, that's… a lotta water for this early.*

"Temperature ain't been over sixty in weeks, but I gotta keep drinkin'. Doc's orders an' shit." That last line was a bit more contemptuous than it should have been, but to be fair, the man had almost died a few weeks into the program. You don't just snap back from that. The drill sergeants' perception was that Evans was lacking the requisite fitness to successfully complete the course. And they were right: he barely met the Army's minimum standards for completing basic training. Now, after passing out during an intense workout session, it seemed that this trend was continuing, and Evans' place in the course was likely in jeopardy.

Seeing a chance to strike a deal, Knight told Evans about his talk with Drill Sergeant Shrieves. "Tell you what," he concluded. "You get me through these academics, and I'll help you with the physical training parts. I'm from Georgia; we've been dealing with dehydration for centuries. You just need to know *when* to drink, not necessarily how much. Did you hear about what happened in the Air Force a couple months back?"

Evans shook his head.

Heh. Reading that copy of The Army Times *paid off,* Knight thought to himself.

Knight continued, "Some kid died in their basic training because he drank *too much* water and no one could see the signs. They autopsied him, and the poor bastard had four gallons in his system. We've got a field exercise next month, so space out the water, and don't overdo it out there. If you die, they'll probably kill me, too."

"Sounds easy enough." On instinct, he took another sip. "So what's holding you back in class?" Knight explained to his classmate what had happened over the last few weeks. Evans listened intently, silently composing a plan of action, and then arranged a standing study time for the two of them. "There's really only one thing you can do at this point," he told Knight. "You gotta dive headfirst into the hardest parts of this course, and then, when you think you're at the bottom? Dive even deeper."

"I don't know how much deeper I can dive. I'm studyin' every night, doin' drills on procedures, and it's just not workin'. I mean, Shrieves gave me a warning, and I told him I'd do what I had to... but I don't know what else to do."

Evans' expression said that he did. "Look here. From here on out, you and me are gonna work one-on-one on everything, inside and out. Can't be no halfway. That last lesson on the Posse Comitatus Act is kind of like the infield fly rule—you either get it, or you don't." Being a baseball aficionado, Knight saw the wisdom in his friend's comparison, and resolved right then and there to emulate Evans' approach, but with a twist.

"You're right, man. Okay, let's meet right after chow, and we'll start with everything we learned since this block started. We'll throw in some push-ups every thirty minutes and, that way, both of us get something out of it."

Evans cut Knight a look before closing his eyes and shaking his head, realizing he had sort of shot himself in the foot by offering his assistance. Now he would have to work out. "Not much to do but accept." He placed the cap back on his canteen, secured it in the pouch on his web belt, and glanced at the clock. "Shit! We got about a minute before the whole platoon's in front-leaning rest, and I don't wanna puke all over everybody."

"Good call."

Both men double-timed it outside and arrived with only seconds to spare before the group was directed to form up by the class leader and began heading back to class. It was time to buckle down.

MONDAY, 17 JANUARY 2000

Courtesy of Evans and, most surprising of all, Cathell, Private Knight successfully completed the course and was on the cusp of graduating from the most difficult thing he had ever attempted in his life. While his colleague from New York guided him through the minefield of the academic side of the course, it was Cathell who had mastered the hands-on portion of weapons management and imparted that wisdom to Knight. So good was Cathell at field-stripping and reassembling his rifle that he actually bested one of the instructors in a side-by-side race. Only days remained between now and the march across the parade field, thus culminating his time at Fort Leonard Wood. Morale was high among the remaining 139 troops, and today was the day that many had looked forward to almost as much as leaving: assignment notifications.

Sergeant Wilkes took her position at the front of the same auditorium they'd gathered in five months before, and congratulated the class. "Well done. Based on data from the instructor team, the course supervisor and with the approval of Colonel McLaughlin, I can say with a degree of pride that every one of you in this room has successfully completed the program." Her comment led many in the room to express their exuberance as quietly as they could, but some were so elated that a cheer could not be held back. Wilkes continued, "Now, I won't lie to you. Some of you had me more than a little worried. I'm looking at you, Cathell," she said with one eyebrow raised. Undeterred and unable to stop smiling, he received several pats on the back and audible praise from his fellow classmates.

"But you made it. All of you did, and no one can ever take that away from you. Effective Friday morning, each of you has earned the Military Occupational Specialty of 95 Bravo. You *are* military policemen." Knight breathed a deep sigh of relief at hearing these words, closing his eyes as they played again in his mind. The fist bumps and silent gestures continued as she made her way back to the podium and retrieved a camouflage binder, opening it with poise and turning to the first page. "I need everyone to remain completely silent for the next ten minutes. I got a lotta names here and lots of assignments. When I call your name, sound off, and I'll tell you where you're going. Yes, these are final; and no, neither you, nor I, nor your daddy who is a general can change 'em, so don't ask. We clear on that?"

The class responded in thunderous unison, "Yes, Drill Sergeant!"

"Then let's do this. Adams!" She ticked off the list of names and their corresponding bases, cycling through A and finally arriving at K, though Knight was fairly confident in his destination. He had done some investigating, and few in the class claimed to want any installations in the southeast, so an assignment to Fort Benning or Fort Jackson seemed all but guaranteed.

"Knight!"

"Yes, Drill Sergeant!"

"Fort Lewis, Washington state. Bring an umbrella. Kraminski!"

Shit. Shit-shit-shit-shit! How the balls did that happen?

The process continued for another five minutes, though the rain Wilkes had alluded to already seemed to be pouring over Knight's disposition. This was not how he wanted to end his time at school.

"Zwan!"

"Yes, Drill Sergeant!"

"Vicenza, Italy. Lucky bastard." She closed the binder. "And that's it. Now you know where you're going, but don't ever forget where you've been. At some point in the not-too-distant future, a few of you will come back here as instructors, and then, it'll be your turn. Try to look at it from our perspective: we spent the last five months training our replacements. Wouldn't you also want to be trained by the best?"

Many nodded in silent agreement with their leader, and it was hard to argue with her wisdom. Knight took a moment to think of how Shrieves had set him on the path to success by speaking to him before the bottom fell out of his grades completely. Shrieves was once a student like him, and now, he was among the greatest in his field. That was truly something to ponder.

Were it not for him, I wouldn't be here right now.

"Class leader, we're done here. Take 'em back to the barracks."

FRIDAY, 21 JANUARY 2000

The crisp winter afternoon on the base was unmatched by any before, as though Robert Frost himself spoke the day into existence. Class 14-99, decked out in their green dress uniforms and anxiously awaiting Drill Sergeant Wilkes' direction, stood at rest on the parade field, having executed their portion of the graduation ceremony perfectly thanks to hours of rehearsal and Wilkes' verbal motivation. Colonel McLaughlin delivered his closing remarks from the lectern, thanking the instructors and those in attendance, before turning control of the formation back to the staff. "Drill Sergeant Wilkes. Dismiss the class!"

She snapped to attention and faced about, her inscrutable demeanor hiding the fact that her eyes were alight with pride and respect for the professionals before her. "Class 14-99... fall out!"

The soldiers smartly faced about in unison as the crowd erupted with cheers, the enormity of their accomplishment finally sinking in, and all of them made their way toward the bleachers. Knight picked up his pace and easily spotted his parents, Thomas and Michelle, near the left side of the seating area. His father, forty-eight years old and dressed in a suit as always, held his arm around Knight's mother as their son made his way over for a deserved reunion.

Michelle smiled through a tear and said, "Son, that was really something. Your father and I could not be more proud of you." She briefly hugged her youngest child, taking a moment to admire the crossed flintlock pistols on his collar—the branch insignia of the Military Police Corps. Michelle was petite for having had four children, and she wore the gray in her hair like a badge of honor. Thomas shook his son's hand and was similarly affected, but managed to keep it together by offering to take everyone out to dinner.

"Sounds like a plan, Dad. The chow halls are one thing I won't miss about this place. Well, that and the weather, but I'll have to get used to that in Washington, too, I guess."

"Oh, right. Fort Lewis," Thomas lamented. "It may not be what you want, but there are far worse places to be stationed. When do you have to report?"

"No later than March fifteenth, but I can sign into my unit at any point before that if I want. Sergeant Blankenship approved me for Recruiter's Assistance. I'll get a few weeks back home while I do that, and I'm taking another week off when it's done." He looked at his watch, checked the time and continued, "I'll tell you what... I gotta deal with some more paperwork and say goodbye to a few friends, so why don't we get both of you back to the hotel while I do all of that. Then I'll change clothes, and we can head off base for a nice dinner. I've been wanting to try this steakhouse just outside the main gate for the last few months. How does that sound?”

“Well, as an officer of the law, I think we had better follow your suggestion,” Michelle said proudly.

Man, I hope this feeling never goes away. I haven’t seen Mom this proud since Sarah graduated from college.

“Great. In that case, I’ll see you in about an hour or so. I love you... very much.”

“We love you, too, Son. Your mother and I... well, you know.” His throat was tight, but he managed to hold it together again. Thomas had done his time in the Army in the early seventies, but never went to war. He was a man who rarely showed that kind of emotion, and seeing it was something Knight would never forget.

“I know, Dad... I know.” Knight turned and headed toward the administrative office by the schoolhouse, grateful that no one saw him wipe away his own tears.

I am a Military Policeman.

FRIDAY, 24 AUGUST 2001

“Zero-six on the dot. Time to head back,” said the exhausted driver.

“No objection, your honor,” replied Knight, suppressing a yawn. At the wheel, Specialist Dante DeVaughn dropped the gear into drive and maneuvered the patrol car through the family housing neighborhood and back toward the main road, finishing his can of Red Bull in the process. DeVaughn was a personable guy from Pennsylvania who was always dressed to the nines when not in uniform. It was not enough for him to wear a tuxedo to his own birthday party—he also wore a top hat and carried a cane, but he pulled it off brilliantly. He lived on the same floor as Knight in the MP barracks, and they occasionally hung out together during their time off, attending Seahawks games and playing on the company softball team. DeVaughn enjoyed watching sports, but preferred playing them even more.

Knight downed the last few drops of his coffee, and tossed the cup and can into a plastic bag on the floorboard, a practice drilled into them by the Platoon Sergeant on a near-daily basis. He took the clipboard off the dash and ran down the list of incidents they had addressed during the shift, pausing to smile at just how dumb some people could be under the right conditions, most of which involved liquor and poor judgment.

"D., you think that pilot will get counseled?" Knight asked, recalling an earlier incident when they had been called to the Officer's Club.

"Well, he *did* get drunk and hit on a brigade commander's daughter. Might not have been as bad if he hadn't also hit on her mother... with the colonel standing right there." Silence. They both burst into laughter as the sun began to slowly creep over the horizon and into view, the men lowering their shades in response. "Seriously," DeVaughn continued, "I understand the daughter, but the wife?"

"Hey, someone came up with the concept of the 'MILF' for a reason," Knight quipped, proud of his logic.

"Yeah, well, it wasn't because of her. Oh, and speaking of things to avoid, are you going to the captain's farewell next week? The change of command's Friday morning."

With a smile that seemed to go on for days, Knight glanced over at his colleague and beamed. "Not this time. I've got two weeks of leave coming up, and they will *not* be spent here." He could practically taste the peaches as he savored the thought. After nearly eighteen months in the Pacific Northwest, he was more than a tad overdue for a visit to his beloved homeland.

DeVaughn scoffed and replied, "I keep forgetting how much you hate it here." He shook his head. "You do know that Lewis is *the* most requested duty station in the Army, right? Like, more so than Germany."

"*I* didn't request it, and I don't exactly *hate* it here. The unit's fine, work's fine, but I'm freezing. Look at this—it's August, and I'm already wearing *these*." He held up his gloved hands as proof of his first-world struggle.

DeVaughn merely shrugged. "Can't help ya there. I'm from Philly, so this is nothing."

"West Philly?"

"Born and raised," he added, rolling his eyes as he recalled the familiar tune. "Need a lift to the airport?"

"Yeah, thanks. My plane leaves on the twenty-eighth at noon."

"I'll make sure you get there on time."

DeVaughn guided the car into the MP station parking lot, and both men exited, gathering their belongings and heading inside to officially end their shift. Ammo, returned; radios, checked back in; forms, signed. Breakfast, barracks and bed awaited.

TUESDAY, 0545 PACIFIC DAYLIGHT TIME

After two weeks of soaking up the warmth of his beloved home, Knight drove onto Fort Lewis from Highway 5 back from his leave. Knight exchanged a smile and a nod of respect with the MP on guard at the main gate before flashing his military ID. It was Rabinowitz, a soldier from the south side of Chicago, and one of Knight's closest friends. The two were assigned to patrol duty last Christmas, and they'd made the best of it by dining on MREs that Rabinowitz had in the trunk of the car. Eating MREs on Christmas. It was not quite the feast of turkey and ham that he wanted, but with even the gas station on base closed for the holiday, they had few options... and there was some brisket, courtesy of his colleague's reform synagogue.

"Hey, Rabbi. Did ya miss me?" Joshua Rabinowitz was far from observant, but he had been gifted his moniker after breaking up a fist fight in a barracks over the summer. One of those arrested, a soldier who was completely out of his mind on cocaine and now no longer in the Army, misread his uniform and called him "Rabbi" by mistake, and the nickname stuck. Being one of the few members of the Jewish faith on the entire base, he was quite amused by the drug-addled suspect's failure at reading his name and thoroughly enjoyed this new honorific. Chaplain Goldstein, however, did not appreciate the competition.

"Knight... good to have you back, man. How was leave?" the guard asked, genuinely curious.

"As usual, a little too brief. Parents are okay, it's still hot as hell in Georgia, and the Braves might make it to the playoffs again. Who knows?"

"*I* know. The Cubs will have something to say about that. This is *our* year!" He gave Knight a firm fist bump before returning the ID card. "Welcome back. I'll see you around," he said, waving the next vehicle forward.

"Good to be back," Knight said to himself as he pulled ahead toward the station, the familiar sites of the base coming into view: the childcare center, the hospital, soldiers running along the road in formation past the Burger King... just another day in the Army. He made his way through the intersection and then left on Benavidez Avenue before turning into the parking lot across from the water tower. The sign outside his work center had been changed in his absence. It now read:

44TH MILITARY POLICE COMPANY
CPT CHRISTOPHER D. LLAMAS
1SG KELLY O. TRAVIS

Right. The old commander left, and the new one took over. I should introduce myself at some point. Man, they already had the sign fixed while I was gone. The theater marquee still has Planet of the Apes *listed as a coming attraction, and it could be the one from the sixties!*

Knight shut his car off, donned his patrol cap, and made his way inside the station. Producing multiple IDs, he pressed them against the glass partition. The guard here, like others in the office, was focused on a television to her left, so Knight cleared his throat to get her attention. Startled, she jerked her head toward him and acknowledged his card collection with a barely-there wave of her hand, then moved back toward the monitor.

"Can you hand me the roster? I gotta sign in from leave," he said.

The soldier groped around the desk and produced a clipboard with an attached pen, blindly handing it to Knight. He autographed the first column of the paper, and the next two columns would follow easily enough.

First day of leave... that was... twenty-eight August. Last day of leave is... today.

"Hey, Ritter. What's today's date?"

The soldier, her eyes still riveted to the screen, never moved her head as she replied back, "It's the eleventh."

"Eleven September. Too easy. Signed and done." He slid the clipboard back over the counter.

Turning his attention to the desk clerk, he nonchalantly asked, "I know it's probably a slow day, but what's going on?" No response. Knight's curiosity ushered him around the corner and into Ritter's cubicle, where he finally saw what had transfixed her attention on TV. The banner headline spoke of trouble at the World Trade Center, and then the giant gash in the side of the North Tower came into his view for the first time; the dark smoke billowing out against the blue sky created an unforgettable contrast. "What... the hell happened?" His question seemed completely relevant until a second aircraft suddenly appeared from out of frame and slammed into the South Tower, the resulting fireball causing several in the office to audibly gasp and cover their mouths.

Christ Almighty...

CHAPTER 3

SUNDAY, 11 FEBRUARY 2007

"IT'S NOT LIKE THAT! I just don't feel like it's working here and I want to explore some other options—that's all." The young woman peered into her mother's questioning eyes through the computer monitor and wondered if the silent response came from disappointment or a spotty Internet connection. Jennifer Kowalski, a sophomore at Arcadia University in Pennsylvania, sat on her bed in her pajamas and nursed her evening tea, hoping that this revelation would not further set back their relationship. The image of her dark brown hair and alabaster skin were slightly diminished by the congested network, and her almond-shaped hazel eyes fought to avoid contact with the woman on the screen. She had been dreading this conversation for weeks, but when the Dean made clear how shaky her standing was at the school of fine arts, she had little choice.

"And what other options are you looking at?" her mother asked sharply. "You've only ever wanted to be an actress and we've spent a lot of money to get you there, so I hope you've got a pretty good idea." Evelyn was justified in her concern. Despite having been home-schooled until age fourteen, and with a less-than-stellar social experience in high school, Jennifer had made the grade and earned her way into a prestigious private school. But there, she found the challenge of juggling multiple acting programs and the sophomore classes to be too much. Her grades were slipping, and barring a significant jump in performance on her tests for the remainder of the school year, she would likely be forced to either drop out or repeat the entire second semester of her second year. It was not like she was one of the sorority girls or a fixture at the frat house party scene. So dedicated was she to achieving her dream of acting in Hollywood that everything else, including romantic relationships, took a backseat. The only problem was that her commitment to the craft was not translating into passing grades.

"Mom... I'm looking around. Acting is still what I want the most in life, but right now... I-I don't know, it's just not happening like I thought it would. These other classes are so damn hard, and it feels like I'm drowning every time I'm not rehearsing a scene or learning about Stanislavski's system."

"Who?"

"Never mind. The point is that... I may have to leave school in a few months while I get myself straightened out. I'll finish this year, I promise. And I'll do everything I can to pass this semester, but this isn't as easy as I thought it would be. I don't know how, but I swear to God, I *will* pay you back. The agreement we made—"

"Jen." Evelyn's frustration was mounting by the second. "This isn't about the deal. It never has been. I don't need to remind you just how much out-of-state tuition costs over there, but since you brought it up, you're gonna need one hell of a job to pay us back." She took a deep breath and prepared for the next part. "You're an adult now. You can make your own decisions, but you have got to understand that your choices affect the people around you, and I don't just mean what classes you're taking or whose acting method is best or even where you plan to eat tomorrow night. If you quit this now, then it'll be that much easier to quit something else in the future." She paused, waiting for a reaction, and got it. "Don't roll your eyes at me!"

Shit! I forgot the camera's on...

"Sorry, Mom." Closing her eyes, Jennifer let out a deep sigh and took another sip of her steeped tea before continuing, "Without a degree, there's only so many things I can do... I've been thinking about joining the military." To head off the response she expected, she said in a rush,

"Now you may not be crazy about that, but I've been looking into the different branches and jobs and everything, and I found something that interests me."

Evelyn sat stone-faced, anxiously awaiting what her daughter would say next. "Uh-huh."

"Well, um, the Navy has this thing called 'master-at-arms.' It's basically their version of... Military Police." Her mother's eyes grew larger as Jennifer did her best to allay her fears. "It sounds more dangerous than it is. These people guard... things and check ID cards at the gate. Yes, they're armed, and they work with dogs, and they arrest people... but I think this might be a good choice. It's not like I'll be storming the beaches of Normandy or facing down Rommel's forces. Oh, and it's a fully integrated position, so there are no restrictions on women serving in that field." She watched Evelyn fall silent again, and this time it was clear that it was no technical issue. "Mom... please say something." Jennifer had known this would be a tough conversation, but she did not think it would go quite like this.

"Have you spoken to anyone? Like a recruiter?"

Wow. She didn't freak out or burst into tears.

"I have an appointment tomorrow after class. The guy on the phone was nice. He said—"

"And why the Navy?" It was out of character for Evelyn to interrupt anyone, let alone her daughter.

The question caught her off guard. "Seems like a good choice. I never heard Ethan say much good about the Army, and the other branches don't really appeal to me. Plus, I love traveling, and being a cop on a boat seems like a good way to see the world for free."

"Or a good way to get killed."

"Mom, I know the risks. Not many Navy people have been killed since the war started, but even if they had been, it would still be my choice. Right now, I'm not thinking about that. I'm thinking about how my grades are down and how I'm not where I should be. I'm thinking about having a steady job, paying you back, the benefits, seeing what's out there. With risk comes reward. *You* taught me that."

Evelyn closed her eyes and slowly shook her head, clearly kicking herself mentally for that one, but she ultimately conceded her daughter's position. In any event, Jennifer did say that she was only *talking* to a recruiter at this point. Who commits to joining after one meeting?

Evelyn sighed deeply. "Alright. I won't say that I'm happy about this, but it's your life. Ethan and I will talk it over, and I'm going to look into it myself, but I want every detail." She looked over her shoulder as her husband mumbled something off-camera that Jennifer could not discern.

Great. He's *listening in.*

"Right." Evelyn looked back at her computer. "Ethan says not to sign anything, no matter what. Just go in, ask questions and LISTEN carefully to what they say."

No shit, Ethan. Aren't you a goddamn genius?

"Sound advice. I'll make sure it's a productive meeting."

"One more thing, dear. Why that job? Why do you want that line of work? It sounds so dangerous..." Her voice quavered.

It seemed as though she might lose it, so Jennifer quickly tried to come up with a reason that her mother would accept. "If I join the Navy, and that's a big 'if' at this point, I want to have an actual military experience. I don't want to sit behind a desk and push papers all day, or have some other menial office job. If I wanted that kind of life, I'd go talk to the Air Force." She must have made some kind of headway in the conversation, because Evelyn chuckled briefly upon hearing this. Maybe that did the trick?

"I understand that you want to do more than just sit, but please... take a closer look and really think about this before you make any decisions." Her voice sounded strained.

Jennifer looked down at the corner of the monitor. "I will. I promise. Listen, I gotta go. I have tests all week and a big meeting to prepare for, so I'll talk to you later."

"I love you, Jen. Please let us know how it goes."

"I love you." She waved goodbye, clicked the red button, and her mother's face disappeared from the monitor. Distress washed over her, but it vanished when she glanced out the window and took in the view of Glenside as fresh powder continued to blanket the area. It reminded her of her days as a kid in Illinois. No one enjoyed the winter as much as she did, yet the memories of building snowmen and skiing were fleeting in the wake of that conversation. Evelyn was right about most of it, but Jennifer remained unconvinced of one particular piece.

She's got a lot of nerve to lecture me about giving up on something. If she hadn't left Dad, then Ethan would have no place in her life; he barely has one now. Jesus, I'm not going to become a fucking bum just because I may drop out of college. A lot of people don't make it the first time around, and they end up fine.

The door opened unexpectedly and startled Jennifer, though there was no cause for alarm. It was just her roommate, dusted with snow and walking in with grocery bags looped over her arms. Always the pinnacle of fashion, Alejandra "Alex" Gonzalez's beanie, scarf, and gloves all matched, and each had its own hook on the hat rack near her bed. "Damn, girl. Does it ever stop snowing here?" she demanded of Jennifer. Being from Florida, this was a new experience for Alex, one that she had still not adjusted to quite yet. Some snow fell from her jacket when she hung it up. She placed the week's sodas in the mini fridge and tossed Jennifer a bag of mint Milano cookies, her favorite study snack food, for a much-needed morale boost.

"Thanks." One word was all she could muster, despite the kindness of the gesture.

"Something up? You haven't looked this down since your math final." Alex took off her boots and sat on the bed, positioning herself against the wall to see her roommate.

There was no avoiding this next part. She just had to suck it up and get it done.

"You could say that, yeah." She fell silent again for a moment before continuing. "Alex... there is a very real chance that I won't be here next year." The expression on Jennifer's face was bleak, but Alex was not the type to take things at face value.

"You're transferring? You sure that's a good idea? An Arcadia degree can really open some doors."

That was likely true for Alex, the biology major, but theater? In any case, it would not matter if Jennifer could not do well enough to graduate. "No, it's not that. My grades are down, and I'm not holding up my end of the deal with my parents about helping them pay off the first year. I had to quit my job just to pull a C in two classes last semester and

I was supposed to cover ten percent of the tuition costs. It's bad enough they charge forty thousand a year to go here, but trying to pay that off when you're unemployed is kind of impossible," she added, finishing off her tea.

"What happened to the study group? You've been going every night for over a year."

"Well..." This next part was embarrassing. "I sort of... didn't go. The senior classes put on productions every month, and I went there. Taking notes and learning what I could about acting, trying to get better at it. Helped a lot with my technique." She tried to justify her actions through a look of innocence, but Alex was not having it.

"You blew off studying so you could watch people rehearse plays?" Her look of incredulity said it all, yet Jennifer still felt vindicated in her decision.

"I was just being proactive, okay? I *love* acting. I've wanted to be in movies since I was a kid, but this may not be the best path for me right now." A deep breath preceded her next revelation. "I just got off a call with my mom, and I'm going to tell you what I told her: after class tomorrow, I have a meeting with a Navy recruiter. Depending on how long it takes, I may sign up before the semester ends, or I may try to finish the year, or I may not join at all—I don't know yet. What I do know is she paid a small fortune for me to be here, and now, I won't be able to complete this semester—" She had not said that part out loud yet, and the harsh reality caused her eyes to water and a sob to form in her throat. Jennifer had never encountered failure on this level in her life, and it was nothing she wanted to get accustomed to experiencing.

Alex got off her bed, walked across the room, and sat down next to Jennifer. Taking her by the hand, she offered her best assurances to her friend. "Jen, it's gonna be fine. You will get through this, and I'm going to help you every step of the way. Studying, tutoring; you name it, we'll do it."

Jennifer smiled through the tears at her friend. "Thank you, Alex. That really means a lot." She wiped a tear away and continued, "I still want to see the recruiter, even if it's just to get a brochure and walk out."

"I'll drive you."

MONDAY, 12 FEBRUARY 2007

"There it is. 'U.S. Navy Recruiting.' All of these offices look the same," Alex added, unimpressed with the drabness of the advertising.

"It's a military office, not Forever 21." Jennifer's retort seemed to placate her friend. She took a deep breath and grabbed her purse. "I'll text you when it's over."

"Okay, Jen. Remember not to sign anything, and ask some hard questions."

Fuck... does everyone think I'm a moron?

"I'll do just that," Jennifer said with a wry smile. "Here we go..." She departed the vehicle and entered the building, passing various flags, Navy SEAL posters, and numerous plaques on the walls. If nothing else, it was certainly inspiring to see so many accolades hanging up. Hearing the bell affixed to the door, the sailor behind the desk rose to his feet.

"Yes, ma'am. How can I help you?" The hand-pressed vertical creases running parallel to each other in his black shirt seemed to segue into the ones in his pants, and they caught Jennifer's attention, more so than the rows of ribbons and badges above his left breast pocket. His black necktie was suspended just so near his belt buckle, and his black shoes looked as though he had just walked in from the shining station at the airport. The image was truly striking. And somewhat evocative of Johnny Cash.

Good grief. Do all of them look this put together?

"Um, hi. I-I'm Jennifer Kowalski. I have a meeting at four with a..." she produced a folded note from her pocket, "...Petty Officer Thompson. Is he around?"

The sailor offered a firm handshake to his customer, saying, "That's me. I'm Petty Officer Thompson, and I really appreciate the punctuality.

You wouldn't believe how many people show up here late." His smile and warm demeanor were quite welcoming.

No wonder they hired this guy. He could charm a pit bull.

"However, we've had to make a little adjustment to the afternoon schedule. Your meeting was with me, but our chief is due here any minute for a no-notice performance review, so you'll be meeting with Petty Officer Stafford. She's new to the job, but she's already signed up more recruits in the last three months than me and the other guy combined."

"Actually, it's the last four months." Petty Officer First Class Stafford, with her fiery-red hair and ocean-green eyes, rounded the corner and approached the pair in the middle of the office. Looking as sharp as Thompson and ready for any board meeting, she thrust her hand out to Jennifer and shook it with unbridled confidence. "Petty Officer Stafford. I see you've already met CTI1 Thompson, so why don't we move over to my desk? Right this way, please. Would you care for some water?" she asked politely, motioning toward a cooler near the window. Jennifer declined the offer, but was already on her first question.

"CTI... what's that?"

"Cryptologic Technician Interpretive. They work with foreign languages." Leaning in, she half-whispered, "Bunch of nerds," then looked over to her colleague.

"I heard that!" Thompson fired back as they took their seats at Stafford's desk.

Jennifer was struck again by the number of plaques and letters of commendation suspended from the walls surrounding Stafford's desk. All of them indicated a woman who was certainly on the rise in her career, with a few mentioning her service in the Middle East.

Shit. This chick must be some kind of war hero.

"I understand that you're looking at joining our team. Why don't you tell me a little about yourself?"

"Well, I'm a student. I'm at Arcadia in the acting school, but it's not really working out. My grades aren't where they should be, tuition is insane, and I may have to drop out before the end of the semester." She hated divulging such personal information to a total stranger, but the word "Honor" was visibly prominent on the door when she entered. Their house, their rules.

Stafford nodded in understanding. "Yeah, that does happen. College can be a challenge, and it's certainly not for everyone the first go around. I mean, look at me. I got into UCLA and did two years before I knew my heart wasn't in it, and I was at the top of my class. You have to enjoy what you're doing, or it'll make you miserable. That's why I quit and joined the Navy. Nine years later, here I am."

Jennifer loved being on stage and studying the art and science of film production, but the rest of that package deal made her regret moving to Pennsylvania. Yet here she was. "What about *your* education? You only had two more years to go."

Stafford smiled. "The Navy provides Tuition Assistance—TA, as we call it—to pretty much everyone, and I finished those last two years online." She pointed to a frame on the wall behind her. "Got my degree a few years ago, and I'm about to start a master's program at Purdue."

Jennifer looked closer at the framed diploma, and sure enough, it was from UCLA.

"Are you sticking with psychology?"

"Yeah. I love working with people and helping them with their problems. I eventually want to be a doctor, but that's a long way down the road. And we're here to talk about you," she said, pointing to her client with a vertical hand and all five fingers extended. "The Navy has over one hundred different career fields and loads of opportunities for education and advanced training. Have you seen our website?" Though new to the position, Stafford had an excellent command of how to conduct this process, asking the questions like a pro and expertly guiding the discussion.

"I was messing around on it and a few things caught my eye. The one I'm most interested in is the master-at-arms... job... thing. What can you tell me about that one?" Jennifer tried to seem confident, but her lack of knowledge on the subject was starting to show, though it meant little to those in the office.

"Ah, they're a tough bunch, MAs. They're basically our version of military police in the other branches."

Ha! I wish Mom could've heard that. I do know some things.

"They are the Navy's security and law enforcement professionals, but the rate itself deals with many areas: force protection, securing aircraft, weapons proficiency—" Stafford shifted gears quickly and smiled at Jennifer. "I saw that," she said pointedly.

"What? What happened?"

"I mentioned weapons, and your eyes lit up. Let me guess... you play a ton of *Call of Duty* when you're not in class."

Damn it... how does she know everything? Am I that obvious?

"Guilty as charged. My father and I have a standing date on Saturdays. It's how we keep in contact. We've played together since I was a kid. We still do." She grinned as the memories of their time together came flooding back. Countless hours with controllers in hand and a stream of endless profanities hurled at their invisible opponents, all within the context of digital warfare on a computer server. Good times.

"Well, if you become an MA, it won't be a game anymore. Military police are among the few who carry weapons and live ammo on them as part of their job. It's a lot more involved than just checking IDs and directing traffic when the power goes out. Also, don't forget that the Navy deploys our people around the world constantly. Who do you think protects those ships when they're out at sea?" The question was rhetorical, but Jennifer decided to play along.

"MAs?"

"Bingo." Stafford spun around in her chair to retrieve a packet from the filing cabinet behind her, and Jennifer saw a hint of a tattoo on her neck as she leaned over. From her seat, it looked to be some sort of Asian writing.

A tattooed sailor. What a surprise.

"Take this home and read it tonight. It's got an overview of the MA field, and some basic info about pay and benefits, education, travel, and so on."

Jennifer seemed confused. "Does that mean we're done?" she asked, raising an eyebrow.

"Oh, not even close," replied Stafford, smirking. "We have a *lot* more to cover."

And that they did. For an hour, the two ran down Jennifer's academic record, known medical history, physical fitness routine, family members, past employment, drug use, potential criminal behavior; she even took a practice aptitude test, which she passed with flying colors. Stafford explained that the actual background screening was conducted at a separate location in Harrisburg run by a joint military command. It would take about two days to have everything done.

On the surface, Jennifer was exactly what the Navy was looking for, and as their conversation continued, enlisting was becoming more palatable. The service period would hinder her goal of becoming an actress, but for that matter, academic courses with no relation to drama and stage performance were also holding her back. The most pressing matter right now was how long it would take to actually join if she were to sign the contract. But she had other questions. She asked Stafford what she had done before her new job, and whether she had ever felt restricted for being a woman in an overwhelmingly male branch of service. As it turned out, the office's newest recruiter was a parachute rigger, thrice deployed to combat zones, and her gender had never held her back from anything in or out of uniform.

"We've been at war for five years, and there's no sign of it slowing down. My counterparts across the room have been doing this a lot longer than I have, and they say there's almost no wait between signing the contract and shipping out to boot camp. Wars really expedite things."

Interesting. So, if I don't want to finish the semester, I can get out fairly quick.

"That's good to know," Jennifer said. "Thank you for everything, Petty Officer. I can see why you are doing so well in this job."

I hope that didn't sound weird.

"My pleasure." Stafford drew a business card from the holder on the desk and held it out. "Here's my card. It's got all my contact info, so don't hesitate to give me a call, day or night, if you have any questions. You have a lot of potential, Jennifer. I can really see you in this uniform someday."

In contrast to everything she had heard about recruiters, this one defied all expectations. She placed the card in her purse and drew out her cell phone to text Alex. She stood and said, "Acting is my passion and my dream, but... I'll definitely think about everything you've shared today. I'll be sure to call you in a few weeks."

"Thank you. That's all we can expect."

Jennifer shook her hand once more and let her friend know she had finished up. Then she headed outside to meet Alex, rushing to get inside the heated car before the blast of winter air could do permanent damage. Her thoughtful roommate had a cup of Starbucks coffee ready to help her deal with the cold.

"That's why you're the best." Jennifer broke open the perforated lid and carefully took a sip. The heat from the java instantly filled her with even more assurance that everything was going to be fine.

"So? How'd it go?" Alex asked with mixed emotions. The two had become very close over the last year, especially after Alex's boyfriend broke off their relationship via a drunken phone call over Labor Day weekend. She did not want to see Jennifer go, but she understood her rationale.

"Fairly well. There may be more to this than I thought." Jennifer summarized the meeting on the way back to the Arcadia dormitories. Meanwhile, the flurries gave way to a remarkable sunset that perfectly capped off the day. As they ascended the stairwell, she explained how Stafford had been in a similar position at one point, and how the master-at-arms is far more than just a "Navy cop." She went on for so long that Alex eventually had to butt in.

"It sounds like your mind's made up. Are you really going to join the military *now*?" She unlocked their door and they walked in, with Alex slumping down on her bed.

Jennifer leaned against her desk and struggled with Alex's pronouncement. "I don't know. I wanted to at least try to get through the semester, but now all I can think about is getting out of here." Her roommate's face sank a little upon hearing this, so Jennifer tried her best to calm her nerves. "I will make you a promise right here, right now. I'm gonna sit on this for a few weeks and think about it. While that's happening, you and I will buckle down and study like we've never studied before. I will finish this year with passing grades across the board, even if they are only Cs. I won't make a decision until we get closer to the end of the semester. Deal?"

Alex did not like most of this deal's conditions, but if it meant helping her friend, she had little choice. "Deal. But you need to get ready.

We've only got a few months to get you back to where you need to be, and we're running out of time." She checked her watch. "Grab your books and meet me in the library." She rose to leave.

"Wait, right now? We haven't even had dinner!"

"That's your fault. *You* wanna be G.I. Jane, not me." She took her notebook with her and went down the hall, leaving the door open.

Jennifer could not help but smile, grateful they had been thrown together as roommates.

Alex... I really don't deserve you.

Jennifer stuffed three textbooks, a notepad, and a laptop into a backpack. She tossed in the mint cookies and made her way after Alex. She would think of this as a sort of educational boot camp. The time for perfunctory studying was over.

THURSDAY, 15 MARCH 2007

The next month saw Jennifer spend more time in a library than she ever had before, with Alex right by her side, though it was quite an uphill struggle for the budding thespian. The two spent countless hours each night and on the weekends with Jennifer's theater history and Shakespearean performance coursework. They made occasional forays into the nuance of method acting when they needed a reprieve from the endless sonnets and advanced concepts present in the textbooks. Despite Jennifer's intense disdain for how she was spending her free time as a nineteen-year-old college student, she had decided to power through the rest of the year, even forgoing a return home for spring break so that she could prove to everyone—but mostly herself— that she could commit to something and see it through. Alex, on the other hand, already had her tickets purchased and was leaving for

Florida the next morning. Jennifer understood, yet she did not want to see her go.

As usual, the two were hunkered down in the library after dinner, hard at work preparing Jennifer for what lay ahead in the weeks to come. "Anything fun planned for the break?" The question came out strained, colored by jealousy over Alex's getting to go home and by concern over how her studying would fare in her absence.

"Um, going to the beach, seeing the family, having a few drinks at my sister's house... Not thinking about this place at all." Alex made an immediate "I didn't mean it that way" face, her eyes growing wide. She did not intend to imply that tutoring her roommate was a burden.

Jennifer was smart enough to see through the Freudian slip. Her look said it all. "Hey, I get it—it's fine. No one wants to be shackled like this, studying till all hours, not going out. It used to be just because I wanted to think about acting. Now... it's only because I want to finish the year with my head above water. Thanks to you, that just might happen." She placed her hand on Alex's shoulder, grateful for the help.

"You're gonna get there. I'm just pointing you in the right direction."

"On that note, can we take a break? My brain hurts." They had been going strong for hours, and Jennifer could only handle so much before frustration set in, especially when the topic was the Bard.

"Yeah, sure. We'll come back in twenty minutes and keep going." Alex closed her notebook and rose from the table.

"Can we make it thirty? I gotta call my mom; today's her birthday." She gestured with her phone to emphasize the need.

"Twenty-five. Be ready to pick it up again when I come back." Alex gave her a playfully stern look and walked over to the ladies' room.

Jennifer took a deep breath to calm herself. While calling her mother was certainly nothing new for her, it would be the second order of business, now that her friend had given her some momentary privacy. She fished around in her purse and retrieved a small, white card, typed a text message to the printed number, and held her thumb over the Send button. Closing her eyes and holding her breath, she finally pressed it:

> Hi, Petty Officer. It's Jennifer Kowalski. Can we talk?

MONDAY, 14 MAY 2007

"Suck on that, bitch!" Jennifer's elation at seeing her grades spoke for itself, and she felt completely vindicated in her use of obscenity. Alex beamed along with her friend; tutoring Jennifer had driven her own grades upward and earned her a spot on the Dean's List. But the mutual joy soon morphed into a harsh reality check. "I never thought I'd be this happy to see so many Cs."

"So, that means we're one day closer, doesn't it?" Alex asked, with a look of concern for Jennifer that was not going to fade so easily. "This time next year, you will have *sailed* so many seas."

Nice pun, Alex.

"Yeah. I suppose it does." In the months prior, Jennifer had taken the steps needed to commence the enlistment process. Other than getting poked and prodded by a male doctor after a restless night in a two-star hotel, it was not that bad. Her mother and stepfather were supportive, but she could detect the disappointment in Evelyn when she broke the news to her in a video call over spring break. She had a feeling her mother might put away the better part of a pitcher of margaritas once they hung up. Her father, in contrast, was completely behind her decision, even going so far as to start volunteering at the USO since then.

Tonight, however, there was no room for dreading what the unknown future might hold for each of them. "Hey! No more of that talk for the rest of the day. I passed all my classes, and you got me there, so dinner's on me tonight. Let's head downstairs before it gets too crowded." Having achieved academic invincibility, they settled on celebrating over victory pizzas at the student center.

The atmosphere was an odd combination of somber and joyful, depending on the fortunes of those at each table, but especially so at

Alex and Jennifer's corner booth. They split a half sausage and bacon, half cheese pie (out of respect for Alex's vegetarian diet), while other students in the vicinity likewise enjoyed a well-deserved break from the cafeteria's usual bill of fare. After a few bites, Jennifer tried to lighten things up a bit by drawing her friend's attention to the cute guy working the register. But it was to no avail. Alex barely acknowledged the effort. Things would grow far worse if someone did not say something soon.

"So, now that we're done, how much longer will you be sticking around school?" The question was routine, but Jennifer was desperate to see her friend climb out of this funk.

"My parents said they'd pay for a cruise if I maintained an A average for the year. They'll probably upgrade me to a suite when they hear I made the Dean's List." Her tone softened and her eyes danced a bit with the realization of her prospective reward, but her friend knew another nudge was needed. Jennifer's mind shifted into overdrive, and she glanced down at the receipt from their dinner, the solution presenting itself.

"You know... that guy at the register was checking you out when we ordered. You have his name—" she held up the receipt "—so the first part's over. Why don't you go talk to him?" It seemed a tad unlikely that this would work, but she went for it all the same. Alex had not had much success in the romance department, and it was Jennifer's turn to help her.

"Jen... no offense, but he has a job with his name on his shirt." She continued eating, totally oblivious to what she had just said. Jennifer capitalized on the error immediately.

"Um, in a few weeks, *I* will have a job with my name on my shirt, and even a name tape on my ass, apparently."

Alex's eyes grew wide at the thoughtlessness of her words. "Shit, I'm so sorry, it's just... you're leaving, the school year's over, so much is changing. I'm just not myself right now. It'll pass."

Taking a mock tone of haughty offense, Jennifer channeled her inner actress. "Well, I've *never* been so insulted in all my life!" She continued with all the subtlety of a chainsaw, "I may never overcome this flagrant rudeness and wanton disregard for my feelings! The only way for you to *try* to make amends is to get that cashier's number, and bring it back here as proof. I'll accept *nothing* less!" Her antics drew the attention of some nearby students, who were glad to see that the scorned-friend routine was all an act.

"Alright, alright... I'll get his number. But I won't call him."

"We'll see. Say hi to..." she squinted at the grease-stained receipt, "Dominic for me." And with that, Alex was off to meet the cashier. Jennifer sat back smiling from ear to ear, taking a moment to marvel at her handiwork before finishing off the last of her beverage.

My work here is done.

TUESDAY, 5 JUNE 2007

An authoritative voice bellowed out over the parking lot, "If you are a recruit bound for O'Hare and the ride to Great Lakes, which means all of you to my left, you have approximately ten minutes before you will board the van and depart the area. Please say your goodbyes now, and be ready to go when the driver shows up. Thank you." The Joliet recruiter was considerably less cordial than Stafford, but he had a schedule to keep and a slew of new recruits to ferry to Chicago. Jennifer, in her minimalist attire of blue jeans and a black T-shirt, took the cue and headed over to her father's car for her final words to him as a civilian. The others followed suit, exchanging teary hugs and handshakes with their respective clans.

Mike Kowalski sat in his '91 Subaru, desperate to avoid eye contact with Evelyn across the lot. Even though they had been divorced for nearly fifteen years, he never fully overcame the loss of his marriage to Jennifer's mother. He quickly opened the door as Jennifer approached.

The gravity of the situation brought him to tears as he hugged his precious daughter. He fought to hold them back. "I'll write you every day.

I guess that's one more good thing about being unemployed," he half-joked. He had not worked steadily in a decade, but Mike never let it bring him down. His long-standing friendship with Mr. Johnny Walker kept him on an even keel. While Jennifer could not recall the last time her father told her that he was going out on a date, she did, however, remember him claiming that the chorus to ELO's "Evil Woman" was about her mother whenever it played on the classic hits station.

"Thanks, Dad. I'll write when they give us time, but I don't know when that'll be."

"It's alright, Jenny. I know you'll make me proud." He continued hugging until he felt her start to break away.

"I gotta go say bye to Mom."

Mike pursed his lips at the mention of his ex-wife, but he knew he had to let Jennifer go to her. "I love you, Dad. Thank you for everything."

"Tell her I said hi. Oh, and I won't forget that you came to see me first!" His expression was glorious as he waved goodbye to his child.

"Yeah, I'll be sure to leave that part out," Jennifer mumbled to herself. She hurried over to the other side of the lot toward her mother's Lincoln Navigator, no doubt a gift from her husband.

Real fucking classy, Ethan. Dad's car is almost as old as I am, and you show up in this.

The doors opened, and her mother and Ethan made their way near the vehicle's grill. Her mother's makeup was running from the preemptive tears, and her repeated attempts to fix it had failed spectacularly. "We both love you so much, Jen..." She went off into a weepy soliloquy.

Ethan stood by in his Desert Storm Veteran ball cap and anxiously awaited his turn, finally butting in, "We couldn't be more proud of you for doing this. Joining up at a time of war takes a lot of guts." His attempt to sound like General Patton achieved the same success as Evelyn's cosmetic touch-ups, but Jennifer knew he meant well. It would only be a few more minutes until she was forever released from the drudgery of living under his roof.

"Thank you for helping me with school. And like I said, I *will* pay you back once I can set up the payments and—"

Ethan held up his hand before she could even utter the remaining words. "Don't worry about that. You just focus on getting in there and getting through boot camp. We'll talk about the money later."

God, could you be any more transparent?

"Alright. Later it is."

Her mother continued to weep silently as the van appeared from off in the distance, and Jennifer seized on the opportunity to curtail this show of emotion. "Well, that's my ride," she said lightly. "I just hope they don't charge us for the trip."

Evelyn chortled slightly at this remark, but the waterworks continued to operate. Jennifer gave her and Ethan a final hug before taking her one bag and boarding the vehicle. She looked back through the window as the van left the parking lot, bound for a simultaneously known and unknown destination. With an hour to ponder her decision, Jennifer's mind began to race.

This is it. No more bullshit, no more waiting. I am in the van, and we are headed to the airport. Please... let the next two months go by quickly. I hope I hear from Alex first, so I can hear more about Dominic. She said she's never been with a guy like him before. I hope she likes him. What'll I have? No Starbucks, no phone, no Xbox... nothing. I'll survive. I always have. Not crazy about the group showers, but it's better than smelling like ass the rest of the day. I hope the instructors aren't too insane. The last thing I want is that guy from Full Metal Jacket *running things. I can't wait to handle those weapons and do something tactical! I need to write to Stafford, as well. I may be shipping out under Petty Officer Stane, but she'll always be my recruiter.*

She dug her iPod out of the bag, plugged in the headphones, and closed her eyes, calmed by the melodic tunes of her favorite artists. She then untied her shoes and slipped them off, hoping that she would awaken in time to quickly put them back on once they arrived at the passenger loading zone. A mere five minutes had lapsed since the van took the on-ramp and made its way toward the Windy City.

Let's do this.

CHAPTER 4

FRIDAY, 24 JANUARY 2003

THE AFTERNOON AIR was chilly on Watkins Field as the bulk of the 44th Military Police Company stood in formation, upholding one of the Army's great traditions: the deployment ceremony. In one week, the unit would depart Fort Lewis and begin its year-long rotation at Camp Udairi in Kuwait, supporting the massive buildup of forces preparing to invade neighboring Iraq. The soldiers looked as sharp and crisp as ever, with their pristine service jackets and black berets conveying the image of a crack unit ready to bring the fight to the enemy. Among them stood Specialist Knight, with DeVaughn and Rabinowitz dispersed among the ranks as well.

Captain Llamas stood on the stage before his troops, commenting on how appreciative he was for their sacrifices at the base, and how much more would be required of them. "For fifteen months, our nation has been engaged in a campaign against those who attacked us on our own soil and brought about the deaths of thousands of Americans. To aid in that effort, we have been called upon to deploy to a region known for its hostility to Western forces, as our nation prepares to mount another campaign to liberate a country that cannot liberate itself. The 44th will provide direct combat support to the brave men and women serving on an invisible front line as they prepare for what lies ahead." At this point, he turned to another officer on the stage and continued, "Chaplain Langford, I hope I'm not stealing anything from your benediction, but I am going to borrow a quote from Eisenhower for this next part: 'Let us all beseech the blessing of Almighty God upon this great and noble undertaking.'" The chaplain flashed a hearty smile and a thumbs-up at Captain Llamas.

"Soldiers of the 44th, our task is clear, our mission is clear. Let's get it done."

Those gathered in attendance applauded the captain's speech, and Knight found himself rather motivated by the remarks, though part of him wished he was deploying to Iraq instead. His family, by contrast, was already terrified at the prospect of him going anywhere near an active combat zone, let alone two of them, but as he pointed out to them, he did enlist voluntarily.

The chaplain took the stage next to deliver his closing prayer, and with that, the ceremony was complete. All that remained for the rest of Knight's day was to further prepare for his departure, but he had already checked all the boxes on his list of tasks, so he tried to get his friends to join him at the local watering hole for a drink. "Guys, it's our last free weekend for a year—a year! You can't seriously wanna stay in tonight. D., whaddya say? First round's on me." Only an idiot would turn down free drinks.

"My girlfriend has a special evening planned for us, so, no. Getting laid's more important than getting drunk, especially since it won't be happening for *a year*."

Or not. Smart man.

"Hard to argue with that. And you, Rabbi? Anything fun planned for tonight?" If anyone was up for a wild Friday night, it had to be Rabinowitz. The guy had once drunk so much that he tried to set a personal best for breaking as many of the Ten Commandments as possible in one sitting. It was a night to remember—just not for him.

"My temple is throwing me a farewell Shabbat dinner tonight, so I'll be there. They should have some Manischewitz if you want."

The invitation was thoughtful, but Knight was not a fan of anyone's wine, no matter how culturally relevant. It seemed that the evening was open to all manner of skullduggery, so he accepted his friends' justifications and began to envision a spectacular final hurrah involving himself, a bar, and, ideally, some good times that he would likely have difficulty recalling. It was not normal for him to be off on a Friday *and* Saturday, so Knight was eager to take advantage of the occasion. Since General Order Number 1 forbade the consumption of alcohol while deployed, he had an additional impetus for wanting to cut loose.

Looks like it's just me.

He left the parade field and made his way back to the barracks to change clothes and begin his quest for diversion, stopping at the chow hall for a quick takeout plate on the way. Though made by the Army, the food was still free, and Knight was no millionaire. He ate in the lounge on his floor and called the on-base cab service for a ride to Callahan's, a pub about two miles away and his favorite haunt. Leaving a generous tip for the driver, he closed the door, drank in the sight of the neon-green marquee, and could not help but chuckle at the motif. The name implied a sort of Irish atmosphere, especially with a shamrock serving as the apostrophe and the waitresses dressed in short kilts, but it was also the kind of place that had "Taco Tuesday" every week and was owned by a Japanese man named Yamato. At least the bartender was incredibly hot, and she seemed to enjoy his company.

He made his way to the door and greeted the hostess with a look of confidence, explaining that he would be sitting at the bar, and he took a seat by the support beam. Sure enough, that bartender was working the early shift, and she was looking as ravishing as ever, though her duty of slinging drinks meant that she did not have to wear the official tartan of Clan Callahan. She was decked out in solid black from head to toe, her satin blouse concealing what Knight imagined as the pinnacle of physical perfection. The top two buttons were unfastened, and her jet-black hair was expertly pulled back with decorative chopsticks, the combination of which was so alluring that he had to force himself not to stare. His previous attempts at securing Amy's number had all failed, but for some reason, tonight felt different. He ordered a shot of tequila with salt and lime, threw it back with ease, and requested another, thinking that she might be impressed with his ability to hold his liquor.

She's a bartender. Think harder.

"Amy... you're looking as lovely as ever tonight. How have you been?"

"Not too bad. The manager took me off second shift, so now I won't have to be up all night. I can't complain." She multitasked their conversation like a pro, making numerous adult beverages and cashing out two customers' tabs as they wrapped up their evenings.

Knight could not help but be impressed with her prowess, but his mind was still elsewhere, and the night was young. How would he get this woman to talk to him about more than just work and cocktails? Thinking for a moment, he tried a new approach.

"Care for a drink?" he asked.

"I'm pretty sure that's my line, Rick. How's work been? You arrest anyone lately?" Her concentration on pouring drinks and remaining completely unattainable must have required immense practice, but she pulled it off as though it was as normal as breathing.

This would require a herculean effort if he was to add "bedding a stunning bartender" to his list of pre-deployment undertakings, and he was certainly willing to take on the challenge. How could he not be? Amy had been the focus of his desire since he saw her on his twenty-first birthday late last May. That she was a few years older than him was not an obstacle in his mind.

"Not since Thanksgiving break, but you never know. Someone could cross the line before next Friday." He paused, then added, "Did you hear that my unit is heading out soon?" He tried to add an air of mystery to his question, looking away as he uttered the words and hoping she would be the slightest bit intrigued. Yet, when he looked back, her eyes were glued to the glasses in front of her that would soon hold the Long Island Iced Teas ordered by table six.

Wait, did she pause? Her hands stopped moving, and she glanced over here for a sec.

"You're leaving? No, I hadn't heard that." She placed the drinks on the counter and turned her attention back to him. "Does that mean you'll end up in Iraq at some point?" Her eyes softened momentarily as concern grew for this man and his company. Knight was not one to try the "I might not make it back" routine, especially since his destination was hardly a haven for Saddam loyalists, and Amy was a very intelligent woman. This current path *might* be the right one.

"Kuwait. It's a one-year tour, but who knows? Maybe they'll need to pull a few of us north for support. Pretty much everyone is going to Kuwait to start with, and then the front-line units will cross into Iraq at some point, if the war actually kicks off, that is."

"If?" She raised an eyebrow at this point. "You don't think it'll happen?"

"Just trying to be optimistic. Even if the whole thing is called off, they may move us over into Afghanistan to help out there. Either way, I'll be without the services of the world's most beautiful barmaid, and that's more than enough to make me want to stay here a little longer," he said with his gaze lingering on hers. She returned his compliment with a brief laugh. He could have been wrong, but it seemed as though something was hidden behind her expression.

"Well, Specialist Knight—Specialist, correct?" He nodded in affirmation. "You're stepping up to the plate and heading out to fight for us, so on behalf of a grateful nation, you have my thanks," she said, gently placing her hand on his as her ruby lips parted to reveal the brightest smile he had seen in years. Her hand remained on his for longer than he had expected. "Now, if you're looking for some companionship before you go, there are two girls from Alpha Delta Pi over there, and I know for a fact that the blonde is *really* into Army guys." She motioned with her head toward the jukebox at the duo doing shots and laughing. Knight could not help but appreciate her attempt to be his wingman, even if she did not immediately take the bait. After all, the blonde was quite a looker, with her tight shirt, even tighter jeans, and perfect, college-girl figure. Was Amy really not interested in him, or was she making him work harder? Knight was hardly a Don Juan, but the last year had seen his most successful period in the dating game in his young life, and yet this lady had eluded him since they met.

"I'll keep that in mind, but I'm not interested in her." The direct approach. This will work.

"I know." She had the allure of a Siren. "You're a nice guy and you always leave a good tip, but soldiers just aren't in the cards for me. You show up, you stay here for a couple of years, and then you're gone. And don't even get me started on the guys who are here just to bag the barkeep. I mean, look at you—you're about to leave, and you're trying to take me home and fuck me."

"Hey, give me a little credit, okay? I was hoping we could go to your place because my roommate would make things a tad awkward." He hoped his smirk and jocular tone would smooth things over, but she seemed as though she had had this exact conversation before, and more drink orders were pouring in. She grabbed a bottle of Patron and leveled off a shot in a matter of seconds.

"Rick... it's not going to happen." Her tone was consolatory, but also sounded fairly final. "Here. This one's on me." She handed him the shot glass, gave him a final smile, and walked through the double doors to the kitchen as another bartender took over.

This one was nothing like Amy. And it was a guy.

Well, that sucks.

Knight took the shot glass and finished off its contents in one go, placing it inverted on the bar and making his way toward the jukebox. Striking out was nothing new for him, but when you have had a chance to bat in the big leagues, nothing makes you want to play anywhere else again... except maybe that blonde with the military fetish. Even after three shots of tequila in a fairly brief span, he had yet to feel the full effect of his choices, but something was keeping him tied to the bar, some unseen force telling him to return to his seat, so he walked back over and sat down. He kept his eyes focused on the door to the kitchen, ever hopeful that she would return, but he also glanced over at the sorority girls every so often. He may have failed with Amy, but he was still human, and they were still quite lovely. After another round of conversation and Long Islands (as it turned out, this was table six), both of them were living the high life, and Knight began to wonder where they would go next. That was, until, the blonde apparently hit her limit and had to run to the ladies' room with her friend in tow. He could only imagine what was going on in there and he certainly did not want to dwell on that image for long.

It was then that Amy returned from the kitchen and saw Knight, still seated and waiting for her... and then she smiled like she had before when she touched his hand. He returned the gesture, hoping she would pick up on the fact that he had turned down what was, no doubt, a sure thing in favor of more time with her, even though it would lead nowhere.

No words were exchanged, but he could tell that it meant something to her.

Knight remained at the bar for another hour, ready to call it a night, when he felt a hand on his shoulder. A familiar face leaned in close to his ear, and a dusky voice whispered, "Meet me outside." He looked back in time to see Amy walking toward the door with her purse in hand and, understanding the importance of following orders, he hurriedly paid his tab and departed Callahan's for the final time that year.

SATURDAY, 25 JANUARY 2003

Knight's eyes struggled to remain closed as the morning sun broke through the blinds in the bedroom. He had little recollection of where he was or how he had arrived there. The bed was certainly larger than his, the blankets were much frillier, and the warmth of the body next to him was a welcome change of pace compared to his average post-sleep routine. The desire for more rest competed with flashes of what had happened after he left the bar: following Amy to her car, cracking jokes on the way to her apartment, drinking Jack and Coke as she tried to catch up to him.

He gingerly sat himself up against the headboard and took note that she was still asleep and was probably still undressed, though he did not pull the covers back to verify. Desperate not to ruin the moment, he kept his eyes closed and slowed his breathing as more scenes from their time together began to form. The next parts were even hazier, though he definitely remembered his cock in her mouth, him tearing her bra off and tossing it across the living room... then the bed, and he recalled the way she moaned as she rode him to a long-overdue release, her legs shaking in its aftermath. He hoped that other events from the evening would become clearer with time. Regardless, it was a night he would relive in his mind for years to come.

He could feel the headache beginning to intensify, so he quietly retreated from the bed, put on his shirt, and tiptoed to the kitchen, where he poured a glass of water and slowly sipped it down. He filled a second glass from the cabinet and found some aspirin, taking two for himself, and brought the rest back to the bedroom. He placed the glass and pills on Amy's nightstand as she began to stir.

"Thanks. I like it neat," she mumbled, her eyes barely open. Then she began to rub her temples with both hands, so Knight handed two pills to her, and then the glass, though she needed to sit up to take them. She pushed herself up in the bed, and the blanket fell from her torso, exposing her flawless breasts to the chilly air in the room.

Knight's eyes nearly popped out of his head. No blurry vision or residual alcohol could possibly cause him to forget that sight. "You are so fucking sexy..." That was all he could say under the circumstances. Between a hangover, having mental access to mere flashes of his greatest sexual escapade, and anticipating a long "this was a mistake" discussion, he could only come up with the most pedestrian of statements, even though he had just made love to Venus herself.

Despite their physical connection the night before, she still felt compelled to keep herself covered in his presence, and quickly drew the blanket up and over her body.

"Thanks," she said, simultaneously demonstrating gratitude for and rejection of his compliment, most likely a side effect of her years tending bar and dealing with drunken patrons. She swallowed the pills and downed the water quickly, then asked if he would get her another glass. He returned a few moments later with the glass full, and this one had a drinking straw from the receptacle near the sink. She sipped slowly and closed her eyes, laying her head back on the headboard as what Knight supposed was guilt and shame overtook her for facilitating what had happened.

He tried to head off the second-guessing. "Listen... I know you have your rules, and I-I get it. But something happened here. It was... I've never felt it before, and I have a feeling that you felt it, too. Something... different."

Her eyes remained closed as he poured himself out to her, though she managed to pry them open after a moment, struggling to look him in the eye. "Rick... last night was fun, but... don't get your hopes up. What I said still stands." She went back to the straw and continued rubbing her left temple as she sipped on the cool water.

Even after that rejection, Knight could not take his eyes off her, though his heart did ache hearing her words. It could have been because she still looked as appealing as she did the night before, but it was really because his feelings for her were more than just physical at this point. He maintained a calm demeanor while enduring both the throes of his condition and her preemptive breakup speech. He knew this was a one-time deal. But it was hard to take her comment seriously, knowing that he had brought her to climax on three separate occasions nine hours ago. "I know. I just... wish you'd reconsider, is all." He moved to the foot of the bed, placed his hands under the blankets, and began massaging her feet. "Just know that, for me, last night was incredible—the parts I remember, at least." He grinned through the headache and continued his task. She closed her eyes and smiled at his generous act. Though both knew it would not go anywhere, neither really wanted this moment to end, Knight especially. But it had to end.

They talked a little longer about what they remembered, like how she had changed her mind about taking him home when she touched his hand, and how she may have spiked the sorority sisters' drinks with a small spritz from her inhaler to engineer their departure, but she would not definitively admit to that one.

A light breakfast of toast followed, but both found it difficult to eat their entire portion, so they forced down more water instead. Knight finished getting dressed while Amy took a shower, and he took in the sights of her apartment, impressed with himself for finally making it inside. She worked at a pub near the base, but she appeared to be doing well for herself, much better than he was, at least. Maybe she had a second job? Did they discuss that at some point? He thought she had said something about a lawyer, but that was multiple drinks ago. Her living room was quaint but well-furnished, and her bachelor's degree in sociology was displayed prominently on the wall leading to the bedroom. She emerged from the bathroom fully dressed, including her shoes, and both were out the door within minutes.

As she drove him back to Fort Lewis, Knight continued to pursue the prospect of them working as a couple one day. "So, this rule about soldiers... how firm are you on that?" He kept his tone light, so he could claim it was a joke if he had to.

"Very. It's not that I don't have the time for it, but you're twenty-one and you're about to leave the country. It only underscores what I said about us dating. I work two jobs, I'm paying off all this college debt... it just won't work, Rick. I'm sorry."

We could be great together, you know.

Knight sighed. "Alright. I still think you're wrong about that, though."

He signed her onto the base, and she dropped him off in front of his barracks, offering him a goodbye kiss on the cheek as a parting gift. Then she said farewell and drove away. Knight watched as her car disappeared down the street, wondering if she had a good time and was trying to play it cool, or if she was truly upset with herself for caving. In either case, he was ready for his first deployment to an overseas location. And while nothing stood between him and boarding the plane, he still had a persistent urge to see her once more.

THURSDAY, 1 MAY 2003

"God in Heaven... I thought *Georgia* was hot." Knight was still struggling to adjust to the desert climate a full three months after arriving, but he was not alone in that regard. Many of his colleagues from Fort Lewis, accustomed to the temperate conditions of Washington, were also contending with Kuwait's extreme temperatures, and some had even become heat casualties. Spending time in the medical tent was no picnic, however, as the boredom of life at Camp Udairi for a troop not entering

Iraq could often be worse than suffering through the hundred-degree mornings.

"Didn't you say Georgia was as hot as Kuwait?" Ritter's question was explicitly intended to get under Knight's skin, and so far, she was right on the money.

"I did, thanks. And I regret that statement entirely."

It was approaching 112 degrees, and his shift was nowhere near done. Knight removed his boonie hat, poured some water from his canteen over his head, and took a huge drink. The sun continued to pound him and Ritter while they maintained a watchful eye on the flightline. Several rows of U.S. Army helicopters stood at the ready while others transited to and from the base, off to undisclosed destinations to support the warfighters to the north, and to ferry back some of the wounded. This was one of many tasks that Knight and the rest of the 44th Military Police Company performed daily, as they had done since their arrival. It just so happened that on this day, he was pulling security on aircraft in one of the more exposed locations on the base.

Ritter, now also holding the rank of Specialist, gazed upon one of the Black Hawk helicopters as its rotors slowly sprang to life and the flight crew prepared the aircraft to depart. "You think it's supporting us, or the Marines?" Speculating on where these birds were heading helped generate conversation and made the day go by faster.

Knight pondered her question for a moment. "Marines, this time. They're operating east of Baghdad. Let's just hope he gets there in time."

"No kidding. We lost six more people in the last week." Her tone was somber. They watched the helicopter taxi down the runway and fly off into the distance. "More than half weren't even in combat," she added. Due to her computer skills, Ritter had the unfortunate duty of assisting the casualty notification network, and this gave her immediate access to Red Cross databases and field reports from the front.

"I was on gate guard when the first brigades rolled out toward the border," Knight began. "Part of me was jealous that I wasn't going with them, but then I hear stories like that. Kind of makes me grateful to be on this side of the wire. I'm trained for it—hell, we all are—but I don't know how I'd handle it. Huge firefight, explosions everywhere, just... chaos. I don't know how they do it." His own introspection caught him off-guard, and he realized how cowardly he sounded, but Ritter knew what he meant.

"I think most of us feel that way, even if we can't admit it. For all the training and preparation and shit, we're not Rambo," she said.

"Amen to that."

They continued to man their position and perform their hourly perimeter walk as the hours ticked by and the temperature rose. More choppers returned, and fewer left. It seemed that operations were leveling off for the day. Their shift ended at 1800, and they were replaced by Rabinowitz and Wilson, a soldier from Nebraska who had planned to leave the Army once his four years were complete but was forced to remain in uniform when the Afghanistan War commenced. He had no qualms about letting anyone and everyone know of his ordeal, but everybody had a story, and his was no more or less compelling than the next soldier's.

After a filling dinner at the mess tent, Knight entered the recreation center and registered for a thirty-minute session on the computer, grabbing a bottle of water out of the refrigerator on his way to the Internet café in the corner. For all intents and purposes, this "café" consisted of half a dozen desktop computers, each one positioned back-to-back on a conference table, with a connection that could be described as inconsistent at best. He fired up the system, logged into his civilian email account, and set about the task of updating his friends and family about life in Kuwait.

The war did officially kick off in mid-March, in contrast to his naïve optimism, but significant progress had been made thus far throughout most of the country. Baghdad had fallen into the hands of coalition forces, and while there were losses among allied troops, the situation was still under control. Best of all for Knight's family, his duties kept him confined to Camp Udairi and its immediate vicinity, so their fears of him becoming a combat casualty were largely tempered. He continued clicking through messages until one caught his eye. It was a week old and sent from Amy's personal email. The subject line gave him pause: *"Goodbye."*

The word jolted him from his relaxed state.

What does that mean?

In addition to her phone number, Knight had managed to secure her work email address, and he had remembered to drop her a line whenever he could. All of their correspondence had been limited to generic catch-up messages and brief words of encouragement, but he had not heard from her in some time. He assumed that she was busy with her real job and did not want to intrude on her personal business. He clicked on the message and felt his heart stop momentarily as he read her words.

Rick,

It's taken me two hours and multiple tries to write this, but I think this is the best version. The night we spent together was great for me because it had been a long time since a guy pursued me like you did. Men hit on me for free drinks and they even try to cop a feel on the nights that I have to wait tables, but you never did. Before that night at the bar, I didn't think you wanted anything long-term, which was fine, but when you told me about your deployment, it stirred something in me that I couldn't explain, and it only became stronger when I touched your hand. It was then that I knew I wanted to be with you, even if only for one night.

After you left, I went about my life and tried to forget about you, but something wouldn't let me forget. Eventually, I started feeling strange, which I thought was just me missing you, but it was something else. I went to a doctor and found out that I was pregnant, and since you're the only guy I had been with in months...

I'm writing in the past tense because I went ahead and took care of it a few days ago. I'm sorry, but I am just not ready to have a child with someone I don't really know and who couldn't even be there for the delivery. You're a good guy, but this was something I simply could not do. I hope you can understand one day.

You will eventually come home next year, but when you do, I have one request: forget that you ever met me. I just can't handle it anymore. Don't come back to Callahan's and don't try to see me again. I broke one of my rules to be with you and it came back to me in the worst possible way. Please... just let me go. It's hard enough writing this. I don't know what would happen if I were to see you again, but I do know it wouldn't be good for either of us.

I'm sorry it has to be this way.

Knight sat frozen in his seat, his stomach in knots, sweat pouring down his face, his mouth dry, his mind unable to form words. Did he just read that? Was she really...?

Jesus Christ...

The room began to spin, and he fought to maintain control of himself. He tried to drink some water, but he could not get the cap off the bottle. He stumbled out of his chair, made his way to the side of the table, and tripped over the trash can, tumbling to the floor and startling the onlookers. One of the soldiers in the tent, a medic, rushed over to his side. "Hey, are you alright? What happened?" He began checking his pulse and placed his hand on Knight's forehead.

He struggled to get the words out. "Yeah, I-I'll be okay. Just got some... bad news from back home, that's all." He did his best to hide the emotional agony he was enduring, but the medic was not buying his performance. He helped Knight into a nearby chair, unfastened the buttons on his top, and began the procedure for cooling off a heat casualty, asking him the requisite questions about hydration and his work routine. Knight was in no condition to argue, even though his current state had nothing to do with the weather. His heart was the source of the problem, not his core temperature.

He continued to sip from the water bottle with the medic by his side. The fellow eventually accepted that he was not about to overheat and helped him get back to his feet. Knight thanked him and returned to the computer, where the window was still open to Amy's email. He read it again and again, processing what she wrote, yet he was still unable to organize a coherent thought. He took another drink of water, closed his eyes, and forced himself to focus.

She was pregnant... we used protection... she never told me... I would've helped her... why didn't she tell me? We... could have... I mean, it was her call... but... Amy...

His eyes still closed, Knight rested his head on his hand, still taking in the gravity of her words and wondering what this meant for him. What he was looking forward to the most was a celebratory night out at Callahan's upon his return home. But now, he could never go back. Never again would he close down the bar with his friends or compete in the Wednesday night trivia contests. Worst of all, he would never see the one person he wanted to see most in the world.

He saved the email to a folder and logged out, unsure if he would ever be able to forget what he had read.

THURSDAY, 12 JUNE 2003

Six weeks had lapsed since Knight had read Amy's email, and the burden of this knowledge had not subsided in the least. In fact, his condition had only worsened since he left the recreation center and resumed his duties around Camp Udairi. On one occasion, he conducted his entire patrol with the safety off on his rifle. On another, he very nearly forgot to sign a chain of custody form when a soldier tried to smuggle an enemy AK-47 out of Iraq. Thankfully, no one had witnessed his absentmindedness thus far, but he knew it would eventually happen if he did not get his head together, and fight through this pain.

This week's duty roster saw him working at the post office. In addition to American forces attempting to collect wartime souvenirs in the form of Soviet rifles, their families often tried to send them contraband, like alcohol and pornography. When there was suspicion of such items in a package, the MPs were tasked with supervising the opening of the box in the presence of the addressee. It was then up to them to confiscate anything illegal for orderly disposal, and they were expecting just such an item this week. A soldier was caught drinking in his tent recently, and he had confessed to Captain Llamas that he would be receiving another shipment in time for the weekend. So, Knight and Wilson were on hand when he opened the box and removed its contents. Inside were medium-sized mouthwash bottles, about thirty ounces, and while three of them looked as though they held the mint-flavored hygiene product advertised on the label, they were actually filled with a clever concoction of vodka and blue food coloring. The fourth likely contained plain vodka. Knight took the caps off of each and smelled the contents. He was tempted to take a swig to confirm that it was alcohol, but refrained; too many prying eyes were in the area. Wilson checked the rest of the box for unauthorized items, found none, and handed the remaining contents to the soldier, walking him back to the police tent. Seeing an opportunity, Knight told the postal clerks, "I'll take care of this." The procedure for disposing of alcohol was simply to pour it into the sand in a secluded area, so it would not look out of place for him to do so.

He took the four bottles and placed them in a small box provided by the clerks, and then made his way outside toward the chapel. It was 1045 on a Thursday morning, so the tent would likely be devoid of worshipers, though the staff may be around. Knight squatted down outside the northwest corner of the tent, opened the first of the three mint bottles, and carefully poured each into the Kuwaiti desert, chuckling at the irony of the act. In a land where alcohol is strictly forbidden, here he was contaminating its soil with a prohibited substance, and he was doing so voluntarily. The second and third bottles followed easily, but there remained one more. He took the fourth bottle with the crystal-clear vodka, made sure that no one could see him, and then upended the entire container into his empty canteen, making sure not to spill any before sealing it with haste. He took several handfuls of sand and spread it over the blue liquid, covering his tracks as best he could, and then made his way back to the police tent with the bottles in the box. All he had to do now was sell what he had done.

Entering the tent, he acknowledged the desk sergeant and made his way toward the operations division, placing the box on the desk and holding up the four bottles. "These were in that guy's mail from earlier. Wilson escorted him over here after we checked for other contraband, but he was clean apart from this."

The sergeant examined the box and looked back at Knight with mild dissatisfaction. "Why are they empty?" His tone was neither accusatory nor civil, but it gave Knight a jolt.

"I— poured them out near the chapel. There's a pile of blueish sand by one of the corners. I can take you there if you want." He hoped that would suffice, considering he had a canteen full of hard liquor suspended from his web belt inside the police station.

The sergeant looked down at the box and back at Knight before shrugging and saying, "Okay. Sign here." He handed Knight a clipboard with a form attesting to the disposal of the beverages, and Knight placed his John Hancock on it without even the slightest hint that he had engaged in nefarious conduct. The sergeant took the box and handed it off to another soldier to process as evidence.

Then, as though it were any other day, Knight returned to his post with Wilson. Both men made small talk on the way there, theorizing what would befall the troop once his case went forward, though Wilson was keener on mentioning how he was supposed to be out of the Army at this point.

For fuck's sake, man. We get it—you don't wanna be here.

Knight completed his shift with the evidence still on him, thankful that he had purchased a Camelbak hydration system before he left for Kuwait. He had had his fill from the water pack on his back as he worked, preserving the canteen for later. A smug sense of satisfaction came over him as he headed toward his tent in zone one.

After securing his rifle in the locker, he walked back to the dining facility for chow, and then made his way back to the recreation tent for another look at Amy's email. Maybe she had written him back since then?

He logged in and saw that she had not sent him anything in the interim. He sighed and lowered his head in disappointment, mocking himself internally for thinking she might reach out again. She had titled the email, *"Goodbye,"* —why would she follow that up with anything? The overwhelming finality hit Knight all at once, and he fought back a tidal wave of rage and tears as he read her email once more. The outcome certainly undercut how much their night together had meant to him. If there was ever a time for a drink, this was it.

He left the tent and reached for his canteen, eager for some way to kill the pain that he was feeling. The lukewarm vodka hit his tongue with the force of an artillery shell; it tasted like lighter fluid. His face twisted as he struggled to down the delightfully illegal drink, but he took no joy in the criminality of his act. His flagrant disregard for a military-wide direct order was meant to be therapeutic, not an exercise in willful disobedience.

He continued to sip from the canteen as he pressed onward to his tent, desperately hoping that he would not pass any of his colleagues on the way there. Knight had not consumed any alcohol in months, and even the combination of a recent meal and hundreds of ounces of water in his system did not prevent the drink from going straight to his head within minutes. His concentration on walking straight and presenting a professional image was pushed to its maximum as he finally entered the tent and sat down hard on his bed.

The air conditioning aided his physical state, and he alternated between drinking from the canteen and the Camelbak for the next twenty minutes. But that did not help him in his quest to forget Amy. Throwing caution to the wind, he put his head back and turned the canteen practically upside down, guzzling the vodka and swallowing a few tears once it was empty. He capped the container and tried sipping some water as he lay down on the bed, still wearing his boots, and already regretting the idiocy of his actions. He knew he would be in for the mother of all hangovers in the morning, but for now, he did not care. He was thinking only of going to sleep, determined to avoid thoughts of the raven-haired beauty who tended bar at Callahan's.

FRIDAY, 13 JUNE 2003

The ringing in Knight's ears could have been an air raid siren or the simple beeping of his wristwatch sounding its daily alarm. At this point, either one seemed plausible. He struggled with all his might just to will his head off the pillow, but his first attempt failed. He could only imagine how his breath smelled after drinking more than a fifth of liquor in under two hours and then falling asleep, but right now, that was the least of his concerns. He had about forty-five minutes to shower, shave, get dressed, and report to the post office for his shift. And he had already wasted two minutes just trying to raise his head six inches.

Hearkening back to previous hungover mornings, he closed his eyes, felt around so that he would not injure his head, and managed to sit on the edge of his bed, his eyes still sealed shut. If he was going to do this, it would require more than he could muster at this point. Knight carefully removed his boots and socks, fighting the urge to vomit. He continued to slowly peel away the layers of his fatigues, then changed into his workout uniform and shower shoes. His sunglasses were a lifesaver as he fought his way toward the shower and made his entrance, the other soldiers tending to themselves and paying him no mind. He undressed and stood under the cool water, forgoing the usual heat in the hope that this would shock him back to his senses and help him overcome this self-imposed prison of post-intoxication.

Ending his shower, he dried off, dragged a razor across his face, and slowly returned to the tent. There, he donned a clean uniform from his wall locker, patting himself on the back for keeping a consistent laundry schedule. With his rifle slung over his shoulder and everything else ready, he took a final look in the mirror and saw just how rough he appeared. His eyes were bloodshot, the bags underneath them looked darker, and the look on his face was that of a man in dire need of help. But that would have to wait.

Knight left the tent and began the ten-minute walk to the post office, drinking as much water as he could. Near one intersection, the full scope of his poor decision was realized as he vomited into the sand, with a force so great that it drove him down to one knee. He heaved so long and so hard that his vision blurred and the only thing he could taste was stomach acid. Woozy, he spat into the ground, then rinsed his mouth with water as best he could, nearly convulsing again, and when he was finally done, he sat down and breathed deeply. Dehydration could be remedied; his preoccupation with Amy, who was still at the forefront of his mind, could not.

Silently vowing never to subject himself to this again, Knight strained to pick himself up off the desert floor, leaning the butt of his rifle into the ground for balance and finally making it to his feet. He kicked some sand over the evidence of his misconduct, sipped some more water, and continued toward his post. He could not see 100 percent clearly and nearly tripped over a tent cable, but at least he was still moving forward.

The relentless desert heat maintained its onslaught as Knight soldiered on. The post office was in his sights as he began to cross the street, but he never saw the speeding Humvee as he took his initial steps into the road. The driver swerved to miss him, catching a deep hole in the tightly packed, synthetic sand, and flipping the vehicle over twice. It landed on its side with a bone-jarring *crunch*. Knight, having recoiled from the road to avoid the collision, took measure of what just happened and hustled over to the windshield to see the driver unconscious in his seat, a trail of blood running down the side of his head.

Good God. This can't be happening.

His body suddenly cold and clammy all over, Knight grabbed the radio on his uniform and requested medical support, barely able to form the words. Others in the area who had heard the wreck flew from their huts to offer aid. Minutes later, another Humvee with medical personnel arrived, and they began to extract the soldier as Knight gave a statement to one of his colleagues about what happened. He continued to watch, even sicker to his stomach than before, as the men carefully hoisted the driver out of the open door and onto a stretcher, then placed him inside their own truck for transport to the hospital.

Is he alive? They didn't cover him...

The knowledge that he was responsible for this tragedy completely overrode the effects of the vodka. Knight knew better than to wander around the base without looking where he was going, but it was not as if there were stoplights or crosswalks out here. Massively shaken, he left the scene and made his way toward his place of duty for the day. He was not going to be much good for anything.

Knight walked into the post office to be greeted by Captain Llamas and First Sergeant Travis, the senior enlisted leader of the company. This would probably not bode well for him. The three were allowed access to a private room, and each took a seat at the table inside. Llamas and Travis both looked concerned for him, yet there was something else going on behind their eyes, something that seemed to indicate an awareness of what Knight had done, and he mentally prepared for the worst.

Llamas spoke first. "Sauerland gave us a brief on what happened. My first question is, are you okay? Did the truck make contact with you at all?" The questions were direct but sincere because he was truly worried about the welfare of one of his men, like any good leader would be.

"No, sir. I stepped out to cross the street, and he swerved at the last second. I don't know how fast he was going or—or what happened next. But the damn thing flipped over and landed like so." He reenacted that part of the incident with his hand on the table. Then, dreading the answer, he asked, "What about the driver? Will he be alright?" Knight's mind was racing about a hundred miles per hour as he fought off fear, anxiety, doubt, and the lingering effects of alcohol. He could not help but wonder whether he would be court-martialed for his part in this debacle.

Travis spoke this time, saying, "We don't know at this point. He was wearing his seat belt and his helmet, but he was going way too fast. Did you not see him when you went to cross the road?"

"To be honest, First Sergeant, I didn't see a thing." It was true; Knight's vision had dimmed. "I started heading toward here, and then he was just there, and... I saw him jerk the wheel, and then he flipped over." He kept his eyes on hers as he recounted what had happened. Leaving out the previous ten minutes when he was projectile vomiting what he had consumed the night before, he told them the full truth. Llamas and Travis exchanged glances before the latter offered some further insight.

"We just wanted to make sure you were okay. You really dodged a bullet."

Llamas piped up, "No shit. I mean, we're not exactly in the thick of it, but this was damn close to being a friendly-fire incident. I can't imagine a worse way of going out—getting taken down by one of your own." He shook his head at the notion before looking back at his assistant. "Top, you got anything else?" She said no, and both of them rose. "That's all for now, Knight," Llamas dismissed him. "Try to shake this off as best you can, but we will need you to come back to the station and fill out some more paperwork." He walked over and extended his hand to Knight, who stood and took it, providing a firm shake.

"Thank you, sir. I'll head over during lunch."

Llamas' face changed momentarily as Knight uttered these words, and he took a slightly deeper breath before releasing his hand. He looked over to Travis and nodded to his subordinate, and both left the building.

What was that about? Did I say something wrong?

CHAPTER 5

"HOW DO we address you now that you've been promoted? Are you a sergeant or a captain?" Her mother's inquiry was sincere, but woefully uninformed, especially for someone whose child had been in the Navy for two years. All Kowalski could do was laugh inside and fight the urge to label herself a fleet admiral.

"Master-at-Arms Third Class, Mom. Or MA3. Or Petty Officer Third Class. Or just Petty Officer." Kowalski's annoyed tone was starting to peek through, something that Evelyn did not appreciate yet tolerated, as she was gravely concerned for her daughter's safety. She had survived boot camp in Chicago and the master-at-arms course in San Antonio easily enough, but this was far different than the controlled environments of stateside military training. Her daughter was about to enter a combat zone for the first time, and no amount of words or layers of body armor could possibly quell her fears. So concerned was Evelyn that she had flown in for a week before the ship-out date, even though Kowalski could not get her leave request approved. Now, she was reviewing her pre-departure checklist, a staple of the deployment experience.

"Jen... this is for the family. Everyone is asking me for your address so they can send you things."

"You don't use rank when sending mail to an APO. Just have them send it to 'Jennifer Kowalski' and the rest of the address when I get it. Oh, and tell them I won't have a lot of room, so don't send anything bulky or that I can't eat."

"Right. And an APO is... what, exactly?"

"Not a clue. It's just what we use to send mail overseas."

"When will you have that?"

Jesus, mom, I have no idea. Can we please talk about something else?

"It'll be among the first things I do. They'll process me into the unit, show me to my tent, and give me my address. I'll find an Internet café on the FOB and fire it off to everyone. I'll even include Nana, for good measure." Kowalski's grandmother was nearing eighty years old and had not used a computer in years.

"*FOB*. What's that—?" This was getting ridiculous.

"Forward Operating Base," she interrupted, exasperated. "Think of it like flying out of a local airport instead of O'Hare." She hoped that analogy was clear enough, as these questions were becoming monotonous.

"Jen." The tears began to well up in Evelyn's blue eyes, and she clutched her daughter's hand. "I'm here because I am scared to death that you won't be coming back to us. You said you knew the risks, and I accepted that, but now... I just have a really bad feeling about this. I feel like something terrible is going to happen, and you're going to be gone for so long..." Her voice trailed off as she reached for a paper towel. Kowalski's barracks room at Naval Base Coronado was a far cry from their well-appointed home in Joliet, but her mother could not have cared less. She dabbed at her eyes and looked up at the ceiling, taking a mighty sniff as she fought back more tears. "Ethan and I have been watching the news every day since you told us you were deploying, and we're just worried, that's all." Her smile was there, exactly like countless others that Kowalski had seen before, but it seemed as transparent as Ethan's attempts to befriend her when they'd first met. Perhaps a more realistic approach was needed to bring things into perspective.

"Well, it could be a hell of a lot worse." Kowalski walked over to the refrigerator and withdrew a light-blue pitcher from the door. "When the war started, the Army was sending people on eighteen-month rotations. Imagine celebrating two birthdays over there!" Kowalski poured a glass of tea for her mother and handed it to her with a grin, hoping to God that this would somehow calm her down. Evelyn took the glass and pondered for a moment, sipping the cool beverage before placing the glass on the small kitchen table and reaching for the paper towel again.

"We're going to miss your birthday, aren't we?" The tears gave way to sobs as she buried her face in her right hand, her elbow propped on the table.

Way to go, Jen. Figure this out, she thought.

She tried to think quickly about how to fix this, but nothing came to mind. Evelyn, once again, was right: her daughter was two weeks from touching down in Iraq, the threat of death was around every corner, and hers was already a dangerous field in the military to start with. To make matters worse, she was going into the lion's den because she had *volunteered* for the assignment. For once, through her mother's tears and reasoning, she finally saw things through different eyes, and felt the emotions of the moment setting in.

No, no, no. I am not *doing this right now. Unless...*

Kowalski slumped down in the chair opposite her mother and, at long last, wept over her pending departure. Evelyn shifted her chair closer and placed a reassuring hand on Kowalski's shoulder, doing her best to offer comfort as her daughter cried into her own arms. Minutes passed before she lifted her head, partially dismayed at the act of shedding tears in front of her mother, and prayed for a quick end to this afternoon.

"Jen, I am so sorry. I didn't want it to go like this." She had to wipe away her own tears again before continuing, "You mean so much to me and all I want is for you to come back to us. I just can't shake these feelings I've been having..." She trailed off again.

"I know. I shouldn't have acted like that and I'm sorry, but we knew this could happen." She paused, taking a deep breath. "I have to do this."

Evelyn remained silent as her daughter made her case. She knew that there was nothing, not even her words, that could sway her daughter at this point. She could only nod, her lips pursed, before saying, "Okay. Okay... um, it's almost five. Why don't we go into town for a bit, and I'll take us out to a nice dinner? You said San Diego has a lot of great places to eat, and... I don't want to keep going like this anymore." She pursed her lips again. Her daughter sniffed and rubbed her eyes.

"That sounds like a good idea. Thank you."

Relieved, Evelyn rose from the table and wrapped her arms around her child, kissing her temple before saying, "Alright. Let me get cleaned up a little and then we'll head out." Her mother's glow had finally returned, albeit briefly.

Kowalski nodded in agreement and forced a smile as her mother retreated to the bathroom and closed the door. She rose from the table, tore off a fresh paper towel and stood before the mirror, smiling as she dried her eyes, then casually tossed the refuse into the trash. And just like that, as though nothing had happened, she was back to normal.

Still got it.

WEDNESDAY, 1 JULY 2009

Kowalski awoke aboard the C-17 flanked by all manner of international service members, some of whom were returning for their third or fourth deployments. Seated directly across from her was MA3 Jailah Hawkins, a sailor from Naval Station Norfolk and a woman who was certainly not accustomed to air travel. The flight itself was smooth thus far, but the combination of excessive engine noise, cramped conditions, and the realization that it would be a year before she returned home all made for a stressful experience. As the airborne ark burned holes in the sky, an announcement came over the intercom: "All personnel aboard Bastion Eight-Six, we will be making a tactical descent into Baghdad International Airport due to an increased threat level. Landing in approximately fifteen minutes. Make sure everything you have is secured."

Kowalski removed the headphones from her long-dead iPod and stowed both in a cargo pocket on her backpack. Being no stranger to roller coasters and with advanced knowledge of what this landing maneuver entailed, she had a diabolical smile across her face as she envisioned what was to come. She tapped Hawkins on the shoulder and mouthed 'Are you okay?' while flashing a thumbs-up. The distress on her face and endless beads of sweat dripping down her forehead told the whole story. Kowalski chuckled at her new friend's conundrum. Hawkins' eyes were about as large as the craft itself, and all she could do was shake her head in fear. Kowalski shrugged her shoulders in reply and leaned back in her seat, anxious for the "fun" to begin. She had always been an adrenaline junkie of sorts, but this was her chance to experience it on the government's dime... and over a war zone.

The minutes ticked by, and then the intercom squawked to life again: "All personnel, prepare to land."

The winged mammoth dropped to a sixty-degree dive before anyone could register their own name in their own mind. Kowalski could feel her stomach doing hula hoops around her head as the plane plummeted toward the Earth. It showed no sign of slowing down as many aboard audibly indicated their concern with their predicament, and a few even lost control of their midday meals, but Kowalski was loving every moment. Within sixty seconds, the plane had dropped twenty thousand feet as it made its approach to Baghdad, the pilots keeping her level and never taking an eye off their gauges. That was how it was done. They dropped the landing gear and the tires met the pavement with the familiar screech; Hawkins' nightmare and Kowalski's joyride had come to an end.

The plane taxied briefly to flee the runway, and within seconds, the cargo doors were open and all 134 troops were quickly filing off the plane, bound for various destinations in and around the Iraqi capital. Each was greeted by a blast of desert heat so intense that one man passed out as soon as he set foot outside, though the combat landing may have also played a role in his condition.

Kowalski and Hawkins made their way to the terminal and followed the signs to their staging point by what was probably a café of some kind, though it seemed that an explosion had recently turned it into a gazebo. The sailors were met by a soldier who was far too handsome for life in the Middle East, yet here he was.

He promptly called them out for not following protocol despite the MA patches displayed prominently on their sleeves. "When you're in country, keep a weapon on you at all times. Get your pistols out and holsters on, load and sling the rifles—you're in Iraq! Those fuckers out there don't give a shit if you're a woman." The sailors opened their weapons cases and did just as he said. Kowalski's holster fit snugly around her right leg, and she felt a rush as she smacked the loaded magazine into the M9 pistol. Hawkins followed suit as the soldier further filled them in on their new reality: "We're about to go to Victory, outside the airport perimeter. So, while we're out on the convoy, it's weapon status Red. Keep a round chambered, safety on. Let's move!"

The women sealed the cases, grabbed the rest of their gear, and followed the guide to a motor pool by a side door. The heat was such that the glass doors did little to shield the interior from the humidity. But the protective concrete walls opposite the airport did offer some peace of mind. They loaded their bags into the seventh vehicle and took their seats inside the Humvee, as Sergeant Collins, their escort, took the passenger seat, with the self-assurance of a seasoned veteran. The soldier atop the Humvee in the gunner's turret remained ever-silent as he scanned the horizon, keeping both hands on the .50 caliber machine gun and not even acknowledging the passengers at his feet. The remaining vehicles took on more personnel and cargo before the call rang out on the radio: "All units, this is Hammerhead One. Prepare to depart the area." Collins turned his head to the left. "Get ready." His tone was ominous, as though the Grim Reaper himself lay ahead.

This guy has seen some shit. I hope he gets to go home soon.

The radio came to life again. "All units, move out—proceed to destination."

The lead vehicle slowly moved forward, and Kowalski's truck followed the one ahead, with the remaining fourteen vehicles completing the series of up-armored Humvees, each one ferrying new arrivals to this ancient land. They rounded the first curve, and Kowalski had never felt more on edge as she saw what the war had done to the area: blown-out buildings, the charred remains of vehicles abandoned on the sides of the roads, giant potholes from mortar attacks. The people here could hold elections and no longer had a psychopath as their president, but even something as routine as going to the market now carried the risk of death. If that was freedom, what had life been like before?

The truck rounded the next curve with ease and then mimicked the lead vehicle, picking up speed along the straightaway and barreling toward the next turn. All along the way lay more evidence of an ever-present insurgency. At least they were moving quickly.

Fast is good. They can't hit us if they can't catch us.

The convoy made one final turn to the right, maintaining the steady rate of speed set by the lead vehicle. At the main gate, the guard had the barricade open and ready as the drivers negotiated an obstacle course of concrete barricades and concertina wire. A brief conversation with Collins followed, and as quickly as it had begun, the journey was over—no bullets, no bombs, no blood. Kowalski and company had survived the trip from the airport to the FOB without a scratch, and all that remained was getting settled into their new home.

The convoy dispersed into multiple directions with Kowalski's Humvee proceeding north through a sprawling network of roads, tents, towers, buildings and—what caught her attention the most—a swimming pool. In the middle of Iraq, here was a YMCA-quality swimming pool. Hawkins was more than elated upon seeing that amenity, and her gaze lingered as someone did a backflip off the high dive and plunged into the light-blue water.

Kowalski shared her interest. "That'll be a relief once we get a day off. If our schedules line up, we can go together," she said.

The truck stopped outside a makeshift command post labeled, Naval Support Activity Baghdad, and Collins helped the duo unload their bags and weapons cases before offering his best wishes to the pair. "Welcome to Victory. Don't get killed." They nodded silently in response before his truck drove away, then both gathered their belongings from the desert floor. Hawkins wondered aloud if they would ever see him again.

Never one to miss an opportunity, Kowalski ran with it. "Wow. Twenty minutes on the ground, and you're already planning your first date. I think we passed a coffee stand on the way here, so if you play your cards right..."

Her colleague playfully whacked her on the shoulder and gave her one of those "what do you expect" looks. "...Hello? The guy's practically a model! Did you see his cheekbones? That caramel skin? And he's obviously been here a while. I think I could learn a few things from him." Hawkins tried to play it off as though she meant that in a solely professional context, but Kowalski was not fooled.

Her eyes twinkled. "I played matchmaker in college and those two are still together. Let me work my magic with you, and we'll see how it goes," she said, sporting a look of earned credibility. "If I bump into him again, I'll see what I can do for you." Hawkins seemed mildly embarrassed, but knew her friend bore only good intentions.

They walked inside the hut, reported to the petty officer at the desk, and handed him copies of their deployment orders. He checked the papers and their IDs, matched them against an inbound personnel roster, and said, "Hawkins and Kowalski. It's good you finally made it. We need all the help we can get with security, and two more MAs can't hurt." He grabbed his hat and a large ring of keys before directing the sailors to leave through a door at the back of the hut. Then he led them toward a fortified area west of the Navy headquarters.

Behind a walled-off section with concrete barriers standing twelve feet tall was a tent city, and each shelter was lined with row after row of sandbags that went up to Kowalski's waist. The sun continued to beat upon them mercilessly as they strode through the housing area, finally making it to their section near the corner. Their guide motioned to the door and said, "This is you for the next year. It's a female-only tent, so I'm not allowed inside, obviously. Go in and claim your racks, drop any gear you don't need, and meet me back here in ten minutes. The shower building's over there if you need to use the head."

The ladies entered the tent and found two unoccupied bunk beds in the center, and linen bags marked "Property of U.S. Army" on the aisle side of the mattresses. They placed their sea bags in the accompanying foot lockers, secured them, and then took a moment to soak up exactly where they were, and what was about to unfold. "A year ago, I was in

Virginia watching someone get demoted for underage drinking," Hawkins said, waxing nostalgic. "How about you?"

"Coronado. Checking IDs at the gate and wishing I was anywhere else. I am *so* over that part of the job." She knew she sounded rather uppity, but when you are meant to appear on the silver screen, any other form of employment seems degrading.

"You said it." Hawkins looked around and took a deep breath. "We still have a few minutes." She walked over to where Kowalski was standing and looked directly at her, her tone becoming very serious. "I've been in for two years, and this is my first time overseas. No one else from my unit is here, and I don't know anyone but you—and we just met a few days ago. I don't know what's gonna happen out here, but I'll tell you this: if you watch my back, I'll watch yours. Okay?" She sounded much graver than Kowalski was expecting, but under the circumstances, it made sense. The safety and comfort of their previous assignments no longer applied. Even though the security situation today was better than it had been in 2005, Iraq remained an active theater of war, and people were still dying.

"I've got your six, Hawkins. This is a first for me, too. We'll get through it." She placed a hand on her new associate's shoulder and looked her squarely in the eye.

They stood silently for one more moment before turning to leave the tent. Then they put on their issued sunglasses, opened the door, and stepped out into the blinding sunlight of Baghdad. There, they waited out front for the petty officer to return.

This was it. Their tour had officially begun.

MONDAY, 31 MAY 2010

Thirty days and a wakeup. That was all that remained between Kowalski, and the end of her stay in Saddam's sandbox, though it was hardly fair to say that the experience had been completely awful. She and Hawkins had grown quite close as friends. They had met Arnold Schwarzenegger when he visited the base with the USO, and Hawkins had shared Kowalski's pride in receiving a coin of excellence from the Secretary of Defense when he toured the facility over Christmas. To top it all off, her workout regimen had Kowalski in the best shape of her life—so much so that she actually mustered the courage to don a two-piece bikini in a recent evening by the pool.

Her work as a force protection specialist at Camp Victory had likewise proven fulfilling. While she had occasionally enjoyed what she did stateside as a master-at-arms, her work downrange had yielded tangible results that were above and beyond anything her recruiter had described. Stafford had failed to mention, however, that the twelve-hour shifts were closer to fourteen hours in length. But the fact that she had kept in contact with one of her enlistees helped Kowalski partially forgive her for the sin of omission.

Damn it. I need to let Stafford know I'm okay.

Kowalski's duty day was nearing its end when she met Hawkins outside the Green Beans coffee kiosk during her break, though it was hard to fathom enjoying a hot beverage in the sweltering summer heat of central Iraq. But as her father would say, "It's not about the drink. It's about the company it brings."

Dad was right, but, fuck... it's hot.

Hawkins' work detail that day saw her augment a convoy as it transited between camps to resupply various brigades around the city, then had her return to pull guard duty for some local Iraqi women while they unpacked their wares at the on-base market. They did not earn much compared to their competitors in the U.S., but offering Coach bags for ten dollars apiece ensured that they would sell out within an hour. So, Alex's going-away souvenir was covered. To Kowalski, the bargains meant that Evelyn's birthday and Christmas presents were taken care of, and all the other women in her family would have conversation starters at their offices. Capitalism had prevailed once more.

She ordered an iced coffee for herself and Hawkins' usual double macchiato, which she handed to her friend as both took a seat under the circus tent–sized umbrella at their table. It did little to combat the heat, but it at least provided reasonable shade in a nation that seemed to be positioned a mile from the sun. It was a luxury to be enjoying their beverages with the knowledge that they would soon be getting their caffeine fix elsewhere. Hawkins was excited about their pending rotation back to the states, but she was also trying not to jinx it by discussing it too much, a belief that Kowalski had to actively resist mocking. A polite smile and a quick change of the subject did the job.

"So, what happened yesterday on your shift? I heard you, uh... *witnessed* some things," Kowalski said, suppressing a laugh.

Hawkins could only roll her eyes in response. "Nothing. Absolutely *nothing* happened." She continued to sip her beverage, hoping against hope that her friend was not eyeballing her.

But she was. "I see. It's just that I read the report and it said you were called to the showers during that fight between some Marines... and there may have been a little... exposure?" Her inflection went as high as her eyebrows as she said the word.

She exhaled, mildly embarrassed, before saying, "Yes, Jen, I saw some things. A whole lot of... *things*." Kowalski's laugh was audible and good-natured. She knew that her friend was shy and probably did not expect questioning half-naked men to be part of her deployment experience, but it happened all the same. Now, she had a story that would entertain for years to come.

"Did you recognize anyone?"

"Just one of the privates." Kowalski tilted her head slightly, smirking as she did. Hawkins took note, realizing what she had said. "Shit, no, I mean... it was Johnson." Somehow, she had done it again. "You know what? I think it's time for us to get back to it," she said, praying that would put the nail in the coffin on this conversation. She finally let out a laugh as Kowalski did the same.

Both sailors finished their coffee and started heading back to their respective missions. Before parting ways, Hawkins turned to Kowalski and said, "A little bird tells me next week's bazaar is gonna have Michael Kors and Gucci. Plan your lunch accordingly." She flashed a devilish grin as she turned right at the intersection and proceeded toward her post at the entry control point. Kowalski chuckled to herself as her friend and shipmate walked off in the distance.

Be safe, Hawkins.

Kowalski turned to her left and began walking back toward headquarters, passing two Air Force civil engineers using heavy construction equipment. The noise blunted the sound of the first rocket striking a building fifty feet in front of her.

The force of the explosion threw Kowalski to the ground, the subsequent high-pitched ringing in her ears signaling that she was still very much alive. The sound of sirens blaring across the area broke through. One of the engineers bolted over to Kowalski, helped her off the ground, and ran with her to a fortified shelter near the recreation center. It all happened in seconds.

More explosions could be heard as 107mm rockets and mortar rounds rained down upon the base, seeming to indicate that this was more than just indirect fire. Kowalski and the airman drew their rifles, chambered a round, and took their weapons off Safe as they waited for the "all clear" message to sound... but it never did. Additional rockets and gunfire could be heard across the camp. Kowalski was powerless to do anything about it from her current position, so she sprinted from the bunker toward the first building that had been hit, and heard the desperate cries for help from a man trapped near the rubble. An Army officer was screaming as he lay on his back, his face a bloody mess, with both arms showing signs of injury, and his right leg was pinned underneath a chunk of reinforced concrete.

The screaming continued long after Kowalski arrived by his side. She was not entirely prepared to handle this. "Help me! Get this thing off! My fuckin' leg's broken! Oh, Jesus! Oh, my God!" His cries competed with the cacophony of gunshots and explosions that shattered an otherwise peaceful day. The intensity of her heart pounding skyrocketed as she assessed the horror before her.

"Doc! Corpsman! I need a medic over here now!" Kowalski yelled at the top of her lungs. But between the wounded soldier and the chaos of the situation, no one could hear her pleas. Acting quickly, she withdrew a medical kit and began applying a tourniquet to the man's leg, though his writhing made this a nearly impossible task. She cinched the strap as tightly as she could, but more drastic action was needed. Seeing a soldier running toward the shelter, she called out to him, "Hey! Get the fuck over here! Help me with this guy!" The soldier, dazed at the attack and clearly not a combat troop, ran over to Kowalski and nearly fainted at the sight of the bloodied and broken warrior. She yelled again and smacked him on the head to get his attention. "Look, Perrin, this guy can't move, so I need you to pull that thing off his leg while I get him out from underneath. Can you handle that?" He could not peel his eyes from the soldier's blood-drenched uniform, and his hands continued to shake from the adrenaline. "Hey! Wake the fuck up! *Can you handle that?!*"

"Okay... ma'am, Petty Officer... I-I can do this. I can do this. Just... tell me what to do!" His words were as labored as his breathing, and Kowalski had serious doubts about what was going to happen. To save the soldier, they had to move fast. So, she ordered her assistant to move as much debris from around the leg as he could. His hands became a mess of sand and blood in the process, and he again seemed as though he might faint again over what he was tasked to do.

This was taking too long.

"Okay, Perrin... you are going to pull that rubble off his leg, and I am going to pull him out by his collar! Grab that chunk by the rebar, and pull with everything you've got! Do you understand?" He seemed paralyzed with fear over where this might lead. "Goddamn it, Perrin! We are going to lose him if we don't do something!"

"Alright... I'm with you!" His response did not instill a great deal of confidence in Kowalski. Nevertheless, she pressed forward, driven to save this man, and prevent another life lost.

Perrin dropped to his knees, gripped the bars protruding from the concrete slab, and pulled as hard as he could, gritting his teeth. The rubble began to move upward slowly, and Kowalski could feel the slightest bit of room to move him. She grabbed his collar with both hands and then realized just how heavy this soldier, likely an infantryman, really was. She moved him back slightly before Perrin called out to her, "Hey! This thing is slipping! Hurry!" Bracing it against the ground, he managed to completely clear it from the soldier's leg by several inches.

"Hold that up! Don't let go!" Kowalski tried to shift the man's weight with everything she had, but he would not budge. Just then, Perrin lost his grip on the rebar.

The slab came crashing down precisely on the wounded man's leg with a sickening thud, and his agonized cries became even louder and more violent. He gripped Kowalski's arms before he passed out.

She turned her horror into a reprimand. "Jesus Christ, Perrin! What the fuck did you do?" Her rage with him matched her rage with the insurgents, and she called out again for a medic—or anyone—to assist, but no one came. She scrambled to her feet, ran toward the road, and flagged down a Quick Reaction Force vehicle that was on its way to the main gate. Instantly, multiple soldiers disembarked, and Kowalski gave them a rapid overview of what happened.

The medic attached to them took over and directed the remaining soldiers to lift the rubble once more, an act they easily accomplished together. Yet it revealed the full extent of the damage: the officer's leg had been sheared off below the knee and crushed by the slab. Seeing the mangled and ruined limb, Kowalski marched over to Perrin and almost decked him. "You see that? *Do you?* He lost his leg because of you—*you!* Do you understand? What the fuck is wrong with you, Perrin?"

With his mouth dry and agape, he had no response. His breathing continued normally, but his hands were still shaking, and the vacant look in his eyes said it all.

"I... I'm just... just... a clerk. I work in the po-post office." He pointed off in the distance as his words faded. Then, he turned toward the shelter and slowly walked away.

Kowalski fought the urge to pursue him, and instead scurried over for her rifle as one of the soldiers directed her to board the Humvee. "Get in! We need you up in that tower right fucking now!" He pointed toward a perimeter gate, and within seconds, they both were speeding toward their destination. Skidding to a halt and with sand kicking up all around the truck, they quickly ascended the security tower, and prepared to take up defensive positions inside. But the building was pre-sighted, and incoming automatic weapons fire peppered the outer walls. The two dove for cover on the floor. Kowalski popped her head up briefly to look out the window and saw multiple masked men on a balcony, each armed with Soviet weaponry, motioning toward the tower and prepping another volley of gunfire.

She ducked again and relayed what she saw to her counterpart, and he grabbed a radio from the counter, calmly updating the command post.

"This is Tower 4! We have multiple tangos directly opposite our position opening fire on us. Request immediate fire support, over!" A voice replied that help was inbound.

The insurgents continued to rake the tower. A rocket-propelled grenade whizzed past, missing their position by inches. Broken glass from the window fell to the floor as the pair lay prone, trapped by a faceless enemy.

Kowalski was growing impatient. "How much longer on that support?"

"Give 'em a sec! We're not the only ones getting shot at!"

A few agonizing minutes later, they could hear the unmistakable sound of an Apache helicopter's rotors in the distance. It unleashed a barrage of gunfire on the occupied building across from the camp. The insurgents fired their weapons at the aircraft, but they were no match for its 30mm chain gun. The rounds easily shredded their bodies upon impact, and the helicopter turned and flew off to another location. The pilot came through on the radio to inform them that the area was sanitized, and both troops took up their positions again, remaining at their post until the "all clear" message finally came over the PA system.

Kowalski looked out at the building the Apache had just hit and saw the eviscerated corpses of the enemy combatants who, mere moments earlier, were trying to kill her. Her nerves still tempered and almost forgetting to breathe, she exchanged a silent look with the soldier she had holed up with, then began her descent out of the tower. Taking in the pockmarks from the shots fired into the structure, she wondered how she was still alive. The rounds really were *that* close.

What about Hawkins? Is she okay? How many died? And the officer? Is he alright?

She looked down at her watch and saw the time: 1918. Her shift had officially ended over an hour ago.

AS MIDNIGHT APPROACHED, Kowalski stood motionless underneath the shower, completely alone and indifferent to the fact that she had already exceeded the allotted time by at least thirty minutes. Memories of the day played in her mind: the morning briefing with the battalion commander, listening to the chaplain's Memorial Day message, the hours spent guarding the gate, buying coffee for Hawkins, watching a man lose his leg, avoiding hostile fire, and having to relive it all during a debrief with her chain of command. Without a doubt, an extended shower was certainly something she had earned.

Despite the relief from the steaming-hot water, Kowalski was thinking only of the soldier she had tried to rescue, and how his world was now forever altered by her actions. She probably traumatized Perrin for life over his physical weakness, yet it was she who had failed to extract the man from the rubble when it was her time to step up. The accompanying guilt washed over her like the water raining down from overhead. She glanced at her biceps and could still see the bruises from where the man's hands had clamped down on her like a Vise-grip when the slab fell, and she could only close her eyes as the battle played once more.

She shut the water off and dried herself with a towel, placing a clean physical training uniform on her body as she stared—unblinking—into the mirror, then walked the trail back to the housing area. The night had never been darker than it was then, as though the moon was in mourning for those lost. Kowalski was grateful that no one could see her face. The silence across the camp matched the darkness in its proliferation. The only sound she heard, even with the massive military presence and round-the-clock operations, was her own footsteps as she traversed the gravelly terrain in her shower shoes.

She opened the hatch on her tent and quietly stowed her shower bag in the locker by her bunk... and that was when everything came to a standstill. Hawkins' bed remained empty despite the late hour. She had not returned from her shift.

There was no stopping the tears as they streamed down her face. Kowalski removed the blanket from the top bunk and held it close, the distinctive fragrance of her bunkmate's body soap still present as she inhaled deeply. She placed the blankets on her bed, slipped her legs underneath, and laid her head on the pillow, trying in vain to avoid thinking about her friend. She checked her watch one last time to make sure the alarm was programmed to go off.

The time was 0014. Twenty-nine days and a wakeup.

CHAPTER 6

"SERGEANT KNIGHT'S superb performance and professionalism have significantly contributed to the success of his platoon and reflect great credit upon himself, his unit, and the United States Army," the emcee said into the microphone as the captain expertly clipped the medal to the left lapel on Knight's uniform. The rest of those in attendance stood at attention inside the gymnasium while the base photographer captured the moment.

The commander-directed applause was cursory, but it mattered little to the recipient of the Army's lowest decoration for meritorious service, mostly because he knew no one in the crowd personally. Knight had reenlisted while he was deployed to Kuwait, and upon his return, he received a short-notice reassignment to Fort Rucker in Alabama. Though he had hardly adjusted to life near Tacoma, he was sad to say goodbye to his friends and the familiar routine of Fort Lewis. But most of all, he hated the idea of being further separated from Amy. He honored her wish and never went back to Callahan's, but not a day went by when she did not cross his mind. The pub's website had uploaded a recent picture of all the staff members. Amy was among them, but there was something noticeably different about her.

Captain Palladino, commander of the 55th Military Police Company, walked over to the podium and took the microphone off its stand, preferring the freedom to move around as he spoke. He directed the soldiers to take a seat, and Knight returned to his spot in the front row. "For those who haven't met him yet, Sergeant Knight just recently came to us from up at Lewis, and I can already tell he's gonna do great work with us here at the 'Double Nickel.' His previous unit got back from Kuwait in March, so he should be fairly used to this heat," he said, wiping some sweat off his brow.

A few in the crowd expressed their agreement. The air conditioner was not quite living up to its expectations. For a lesser man, that might be a problem, but Knight hailed from a region not too far from lower Alabama.

Can't wait until it's seventy degrees in December, the way God intended.

The captain continued to speak at this monthly meeting, going over some items of interest with the soldiers and answering questions from the audience. Being an officer who had begun his career in the enlisted ranks, he understood the importance of keeping these functions brief.

"The First Sergeant's on leave this week, so that leaves me to wrap things up. I just got the word from my boss that we are deploying sometime next year; it just depends on who we're replacing. One company is in Iraq, the other is in Afghanistan. So, right now, all we can do is wait and see. I wish I had better info, but I don't, and you all know I believe in transparency."

Knight had just met Palladino a few weeks ago when he signed into the unit, and he was already impressed with him. His father had taught him to be honest with people whenever possible, and his new leader was doing just that at a crucial time, even though the information was scant. At least the troops now had an idea of what was coming and could inform their families.

The meeting was dismissed not long after. Knight began walking back to his car, saluting his platoon leader and plotting his course of action for the remainder of the afternoon before his shift started. This, of course, meant that his mind was going to wander back to Amy, and how their brief relationship had transpired. But like any thought tree, many branches intertwined and led him to contemplate other people he had met along the way. DeVaughn was still at Lewis with one more year remaining before he could transfer. Rabinowitz had married a woman from his synagogue and was planning to leave the Army when his contract ended. Ritter received approval to cross-train into a new job, opting to enter the world of aircraft maintenance, a rarity for women. Her class was scheduled to begin in late October.

The Army's helicopter flight school is here. Maybe she'll get assigned to Rucker?

Then there was Wilson. It seems that he had complained one too many times to the wrong person and the Army had granted his wish of an early departure, though it was under less than honorable circumstances. The last that Knight had heard, he was applying for community college in Omaha, and his success was hardly guaranteed. And lastly, there was Wallace, the soldier who very nearly killed Knight during the Humvee incident and who was then sent home due to a broken leg coupled with a severe concussion. He admitted to driving too fast for the conditions and that he did not see Knight until it was too late. But the guilt over his covert violation of the no-alcohol policy still weighed heavily on his mind. He had no doubt that with a clear head, he would have been able to cross the street without issue. Or would he? There were plenty of vehicles that traversed those roads day in and day out, but that one specific truck was speeding toward him while he was still suffering the aftereffects of intoxication, as though it was some sort of perverted divine providence. Was he supposed to be hit? Was Wallace supposed to be severely injured?

Stop. Gotta shut that down. Work starts in two hours.

He drove back to his barracks and walked up the three flights of stairs to his room, quietly opened the door, and closed it with care. The accommodations were spartan at best: one bed, one wall locker, one dresser, one desk, one nightstand—per soldier. And all of it was as modern as 1983 could produce, but having heard stories of his father's time in the Army thirty years before, Knight was not complaining. Thomas and Michelle had instilled in their children an appreciation of simple things, like a roof over one's head and clothes on one's back. So for Knight, living in a small room with a stranger was just part and parcel of the Army experience. His roommate was his age, but on the opposite shift, so they had to observe quiet hours at all times unless both happened to be awake. Specialist Andrew "Pete" Peterson, of Wisconsin, was nearing a promotion to sergeant and was spending a great deal of time preparing for his review board. Too much time, Knight thought. Unless he was missing something, Peterson was a competent soldier with an excellent record as an MP, but he tended to get nervous when speaking before high-ranking officials, and that had cost him during his nomination for Soldier of the Quarter in March.

Knight was still in a partial haze when Peterson entered the room, his shift complete. "Hey, man. How's it going?" He closed the door, dropped his backpack and began admiring his new 'do in the full-length mirror, running his hands along the freshly shorn sides of his scalp and taking a moment to enjoy one of life's simple pleasures. The two of them were alike in that regard. "Nothing like a fresh cut! I'm telling you, Reggie's the best one there."

Knight seemed to recall seeing this exact sequence of movements with high frequency, but it was Peterson's money. "Weren't you just at the barbershop, like, Friday?"

"Every two weeks. Gotta maintain standards. Speaking of, you might wanna..." He motioned with his index finger at Knight's head, prompting him to glance over at his own mirror and see that he was coming due for a trim himself. The sides had to be taken care of regularly, but he liked to leave some on top for the ladies... even though he was not exactly looking for anyone at this point. He took on a pensive demeanor before saying that he would visit the barber tomorrow before work, and his colleague took note. "It's her again, isn't it?" Knight had only given him some meager background information about Amy, but Peterson was perceptive, as all MPs are trained to be. "Look, I know we just met, but if you ever want to talk about it, I'm here." His brown eyes told only the truth of what he had just said, and his tone made clear that this was no attempt at locker room talk or a body count comparison.

"Yeah. Sure. We can do that sometime," he said, looking up at his new associate. On a deeper level, Knight was inordinately grateful to have someone to talk to about Amy. But he was not ready to go there, at least not with someone he had never met until last month. Both still had plenty of time on their contracts, though, and with a pending deployment, they would get to know each other fairly well in the months and years ahead. Knight rubbed his hands together. "I gotta get ready for work." He rose from the desk and grabbed his black tote bag, placing some personal items inside. Looking down at his watch, he realized he still had ninety minutes before his shift started.

"I wondered when you'd notice," Peterson said. "When's your next night off? And don't bullshit me; this isn't an intervention or anything. I just want us to go out and have a guys' night. Whatever you feel like sharing, I'm listening. The first two rounds are on me, plus dinner."

You really need to get a girl.

Knight answered, "I'm on the next four nights and off two after that, so I'll be free Sunday night into Monday morning." When discussing a night shift schedule, it always helped to clarify these things. "Do I also get to pick where we go?" His tone was mildly sarcastic, but also curious.

"Hell, yeah. And I'll drive."

This deal keeps getting better.

"Alright. But... no Irish places. I'll explain later."

Peterson shot him an odd look, but accepted the terms of their accord. If he was to get to the bottom of things, he would have to accommodate this unusual request.

"Just Irish? Because there's a Scottish place outside Daleville that actually has haggis on the menu." He said this with his eyes alight, as though Knight was supposed to know what haggis was *and* be inclined to order it should they go there.

"Why don't we just stick with something domestic? When I drove here from the airport, I saw a place called 'LZ Charlie' over by a Waffle House. I doubt we'll see any kilts or obscure foreign entrees there." Knight could not help but be impressed with the genius of opening a bar near a Waffle House—or was it the other way around?

By this point, Peterson had his phone out and was inputting the data into the calendar, though it would be unfair to label this device a mere "cellular telephone." It looked like something that could call in an airstrike. "Sunday, July 18th, six o'clock, drinks with Knight. We're all set." He seemed quite pleased with himself for coaxing his roommate into a night out this soon, but he knew something drastic was needed if he was serious about helping him.

"Can't wait." Knight did not mean to downplay the gesture, but he also did not know how the conversation would impact him. "Remind me before Sunday rolls around."

"You got it. Now if you'll excuse me, there's a new movie out, and I hear it's pretty good. Will Ferrell plays this newscaster in the seventies. I'll let ya know how it goes." He changed into civilian clothing, showing off some leg. Being from America's Dairyland, Peterson was taking full advantage of the southern summer by wearing shorts at any given opportunity, even when it was not always fashionable.

"I await your review, Mr. Ebert."

Peterson donned a Green Bay Packers T-shirt, tucked his phone into his pocket, and replied, "I was always partial to Siskel; God rest his soul. See ya around." And with that, he left the barracks and walked out to the parking lot. Knight remained seated at the desk, his mind still awash with memories of his tour at Lewis, as the seconds dragged on. His phone chirped, and he opened it to reveal a message from his roommate:

> Reminder: guys' night out on Sunday at 6.

Knight chortled at the promptness of the message.
I did say before Sunday. He's quick; I'll give him that.

SUNDAY, 18 JULY 2004

"Bombs away…"

Peterson watched his roommate, astonished that he was about to put away his fourth drink of the evening. Knight dropped a shot glass into the tumbler, waited exactly three seconds, and imbibed the entire beverage as though his life depended on it. He carefully placed the two-glass combo back on the table and looked over at his colleague, who had made the wise decision to stick with tea.

"Is that any good?" Peterson asked, eyeing at the glass.

"Not really, but it's hard liquor and an energy drink, which... makes me glad to be alive right now."

Knight's speech was starting to slow, and Peterson knew that the time was nearing when he could broach the topic of his colleague's pain. The buffalo wings they were splitting did little to counter the effects of the alcohol, so it was only a matter of time before the details would come out. They sat at a booth at LZ Charlie, a haven for the service members assigned to Fort Rucker. Garishly decorated with a smorgasbord of flags, unit patches, and other military paraphernalia, the place still maintained a degree of classiness despite the excessive patriotism. The owner was a retired helicopter pilot who had flown missions over Grenada and Panama, and his wife was often spotted running the place in his absence. Knight could definitely see himself becoming a regular there.

In spite of his homespun, Midwestern upbringing, Peterson was growing a bit impatient, so he rolled the dice and went right to the heart of the matter. "So, tell me about her." He hoped this would not cause his friend to order yet another drink, though he had already provided the two he had agreed to supply.

"She was ffff-uckin' gorgeous, man." Knight nearly toppled his glassware as he gestured, which Peterson helped him steady. Almost to himself, he went on, "Five-foot ten, black hair, perfect skin, tits were incredible... and her smile... man, it made me forget my own name once..." He leaned forward, and his voice rose. "But d'you know what her best feature was, Pete? Do ya?" Knight was clearly in a good place now— or thought he was.

"Her ass?" Peterson ventured. He had not mentioned that part yet, so it seemed logical. "Well, sh-ort of, but not really."

"This should be interesting," Peterson murmured.

"It was her *mind*," Knight said decisively, tapping the side of his head with his index finger. "I found out later that she was para-, para-... para*legaling*... she was this paralegal by day, moonlighted as a bartender by... moonlight. Said she was paying off college debt and saving for law school, but I don't know if she ever went. I'll never know..." He blinked rapidly a few times and opened his eyes wide as he did so, seeming to realize just how far gone Amy was from him. When the waitress returned to the table, he ordered two beers, both of which were for him.

"And what happened? She break your heart?"

"Something like that." Knight proceeded to outline, in not-so-linear form, the night at Callahan's, the wild encounter at Amy's apartment, the email she had sent him, the agony of the past year, and finally, an understanding of what could have been. As far as Knight was concerned, the situation would not have been ideal, but he was willing to help her raise the child and even leave the Army if she needed. He loved being a soldier and a law enforcement professional. But he had gotten himself—and someone else—into a scrape, and it was on him to be a man and accept responsibility.

Peterson sensed some righteous indignation beneath the inebriation. "And you feel like she... what? Cheated you out of something?"

"'Cheated' ain't the right word; I don't like it. It was more... like... I had this stupid idea of going off to war, and then coming back, walking into the bar, and schweeping her off her feet, like in some old movie."

"'Schweeping'?"

Knight did not catch the mirth in Peterson's tone. He rambled on, "An' even though she said it was just the one time... it felt like there coulda been more to it... there *shoulda* been more..." He downed half of the first beer and wisely slowed his pace before continuing. "Like..."

"Like what?"

"Like maybe if she'da told me about it, I coulda done somethin' to prove that I'd take care of her, somehow... something. I don't know what, but something." He took another sip from the glass, closing his eyes for a moment, and adding, "I mean... I'm not sayin' we coulda been like my parents or whatever, married for thirty years, but come on..."

His honesty and introspection intrigued Peterson, as did his description of Amy's beauty. It really seemed like they were making some headway.

Knight continued to unspool how Amy had to have felt more than she had indicated because of what she said about touching his hand, and how she potentially sabotaged his chances with the sorority girls so that she could have him for herself. But it was the accident in Kuwait that really captured Peterson's attention.

"You got drunk downrange? And they didn't catch you?" If Knight's drinking was amusing before, it had somehow elevated him to a higher status at this point, and greater jeopardy than Peterson had thought.

"Ain't proud of it," Knight mumbled. "Some dumbass had booze sent to him in mouthwash bottles, and I took 'em for 'disposal,'" he said, making uncoordinated quotation marks with his fingers. "Took one and drank the whole damn thing in an hour or so. I didn't get caught, but believe me, that was a ba-aaaad idea," he added. He detailed the Humvee incident and what happened to the driver. "To this day, I don't know if he woulda crashed or not. There was a, uh, hole in the road he hit, but would he have hit if he hadn't swerved to miss me? I just... I don't know. Fucked that guy up." Knight picked up the stein again and held it in place as he stared into its contents, his eyes going vacant for a moment as he thought of Wallace.

Peterson was not expecting all this. "Knight, man... I had no idea... I never would've guessed you went through all that. Have you told anyone else?"

"Just you. Amy obviously knows about the baby and all, but no one else knows what happened in Kuwait. Pretty sure I got away with it," Knight remarked, not bragging in the least. He finished the beer and placed the mug at the edge of the table, with one liquid obstacle remaining that had been brought before him moments earlier.

Peterson watched him hoist it, concerned at the sheer quantity of drinks accompanying this cautionary tale, but he was merely an ear on this occasion. Knight sipped his final beer, and his friend wisely ordered a pitcher of water for him when the waitress came by.

The two remained at the bar for a few more hours as they went over Knight's story again. This time, it was somehow easier for him to tell the whole thing without stopping or ordering another beverage. He still had to fight through the part with Amy's email, but it was not the emotional slog that it had been earlier that evening; Peterson had engineered a breakthrough. He knew that his roommate was better now than when he walked through the door, but more work remained, and he was certainly not qualified to move him further along. "Have you thought about talking to someone about all of this? Other than the illegal part, I mean.

When my grandfather died, one of the chaplains really helped get me through it—"

"I haven't gone to services in years. My parents still go, but I... it's different for me. I didn't let it go completely, but between everything going on in the world and my fucked-up life, I can't really believe like they do anymore. When I visit them, we go to church and everyone's happy, but I feel like I've been abandoned by God himself. Don't know if that's possible, but it makes sense to me, damn it."

"I didn't mean a chaplain in the religious sense. I just meant someone who has training in counseling and things like that."

Knight was not pleased with this idea, but decided to humor his compatriot. "I'll think about it. Chaplain's okay. But I get mistaken for an altar boy, and it's over."

Peterson did a spit-take upon hearing this, and it was clear to him that the new guy in the unit was going to be both a good source of entertainment and, likely, a good friend. "I'll get you the number for the chaplain's office tomorrow morning." He checked his watch: it was nearing 2230, and while Knight's schedule meant that he would normally be up for a good while, his driver was still on dayshift hours.

"Don't you have to be at work at five?"

Peterson smiled, replying, "Two months ago, I volunteered to work on Memorial Day and pull security for the ceremony at the parade field. So, Palladino gave me an extra day off and I cashed it in for tomorrow. I'm in the clear." He raised his glass of tea and took a sip.

Wow. This guy's pretty cool.

"That's why you asked about my next day off..." Even in this state, Knight could still get the big picture.

"Yep. If we're gonna live together, I needed to know what's going on with you, and this seemed like the best way to get you to talk. Now, we're in a better position to get along. And *that* makes all the difference."

"No shit." Knight could not argue with that. For a man of around twenty-three, Peterson was wise beyond his years. "You're quite the detective."

"I want to be an FBI agent. The Army's just a way to get there."

The two closed their tabs and Knight chugged down as much water as he could before they left the bar and climbed into Peterson's truck.

They chatted about sports and service histories on the way back to the base, comparing assignments and contemplating where they wanted to go next. It was clear what Peterson wanted from life, but Knight's plans were still up in the air.

"Some days I wake up and I'm all about being a twenty-year man. Other days, I wonder if I'm going to finish this enlistment." Knight paused. "I think the best way to sum it up is my plans aren't... concrete."

Peterson saw another opening to help his friend and mentioned what he had recently done to achieve his career goals. "The first thing you need to do, man, is get an education. I've been taking classes—"

"Whoa, hold it right there, I-shaac Newton. My history with education ain't so stellar. I barely made it outta high school, and Leonard Wood was no picnic, either. It took a shitload of tutors and more hours in study hall than I can count to get me to this point. I don't have it in me to get a PhD."

Peterson found this exaggeration humorous, but he also understood where Knight was coming from. "As I was saying, there's a lot of options for online classes, and to say that these things are dumbed down would be an insult to dumb people. And yet somehow, the schools are accredited. You can get a bachelor's degree from an actual university without setting foot inside a classroom, and the classes are fairly short, like, five or six weeks. Bing-bang-boom. Five weeks, three hours of college credit, stuff to put on your eval."

He made it sound way too good for something that Knight had been avoiding actively for five years, but even in his inebriated state, it did jog his memory about something Amy intimated to him last year. Though she liked him on some level, she did seem taken aback that he did not possess any higher education, nor was he pursuing any at the time. Perhaps that would aid in showing the world he was growing up.

Intrigued, he said, "Let's talk about it again tomorrow, okay? I have a feeling I'll be turning in early tonight."

They exited the truck and crossed through the parking lot. Peterson put Knight's arm around his shoulder as they made their way up the stairs, just in case he could not maintain his equilibrium. With their friendship cemented over drinks and stories of heartache, both men retreated to their room on the third floor.

Knight took his shoes off, climbed on top of his bed face-down, and closed his eyes, thanking Peterson again before drifting off to sleep. He had much to contemplate in the weeks ahead.

FRIDAY, 17 DECEMBER 2004

"You wanted to see me, Captain?"

"Yeah, Knight. Come in, have a seat."

Once again exhausted and beyond ready for bed, he entered Palladino's office and sat down in the chair opposite the company commander, uncertain of why he was there. Enlisted soldiers typically did not speak to the boss like this unless there was some sort of issue— and no problems of any kind immediately registered. Knight had been excelling in his role as a security specialist and had recently received a letter of appreciation from a colonel for speaking at her daughter's elementary school assembly about being in the Army. He had also taken Peterson's advice and enrolled in an online university that offered a cooperative program with the military, meaning most of the training he had completed thus far was counted as college credit. He was closer to acquiring a bachelor's degree than he had ever thought possible. At the current pace, he would have the degree completed in about two years, and that would boost the odds of another promotion. Thinking about all of this only further compounded the issue.

Work is going well, college is manageable, the platoon sergeant didn't say anything—what the hell is going on?

Palladino's office made one thing clear: the man was proud of his lineage. Most everything on the walls bore the distinctive green-white-red pattern of the Italian flag. A framed black-and-white photo that might have been the captain's grandfather as a small child sat on a shelf beside some books about Rome and Venice. Even the receptacle holding the pens and pencils on his desk was a replica of the Leaning Tower of Pisa. With any luck, his next assignment would be to the old country.

The captain rose from his desk and shut the door with a nondescript facial expression, though it became serious as he returned to his seat. Knight could feel a knot beginning to form in his stomach.

"How are things with you, Sergeant? Is work going well?" The captain was easing into something. Small talk was not out of the ordinary in a setting like this, especially when the ultimate purpose was to discuss job performance or perhaps relay unpleasant news. Was that why he was here?

"Can't really complain, sir. I really prefer the weather here over Lewis, and, uh, work's about the same. My parents live a few hours from here, so I can see them basically whenever I feel like making the drive, or they can visit me. Oh, and college isn't as bad as I thought. But I just started, and we're deploying next year, so I'll probably need to take a break until I see if I can handle it while we're over there." He felt like those answers were truthful and genuine, but he still could not shake the feeling that something was very off about this entire situation. And he was correct.

"Knight, you're not deploying. The bulk of the company will go, but a few will remain here for various reasons. I thought it best to tell you myself."

Knight sat stone-faced as he listened to the captain, completely unaware that he had not blinked in over a minute.

Palladino continued, "A few weeks back, I got a call from your old commander, Captain Llamas, and he told me about the accident in Kuwait. He also mentioned that you took the lead on disposing of some, shall we say, *contraband* the day before. Does that ring a bell?"

He nodded slowly.

"He thought he smelled it on you the next morning, but he didn't immediately suspect anything. I mean, why would he? He probably thought it was just mouthwash on your breath, and not the scent of the alcohol coming through your pores—alcohol that you claimed to have dumped the day prior."

That's why Llamas got all weird in the post office...

Palladino continued, "Fortunately for you, it's been well over a year since, and there's no real evidence to support the theory that you violated General Order 1. But as the commander of this unit, I won't run the risk of having someone on my team that I can't fully trust." He paused, leaning forward and locking eyes with the serviceman. "I'm exercising my authority to keep you here."

The rage building up inside of Knight was unlike anything he had experienced before. He could not admit to it, and he could not deny it. He was between a rock and a hard place, and he wondered just how obvious it was that he wanted to flip the captain's desk over.

"Sir, what happened in Kuwait—"

"Stop." Palladino held his hand up, palm toward Knight. "I don't wanna hear anything else. I'm already losing a competent sergeant on this rotation; I don't want to lose you for good by hearing a confession." Knight realized that his leader was throwing him a bone by not pursuing an investigation, but his blood was still boiling. Just moments ago, he had ended his rather uneventful shift at the Enterprise Gate, where the most bothersome task had been waiting for a retiree to find his ID card buried in the deep recesses of an ancient wallet. Now he would be stuck here.

"Listen... we all fuck up, okay? Shit happens. I wore stripes for ten years before I became an officer, and believe me, I've made my share of mistakes. You see this?" Palladino pulled his collar to the side and revealed a scar concealed by his uniform. "Bar fight in New York. The guy's knife was *that* close to the artery," he said, spreading his thumb and index finger about an inch. "Nearly cost me everything. But look at where I am now."

Knight tried as best he could, but it was becoming increasingly difficult to mask his ire. He had remained motionless since taking a seat, but his lungs burned as the conversation continued.

"What will I do while I'm here?" The question left his mouth as though he had just run a marathon.

"A few in the company are non-deployable for different reasons, mostly medical. The plan is for the base to augment security with local police officers, sheriff's deputies, and a government contractor company until we figure out what works best. You'll be working with them to spin 'em up on what we do and make sure they keep things running smoothly. You may be working extra hours as a result, but you'll have more autonomy than just about any soldier on the base."

Oh, joy. Everyone else will support the war up close while I get left behind, but I won't have a babysitter!

"Understood. Is there anything else that I can do for you, Captain?" The words left his mouth in as professional a tone as he could produce under the circumstances, but Palladino was not fooled.

"Knight, this whole situation is your fault. I don't know what compelled you to do what you did, but it happened, and these are the consequences. You've been in long enough to know it could be *a lot* worse."

The captain was dead on. The Humvee driver was partly culpable for the accident, but it was also possible that he never would have rolled the vehicle had Knight been in full possession of his faculties that fateful morning. As he had told Peterson, the uncertainty of his role in Wallace's injury, now eighteen months before, still haunted him. Had Llamas acted on his suspicion and ordered Knight to take a breathalyzer test, he would have been punished severely, perhaps even dishonorably discharged, simply for consuming alcohol in an Arab nation. He could argue the inanity of the order all he wanted, but the rule was still in effect, and he had been in direct violation.

"Yes, sir. I… will do whatever is needed to train those guards. When do they arrive?"

"We're scheduled to land at Balad in late May, and I expect the new guys to start rolling in here in April. All of them have experience in law enforcement or physical security, so it shouldn't take long to show 'em the ropes. You'll be instrumental in that effort. I know that doesn't make up for what's happening, but that's life."

Fuck off. I can't believe you just fucking said that.

With a straight face, Knight said, "Alright, sir. I'll make sure it gets done. Is there anything else?" He kept his anger in check, but he was mentally and emotionally drained, and his only desire was to go home and sleep.

"Nah, that's it for now. I'm keeping this quiet, so don't tell anyone why you're not going. When I write the memorandum to identify the soldiers staying here, your justification will be to train the new people and maintain an MP presence for continuity. I won't mention Kuwait." Knight could only nod his head in understanding. "Go home and get some rest. Try not to think about it too much."

Yeah, right.

"Alright, sir. Have a good day." He rose to his feet, opened the door, and walked out of the station, speaking to no one as he marched through the parking lot with all the angst and anger of a grunge song escorting him to his car.

He slammed the door shut, his left leg barely clearing the frame, and then sat staring at the dashboard. Minutes went by before he cranked the engine and drove to the barracks, the radio remaining off during this brief trip. Knight had no interest in music at this point, as the usually soothing sounds could offer no reprieve from the humiliation of this morning's revelation. All he wanted to do was down a quick shot of whiskey, crawl into bed, and forget.

WEDNESDAY, 19 OCTOBER 2005

Five months, one week, and three days. That was how long it had been since Knight's unit had arrived in Iraq for their tour. In that time, they had already lost two members to hostile action: Private First Class Jackson Burke of St. George, Utah, and Staff Sergeant David Chase of Cherry Hill, New Jersey. Burke was taken down by a sniper while supporting a convoy, and Chase died from wounds sustained from an improvised bomb. Six others had been hurt to varying degrees, including Peterson, who had sustained shrapnel wounds when an insurgent hurled a grenade over the wall into the encampment. While Knight was thankful that so few had been lost in that brief span, he could only pray that he would not be tasked with displaying another photograph. And as one of only a few MPs on the base, the task of hanging their pictures on the company's memorial wall fell to him. Truly, it was a loathsome duty.

"Remember the fallen," he said to no one but himself, as he placed Chase's photo on the wall next to Burke's, briefly bowing his head.

As Palladino had explained, new security personnel took over the responsibility of defending the base, and they were a coalition of city, county, and contractor elements. Despite the odd mix, everything was coalescing in perfect harmony. Knight had been paired with a new guard every day since April in order to prepare them for the job, and all had high praise for him. Yet he still longed to be in the desert.

On this particular day, he was working with Sergeant Javaris Bailey of the Ozark Police Department, a nine-year veteran of the force who had also done a stint in the Marine Corps as a radioman. They were seated in an office, going over reports from the previous month and making sure that everything was in proper order. Few people outside the community understood just how much paperwork went into protecting a military base.

Knight asked Bailey whether he had seen any action during his time in the Marines.

"Nah, I don't have any good war stories. I served in this little window known as 'peacetime' when I was in. Ninety-two to ninety-six." He raised a lip and revealed a wide set of white teeth.

"What made you get out?"

Maybe he would have some advice. Knight was more than a little down on his current situation, and as a result, he was starting to explore new career options, including separating from the Army. He knew that remaining at Rucker while his unit was deployed would follow him to the next assignment, which would prompt his new commander to call Palladino about why he was held back, which would start the cycle all over again—or at least that was what he told himself. As far as he was concerned, his time as an MP was likely coming to an end.

"Most Marines only do one enlistment. I just needed some guidance and direction, some money in my pocket, not to mention the G.I. Bill. You got a degree?"

"Next year. It'll be a BA in Criminal Justice." Since he was not dodging bullets and bombs, Knight had time to focus on coursework, and he was on track to graduate well before the end of his contract.

"Perfect! Your time in the Army plus your education makes you a shoo-in to become one of us. Trade that uniform for this one." Bailey's big, toothy grin was truly a sight to behold, as the shine from his teeth contrasted sharply with his dark skin.

Damn. He must brush at least four times a day. Maybe he bleaches them?

"And why become a cop? You didn't want to stick with radios?" It was an honest question.

"Well, I'm a black guy from Alabama, so you can imagine some of the shit I saw growin' up. It makes me sick just thinkin' about it. I wanted to do some good for my community, y'know? And I used to be in that 'Fuck Tha Police' crowd, but then someone told me if I wanted to make a real difference, I'd have to get myself out there and see what it's like. 'Nut up or shut up,' that sorta thing. It ain't been easy, and some people still don't seem to get that runnin' from us makes you look about a hundred kinds of guilty, but I do feel like I've helped people, which is what we're supposed to be doin'."

Knight respected this man even more now, with his forthright explanation striking the right balance of raw honesty and a true commitment to public service. If he were to become an officer, he wanted to be like Bailey.

"Why do you ask?"

"I don't know. Not sure what to do. I have another year and a half or so until I can get out, a degree I'm trying to finish, we're still at war. That's a lot to deal with. I joined right outta high school and wanted to retire at twenty years, but then this happened, and now... feels like my whole world's out of whack."

Bailey chuckled at this expression, saying it was one he had not heard in a while. "Sometimes, you get thrown for a loop—shit happens. I didn't expect for my captain to tell me that I was gonna go from patrollin' Ozark to filin' papers here. I had to roll with it." He went quiet for a moment. "You got a lot to offer and a lot of good things goin' for you. Just think about it. If it sounds good, come by the station sometime and talk to our recruiter. No pressure. Just a conversation." He sounded more like a used car salesman than a peace officer, but something he said took hold.

"It's about noon. You wanna go to the PX? Get some lunch? I do have some questions, but I'd prefer you answer them."

"Let's go."

TUESDAY, 26 JUNE 2007

Crossing the threshold of the gate, Knight surveyed the grounds and was not surprised to see a parking lot, dormitories, classroom buildings, a running track, and a defensive driving area. Everything on the website was right before him, only now, it was no photograph. He made his way around the curve and pulled into the parking lot, taking a spot in the designated section, and allowing the motor to run while he turned the radio off, closed his eyes, and breathed deeply. One career was over, and a new one stood poised to begin soon. He could only reflect on how far he had come since his talk with Bailey.

The "Double Nickel" had completed its deployment and returned to Fort Rucker with five total KIA, but the company received high marks for its performance in Iraq, earning a unit commendation from the Army's Central Command. Sergeant Peterson, despite making a full recovery from his physical wounds, was discharged from the Army within months of arriving home. Their time as roommates came to an unceremonious close, with Peterson leaving in the middle of Knight's shift. Upon the soldiers' return, the extra officers guarding the base resumed their normal lives. With Knight at loose ends, Bailey ultimately convinced him to apply to a police academy before his enlistment ended. The academy had accepted him without question after receiving his résumé, though he still had to complete an interview and a psychological screening.

So, after eight years in uniform, Knight opted to separate and become a police officer. He hoped to bring the same kind of service-driven mindset that his friend Bailey had brought to his community, and armed with a criminal justice degree, he was already ahead of the game. All that remained now was to make it through the next thirty-two weeks of hell.

Twenty-six years old. Army vet. Eight years under my belt. One deployment. Bachelor's degree. In good shape. Been yelled at before. Studied long hours. I know what to do. They will not break me. I will be an officer of the law. I will not *repeat the mistakes of my past.*

Opening his eyes, Knight shut off the engine, and exited the car. With a duffel bag draped over his back and a black folder in his hand, he walked toward the main administrative office, watching as others around him trekked to the same destination. Men, women, blacks, whites, Asians, Hispanics—some younger than him, some older. He was not the only veteran, as evidenced by the smattering of camouflage backpacks and duffel bags in his vicinity, and he relished the thought of being in such company. He would help them, and they would help him.

Approaching the glass double doors, the words printed across them jumped out immediately at anyone close enough to read: SAN ANTONIO POLICE DEPARTMENT TRAINING ACADEMY. He opened the door with a purpose and made his way inside, stopping in front of a long table staffed by three ladies in civilian clothing. He produced a printed copy of orders from the folder and handed it to the clerk.

"Richard Knight, reporting for academy class Two-Zero-Zero-Seven Charlie."

CHAPTER 7

SHE CONTINUED TO RUN, but no matter how fast or how far her legs propelled her, she could not escape what she was fleeing. Her heart rate climbed as her breathing accelerated, and her legs burned with each passing mile, yet she continued to run.

Down the uncrowded streets of Middle America, on empty sidewalks, and through the neighborhoods of Joliet, Kowalski pushed herself as hard as she could toward nowhere, hopelessly trying to run toward anywhere else. Passing the cookie-cutter houses with white picket fences, and with her nerves on edge, she barreled toward another intersection, not slowing down one moment as she raced toward the next, and then the one after that. The laughter of little girls playing in their front yard contorted into the screams of Major Simon Higgins of the 3rd Infantry Division, the man who had lost his leg in a rocket attack just over a year ago, whose name and unit Kowalski had committed to memory, and whose face was indelibly seared into her mind, no matter what she did to forget.

She turned left and kept running, somehow even faster, toward her mother's home on Anderson Street, blinded by tunnel vision as the world around her became a blur. Her drive to keep running as far as possible had sustained her during that final year in the Navy, and if this morning was any indication, it would sustain her well into the future.

Kowalski eventually made her way back to Evelyn's house, turning more than a few heads on the way, and forwent returning Ethan's morning salutation as she shut the door to her room. Grabbing a change of clothes, she trudged into the hall bathroom, turned on the shower, and peeled off her athletic attire. Then she stepped under the water and let it rinse her still-toned body. As the steam began to ascend, she closed her eyes, doing everything possible not to think about Hawkins, how the last image of her was as she walked back to her post in Baghdad with her M4 rifle slung over her shoulder, and how *she* had survived the ordeal, but her friend had not. The drops of water falling from the shower soon merged with the tears falling from her face as she wept silently in memory of her sister. Unfortunately, this had become a daily occurrence for her.

With the shower complete, Kowalski got dressed and crept toward the kitchen, hoping to procure something quick and light for breakfast before anyone else could speak to her, but Evelyn had already anticipated her arrival.

"Morning, Jen. How was the run?" She was firm in her tone and truly concerned for her daughter.

Kowalski had not been the same since Iraq, and the last year in the Navy had been a trying one, to say the least. Despite the difficulties, she eventually crossed the finish line and received an honorable discharge after her enlistment. To aid her transition, Ethan agreed to let her move back in when she began her terminal leave so that she would not have to worry about finding a place to live. But that had been nearly three months ago, and she had barely spoken to anyone since departing the plane from San Diego.

"Good. No traffic. Weather's nice. Any mail?"

"Just this letter. Have you been talking to a lawyer?" She slid an envelope over to her, with an inquisitive look.

"Oh, that's—I just needed a little help with something." She turned the envelope face down and hoped that the subject would change. Her wish was granted.

"Jen..." Evelyn fought to keep it together as she continued, "I will never understand what happened over there, but you can always talk to me—about anything. You and Ethan don't get along, but I'm your mother, and I will always listen to you. I will always be on your side, no matter what." She took her daughter by both hands as the levees finally broke, and the tears began to flow, but Kowalski already had her turn for the day. There was nothing for her to weep over until tomorrow, when the process would begin anew.

"Mom... please don't start. I'm dealing with it—I really am."

"No, you're not! I hear you in that bedroom, I hear the nightmares you have! It's every time you go to sleep!" She clutched her hand into a fist and held it near her mouth, afraid that she would erupt into a giant sob at any moment. "You are not well! I just want you to get better." Kowalski had never seen her mother like this, including when she announced her enlistment, and even when she told her of the deployment. Evelyn was on the cusp of a nervous breakdown when she learned of the attack on Camp Victory, and it took two phone calls from her daughter before finally accepting that she was still alive.

"What do you want me to do?" Kowalski always fancied herself the independent type, and this was no time to show weakness. But Evelyn had some connections in the area through her husband. Now was as good a time as any to exploit them.

"I know a doctor. All you have to do is talk to her. I've already called her office and... she can see you whenever you're ready." The desperation was both heartfelt and warranted, as Kowalski was not fully aware of how bad her own condition had become.

She nodded, looking down at the kitchen counter, and said, "Alright. Alright. I'll—I'll think about it." Wrong answer.

"Why would you even *think* about it? You need help! You barely sleep or eat. I've heard you crying in the shower, you almost never leave that bedroom—you need to talk to someone."

Kowalski did not want to have this conversation with anyone, let alone her mother. "I'm just... not adjusting to civilian life great, okay? I went from structure and rules and all that, to nothing, basically overnight, and it's been a shock to my system. And just like when I quit school, I'll get over this—in my time, on my terms." She did not mean to sound so harsh, but she had hit her limit on parental interference, especially considering that she still had not forgiven Evelyn for leaving her father, even all these years later.

Still, she hated to see anyone like this, her mother in particular. "Just... give me her number, and I'll try to call her at some point."

"You'll try? Promise me that you will." Her inflection indicated a ray of hope for her daughter.

"Yes, Mom. I will call her." She seemed placated enough. "But before I do that... can you give me a ride into town after lunch?"

This was the most the two had said to each other in days. "Of course I can. Where to?"

"The bank first. I need a cashier's check to pay Ethan back for the tuition. I also need to look at getting a car, and then I have an appointment at two."

She mopped up the tears from her cheeks and the counter before answering, "Um... yeah, sure. Where's the appointment?"

"Skin City Ink Shop."

THURSDAY, 11 AUGUST 2011

"Tell me, Miss Kowalski, why do you want to be a police officer?"

The question was one that she had been thinking about for months, even before she left the military, and she had rehearsed the answer countless times. It was time to put those drama classes to good use.

"As a veteran, I feel like it's my duty to continue serving the country wherever possible. And given my background with law enforcement in the Navy, it seems like a smart move. I understand what the law is, how it's enforced, and when it's broken, and I want to apply it to help people in need."

Fuckin' nailed it.

The psychologist seemed unimpressed with this answer, neither smiling nor nodding in response, and she kept her eyes fixed on Kowalski's as she opened the folder in front of her. "That's a fairly stock answer. Why don't you tell me the truth?"

She had not expected to hear something like that, especially since so many departments were hurting to recruit qualified people. What was this lady's problem?

"I had to drop out of college. I wanted to be an actress—I still do, but I had to be real about it. That dream wasn't panning out, so I left school and joined the Navy—"

"I read your file. Here's what I see: you had these notions of stardom, endless riches, but you couldn't hack it in college, so you sought a way out to pay the bills and get your head straight while you put acting on hold. Your work in the Navy proved to be rewarding and more fulfilling than you expected, and now you're torn between trying to achieve your original goal of acting professionally, and recapturing the feeling of accomplishment that comes with wearing a badge. Does that sound about right?" In any other setting, that last part would have sounded inordinately smug, but Dr. Reddy held an MD from Princeton, and she was not messing around.

Kowalski maintained her composure. "I was born to be an actress. The Navy was supposed to be temporary, but it's all I've ever really done. I know I can make it as an officer—but Hollywood... that's a different story." Dr. Reddy continued to read her face, searching for any sign of deception or evidence of malicious intent, but Kowalski simply remained still, looking innocent as the doctor continued the interview.

"I noticed in your records that you have a Combat Action Ribbon. Tell me how you got that." Kowalski's eyes hardened momentarily before she looked away and tried to think of anything other than what had happened.

"They... attacked our base." She could hear the clamor of the sirens as she ran toward the shelter, taking a knee next to the airman once both were inside. "I tried to help a guy get to his feet—" the sight of a bloody, severed leg came into full view "—but someone else took care of him."

"Anything else?"

The oppressive odor of the Humvee was fresh to her senses, as she boarded the truck and it raced toward the tower. "I manned a security tower by the perimeter for a bit." She covered her head and neck as the shards of glass fell to the floor around her.

"So you weren't exactly in the thick of the fight—you were more in the general area?"

The rounds from the insurgents' weapons hammered the structure as she remained on the floor, clutching her rifle as the helicopter appeared on the scene.

"That's... probably more accurate. Close enough to get the ribbon," she said with a shrug.

She stood by the ramp of a C-17, with a Marine standing opposite her, as the burial teams carried flag-draped caskets and placed them inside the cargo hold. Her salute was sharp and crisp as Hawkins' body passed by. The door closed, and those present departed the flightline. Minutes later, the plane taxied down the runway and flew off into the distance.

Back in the doctor's office, every acting lesson Kowalski had ever received and every dramatic method she had studied came to bear as she poured all her effort into remaining straight-faced and emotionless, sitting with a concealed clenched fist in her lap, perfectly erect in the chair. It was the performance of a lifetime, one that would have garnered her the awards she knew she deserved.

"And why San Antonio? You're from Illinois—why not apply there?"

It was a fair question. Most officers elected to work in the cities where they grew up, or at the very least, the same states. She was looking at an eleven hundred–mile move to a city she had not been to in years.

"Well, MA school is here. And even though it was on an Air Force base, I was really attached to what little of San Antonio I saw, and the department here is rated among the best in the country. Plus, Texas loves veterans."

The doctor finally smiled. "That we do." She closed the file and turned toward her computer, typing some notes and clicking away at the mouse before looking back at Kowalski. "I'm recommending you for the next phase of the application process. If you pass that, you'll likely get into the academy's September class. It won't be easy, but you've shown yourself to be quite strong, and we need that. We need women like you on the force: fearless, honest, risk-takers. Bring all of that with you, and don't hesitate to call me directly if you need anything else," she said, handing her a business card.

Kowalski thanked the doctor and carefully walked down the hallway, exiting the building without changing her expression. When she reached her rental car, she closed her eyes and allowed herself a deep sigh of relief, thinking about what she had just done before she saw Hawkins once again. She then let out a terrifying scream that no one else would hear.

WEDNESDAY, 18 JANUARY 2012

"Shooters on the line. Ready... fire!" The range instructor, clad in his distinctive red shirt and tactical cargo pants, bellowed out the order loud enough for every cadet in the state to hear, even with ear protection enabled. His cadre, positioned behind the students, stood at the ready to assist as needed and focused on ensuring the safety of all involved.

Reacting on command, the students drew their pistols, disengaged the safety mechanisms, and opened fire on the targets, aiming dead center. Dozens of live rounds left their weapons and struck the papers on the other side of the line.

"Cease fire! Safety and holster all weapons! Safety and holster all weapons! Staff, ensure all weapons are safe and clear! I say again, ensure all weapons are safe and clear!"

Having witnessed an incident on a range before, Kowalski appreciated the level of safety being observed.

"All weapons are safe and clear. Remove ear-pro and approach your targets. Staff, provide input as needed."

The students and instructors walked over to the targets and surveyed their shots. Most had hit the mark as intended, though some showed room for improvement.

"Prescott, what the hell, man?" Sergeant Ramirez, one of the course instructors, was grilling a student over how off-target he was in his shot placement. "Where did we tell you to fire?"

"C-center of mass, S-sergeant?"

"Yeah, center of mass—not all over the head. Head shots have their place, but until you get your shit together, just focus on the chest. Ya see that *X* in the middle?"

"Yes, Sergeant."

"Aim for that."

Sergeant Ramirez continued further down the line, commenting on a variety of results ranging from mediocre to very good, before stopping at lane thirteen. "Kowalski! Holy shit, look at that! Nice work!" Her grouping was perfect, with only a few centimeters separating the ten rounds she had fired, and if that was not enough, the *X* that Prescott had missed entirely on his target had been obliterated on hers. The rest of the instructor staff came over to admire her handiwork, and even the range instructor was impressed.

"That's some damn-fine shooting, cadet. Where did you learn to do that?"

"The Navy. I practically lived at the range."

"Well, you've got what it takes to hit the target, that's for sure. Can you do that under pressure?"

Undaunted, she accepted the challenge without question. "Every time."

"Then let's see it," he said, pointing at the target, as a few 'oohs' were emitted from the other cadets and staff. "Hembree, go get another target and switch it out. Kowalski, load another ten rounds."

The cadet scampered over to the bench and retrieved a fresh paper from the box. He replaced the original as everyone moved behind to the firing line and Kowalski finished loading her magazine.

"Alright. Instructors, the pressure drill will begin shortly. Cadets, remain silent. Staff, take position. Replace ear protection!" The instructors formed a semicircle behind Kowalski. The cadets stood abreast behind them, while the red shirt stood to the right of the staff.

"Kowalski, you will fire on my command of 'execute' and nothing else—do you understand?"

"Yes, Sergeant!"

"Instructors... begin!"

With that, all five of them began to unleash a barrage of boot camp-style verbal abuse at Kowalski, screaming at the top of their lungs every obscenity and antipolice slogan ever conceived, all to provoke her into a false start. They continued this treatment for a good three minutes before the range instructor yelled out his command. "Execute!"

She reacted instantaneously, but found it more difficult to fire as quickly as she did before, though the rounds were still precise. The first six shredded the target's center, while the next two clipped the white border. She had her finger on the trigger and was squeezing it back when the instructor barked out, "Cease fire!"

She finally completed the action, with the round leaving the weapon an instant after his order was heard. She stared at the target, her eyes afire and not blinking—the same look that was in her eyes from when Perrin dropped the slab on Major Higgins. Her hands had begun to shake slightly from the stress. Blood dripped from the target's chest as the masked insurgent stood before her, wounded but unfazed by her onslaught, staring directly into her eyes and seeming to goad her into firing again.

Then the desert around him morphed back into the firing range. Kowalski stood at the ready, with both hands on the weapon angled toward the floor in front of her.

The range instructor took a look down the line and praised her before the class: "Well, look at that! She did it." He paused briefly before walking up behind her, unseen, and he clapped her on the shoulder, yelling, "Great job, Kowalski!"

Reacting without thinking, her finger jerked the trigger back, and she fired her last round into the floor. It ricocheted toward the back wall like a strike from a cobra, harmlessly hitting no one.

The instructors immediately—and viciously—berated her for what happened. But it was the range supervisor who was most livid. He stood so close to Kowalski that his saliva sprayed her nose. "Get the fuck off my range and report to the commandant's office!" When she hesitated momentarily, he added, "Now! Go! Move it!"

"Yes, Sergeant!" Had there been one more round in the chamber and no witnesses present, she would have used it on him.

Kowalski attempted to engage the safety and holster her weapon, but the instructors ordered her to relinquish it and her belt before leaving the area, which she quickly did on her way out of the room. Flanked by two instructors, she marched through the hallway to the commandant's office in the administrative building, expressionless, and sat in the chair outside his door as one of the cadre spoke to the secretary first. When they received clearance to go inside the office, she reported to her superior, and remained standing at attention while the instructors explained what happened.

The boisterous range instructor soon joined them, and he closed the door as the debrief continued. The commandant, a forty-year veteran of three precincts, listened intently as all three instructors provided the same version of the events that had just taken place. Kowalski remained silent, still wired from the incident, but coming down from the stress of the situation.

"Alright, Kowalski. Let's hear it—what happened?" The commandant gestured toward her, and she finally had the chance to explain her side of things. But with a few dozen witnesses, staff members among them, what else could she hope to add that would aid her cause?

"Chief, it's pretty much what they said. The range supe gave the order to cease fire just as I was in the process of firing what I thought was the last round—"

"What you 'thought' was the last round? You didn't know?"

She could not let on that she was taking down a terrorist from the Middle East, the same kind that had killed her friend with a rocket and then tried to kill her in the tower. No one would understand.

"I had a set number of rounds in the magazine, and there was no directive to keep count; only to fire." She was not sure if he cared about that, but following orders seemed like a relevant detail.

"Go on."

"I ceased fire and stood at the ready, only for Sergeant Schneider to smack me on the shoulder and scream right by my ear. Since the weapon wasn't holstered, I—"

"Did he order you to safety and holster the weapon?"

Holy shit... he didn't say that.

"No, sir. He didn't. No one did." Her breathing became deeper, and her pulse began to slow as she realized the magnitude of that not-so-minor point.

The tone on his side of the desk became incredibly serious in a matter of seconds. He turned to his right and leaned in on his elbow, pointing with a bony index finger and asking, "Sergeant Schneider, did you give her an order to place her weapon on safe and holster it before you startled her?"

His face went as red as his shirt. "No... sir. I didn't." Whether it was shame or rage that caused his skin to change color was unclear, but he looked ready to implode.

"Sergeant Ramirez, Sergeant Green—did *anyone* give her an order to place her weapon on safe and holster it before he startled her?"

They answered virtually in unison, "No, sir."

That was all he needed to hear. "Cadet Kowalski, you had a negligent discharge on the range. But based on what I've heard just now, I can't hold you to blame for that. This will not be reflected in your record, and you are cleared to return to your class. Dismissed."

"Yes, sir." She saluted him, he returned the gesture, and she departed his office. While she was still within earshot, she heard the commandant tear into Schneider for his lack of professionalism.

Despite that, her expression remained cold and dead as she strode through the corridor and back to the range. There, she located her belt and weapon on a bench and returned them to their rightful place on her hips. The other cadets had been given a break to check their recent shot placements and reload, and they did not see her as she joined them.

"Did I miss anything?"

THURSDAY, 10 MAY 2012

The day had finally come. No more pencils, no more books. The forty-two cadets of Kowalski's class were moments away from officially completing their training and becoming members of the San Antonio Police Department. Being on the shorter end of the spectrum, Kowalski was seated in the front row of the auditorium, listening to the commandant speak to the audience about everything the incipient officers had endured over the past eight months.

"The officers seated before me have completed one of the most arduous and demanding academies not just in our great state of Texas, but the entire country. They received a thousand hours of instruction, fired hundreds of rounds at the range, underwent countless written exams and scenario-based training exercises, and a list of other items too numerous to mention here. Every one of them has achieved something that will carry them forward for the rest of their lives." At this point, he turned his attention directly to the front two rows before continuing, "Public safety and public trust go hand in hand. As officers of the law, you are charged with upholding the highest standards of integrity, and you will be held to that charge, not just by me, but by every man, woman, and child walking the streets of our fair city.

"The responsibility placed upon you is immense, but that is why we trained you as hard as we did—to prepare you for what lies ahead. Many of you will finish your careers without ever drawing your weapons. But some of you may be called upon to do just that, and when that time comes, you will be grateful for just how difficult it was to be where you are today. Officers, congratulations on a job well done, and welcome to the San Antonio Police Department."

The roar from the crowd brought back momentary flashes from Iraq, but Kowalski maintained her composure for a picture onstage with Evelyn and Ethan. It was hard to tell which of them was more excited, but her stepfather seemed to be vying for the title. Evelyn had the two of them pose together while Kowalski held up her diploma, an academic achievement certificate, and the award for top marksman.

"Jen, your mom and I are so proud of you. She was a rock the whole way, but it really hit me when they called you up to get this extra hardware," he said, motioning to her framed honors.

Yeah, I still don't like you.

"Thanks, Ethan. That means a lot. So, how about lunch? It may be a bit of a cliché, but there is a Texas Roadhouse right around the corner, and you know what? It *does* taste better in Texas."

The two were in town for a few days to attend the graduation and help her settle into a living space, so both were eager to spend time with Officer Kowalski and aid her in any way possible. Ethan had rented a moving truck and brought her personal items from Joliet to San Antonio, in addition to some household furniture, so that she would not live in an empty apartment. For as much as she loathed him, he did his part to be a good stepfather.

Evelyn was particularly excited about all of this. "We didn't have breakfast, so I'm definitely up for that. But before we go, can you show us around? Maybe do a quick tour?" She had seen military bases, but never a police academy. For that matter, outside of officers themselves and maybe their families, who had?

"Sure. Let's take that door over there." Kowalski motioned toward the stairs that led to the back of the auditorium and escorted her guests to her quarters, the classrooms, and the obstacle course. Afterwards, she drove them past the defensive driving area, and then they left the grounds for lunch. She may not have made it as a student at Arcadia, but Kowalski had completed two incredibly strenuous courses to become a law enforcement officer. Now, she was basking in the glow of the second one, aware of just how hard life was going to become, but even more aware of how much she still yearned to be an actress.

SATURDAY, 12 MAY 2012

"And if you'll please sign right here, that'll be the last one."

Kowalski autographed the form, and the leasing agent, dressed in her high-end pantsuit and pixie-cut blonde hair, collected the document, handed Kowalski the keys, and shook her hand, welcoming her as the newest resident of Sterlington Apartments. The midrange complex lay not too far from her substation and offered the usual in a one-bedroom arrangement. Yet the bathtub was Jacuzzi-style and fairly large, while the floor plan easily accommodated the modicum of furnishings that she brought with her. It was hardly the Hilton, but this place was more than sufficient for what she needed at this stage in life. Kowalski was grateful that, even though she had just earned her badge two days prior, she was not starting out at the bottom by living at home or with a roommate.

"Jen, this place is great!" Her mother eyed every inch of the floorplan, her voice echoing off the bare walls. "You can put a couch right here and your TV against that wall, oh, and maybe an aquarium by the kitchen..." Evelyn was a whirlwind of ideas and suggestions, not stopping once as she laid out her vision for her daughter's new home, to the point that Ethan had to signal to her to take a breath. "Okay, I'll stop for now. But text me tomorrow because that bedroom is the perfect size for this suite I saw at Ikea—"

"Mom... I got this. I've got two guys from my class on the way here to help unload the truck and set things up for us, so all we have to do is get the small things out of the way and let them handle the rest."

"Two guys, huh? Friends of yours?" Her eyebrows could not have risen any higher as she inquired as to who these strapping men were, and if she was interested in either of them. "I mean, they're going out of their way to help you with this, so... you know?"

"Yeah, no, not a chance. I don't see myself dating another badge. They kind of discouraged that in the academy. It's harder to be objective if you're on a case together, you work opposite shifts half the time, never see each other... that's no way to live. Plus, I'm not looking for anyone. I've never met a guy who gets me, or who didn't want to just hook up and leave, so I'll be fine for now. I have some girlfriends from class who are in my precinct. I-I'll be okay."

"Are you sure about that, Jen? Having someone close—close on that level, I mean—might help you with everything... you know... going on with you. I'm not saying it'll fix everything, but just knowing that you have another person in your life who loves you, and wants to be with you, and shares your interests—it really does make things better." She looped her arm through Ethan's as he looked on, both unaware that Kowalski was repulsed by what she saw. She may not have been a champion of relationships, but watching the two of them act that way only reinforced her lack of desire to find a steady man.

"I'm sure. The plan is to throw myself into the job and focus on that. There's a probationary period, so they can still take my shield away if I don't cut it, and there's no way I'll let that happen. The academy was a lot harder than MA school. And since I won't go back to the Navy, this is it for me." The determination in her voice said it all. This was a woman who had been through the fire and came out the other side.

"Hard to argue with that," said Ethan. Noticing something through the blinds, he walked over to the window and glanced down at the parking lot. "I think I see your friends out there. Is one of them about seven feet tall and built like Shrek?"

"That would be Constantine. I gotta go out there and let them know where we are." Kowalski walked to the door and placed a hand on the knob, pausing before turning around. "And no discussing anything other than furniture placement and how hard the academy was, understood?" She pointed her index finger at the pair, dead serious, but still in a playful manner.

"We'll be good," Evelyn said. "I promise." If there was any doubt where Kowalski acquired her smile, one need only look at her mother.

"Alright. I'll be right back." She walked through the door and met her friends outside.

MONDAY, 14 MAY 2012

"Well, we made it." Officer Rachel Ward, another graduate of academy class 2011-C, expressed her exuberance in the precinct briefing room.

The seven new officers about to begin their first shift as keepers of the peace looked absolutely immaculate in their uniforms, eager to begin this new adventure—especially the one seated at the very end of the row on the right. Officer Kowalski, a U.S. Navy and Iraq War veteran, had been the first to enter the room that evening, taking her seat and reviewing notes from the academy about handling the first day on the job. Apart from doing something that would see her fired, the last thing she wanted was to be killed during her first shift, and she had been wearing her vest for two hours before she even put on her uniform. Was she paranoid, or just prepared? Even she did not fully know.

"Thank you again for getting me through that block on working with the military. Without you, I probably wouldn't be here." She owed a lot to her new friend. Kowalski had set her up with no fewer than eight guys over the course of the academy, and it seemed that Ward wanted to keep that arrangement going for the foreseeable future. It would have to wait, though. Tonight was all about business.

Kowalski took inventory of the other officers standing near the front of the room, milling about and chatting with each other, sipping Red Bull, and seeming to ignore the crop of fresh-faced rookies before them. Except for one. He was standing in the corner by himself, a large cup of coffee in one hand and a clipboard in the other, positioned just below his eyes as he surveyed the front row. He started with his right and continued slowly, glancing down on occasion, and taking a sip from his coffee when needed. What was he doing?

What is with this guy? Is he betting on who cracks first?

The creases on his uniform were like knife blades protruding from his biceps, perfectly placed down the center of both sleeves, and his boots looked like mirrors. He had actually taken the time to polish the footwear that would no doubt become scuffed beyond recognition over the next twelve hours, and he had applied black edge dressing to the heels for extra effect. His brown hair had just been cut and it perfectly complimented his overall appearance—that of a consummate professional.

That same officer lowered his clipboard the moment the captain entered the room, and exchanged a polite greeting with his superior.

Captain Justin Daniels made his way to the podium and placed a binder on top, instantly assuming control of the room. His twenty years on the force had taken their toll on him, personally and professionally, but there was no outward indication of him slowing down.

The new officers sat with their backs off the chairs, a common side effect of being right out of the academy, while the captain welcomed them to their initial night on the job. "I'm Captain Daniels, the night shift supervisor, and I'd like to welcome you to the 24th Precinct. The academy's over, but the real training is about to begin. Think of the next year as a very long job interview that you can absolutely fail at any moment for a variety of reasons, one of which is not having cuffs on your belt—I'm looking at you, Davis!"

Officer Davis grimaced at the call-out.

Daniels continued, "To give you the best possible shot at success, we're pairing you with a field training officer to help you until you figure it out. *Listen* to them. *Pay attention* to what they have to say, because they will teach you things that you didn't learn in class, and that just might save your life one day. Listen up for your name: Benitez."

"Yes, sir!"

"You're with Corporal Walters. Davis!"

"Yes, sir!"

"Once you get a set of replacement cuffs, you're with Sergeant Gagner." He continued down the list alphabetically, and it did not take long before a familiar name was called.

"Kowalski!"

"Yes, sir!"

"You're with Corporal Knight." As he continued to read off the remaining assignments, her mind began to race.

Which one's Knight? The name tags are too small to read from here. Tattoo guy? The chick with the glasses?

Daniels spoke again. "That'll be all for now. Rookies, good luck. Officers, you know what to do."

That same officer from before exchanged a respectful nod with Daniels as the captain departed the area and the rookies stood to meet their trainers. The veteran officers began walking over to their assigned trainees and introducing themselves, though Kowalski remained alone.

Okay, is this dude not here or something? What the fuck is going on? I swear, I'm gonna kill this guy...

Frustrated, she sat down, opened her notepad and scribbled a reminder about getting milk on the way home before she received a tap on her shoulder. It was the officer with the flawless uniform and highly polished boots, the fresh haircut and the clipboard.

This was her trainer. This was Corporal Knight.

CHAPTER 8

"TELL ME MORE ABOUT BEING A COP," her breathy words came between the kisses that she was planting on his neck and lips as they struggled to get into Knight's apartment. He, too, underwent his own issues trying to focus on his companion and get the door unlocked as both nearly tripped on the way inside. But he eventually secured the residence and resumed his quest to familiarize himself with his date's figure.

Corinne Campbell was his barista of choice at the Starbucks on the way to his station, and he saw her almost nightly when he pulled into the drive-thru on his way to work. Yet he had waited a month before he tried to get a date with her. Considering that her tongue was down his throat within minutes of dinner ending, tonight seemed to be going pretty well for him.

"You'll have to be more specific. I was a cop in the Army, too." Knight matched her actions with his own, pressing her body against the wall with just enough force to let her know how much he wanted her in that moment, as she dropped her purse on the floor and kicked off her flats. Her dark hair terminated just above her shoulders, and it complimented her face quite nicely, which he kissed with meaning. He dropped to his knee and began removing her jeans, kissing her taut stomach and exposing pink satin panties. His smile took on a lustful quality.

"God, that is so hot." She followed by removing his shirt with one quick pull, and he stood up to return his lips to hers, sliding his shoes off and assisting as she relieved him of his pants and socks. He had her shirt and bra on the floor seconds later.

Their coordinated movements carried over into the bedroom as their bodies locked together in a fiery embrace, with both Knight and Corinne completely engrossed in their mission of mutual carnality. Spent by the end and lying together under the cool air of the ceiling fan, they discussed what had just transpired.

"That was a perfect way to end a really shitty week."

"You mean that last position, or—"

"You know what I mean," she said, laughing and recounting the exact way they had tied their bodies together. "Though to be fair, I haven't done that one before," she said, leaning in for another kiss. Knight gently ran his hand over her shoulder. Her light brown skin and dark hair made her amber eyes that much more inviting, and, standing five feet, eleven inches tall—when not in bed—she was certainly a woman who was not easy to forget.

"Well, I enjoy teaching people new things, so this could be a pretty good arrangement for us," he said, hopeful that she would pick up on what he had implied.

But she did not appear to be on the same wavelength.

"Rick... I, uh... I have to leave."

A look of surprise overtook his face. She gave no indication that she had had a bad time, and if her climax was half as intense as he thought, it was the best time she had had in months. "Um, is everything alright? I thought we were having some fun here..." He was not accustomed to being on this end of the conversation.

"Don't get me wrong. The sex was great—"

Always good to hear.

"—but I don't stay long after the fun is over. Call it a personal rule." The glow she had enjoyed was slowly fading into a veneer of normality, and while Knight nodded along as she spoke, he was also mentally calling her out. The chemistry between them had been undeniable, and he sought to capitalize on it right away. She was inordinately drawn to him for being a police officer, but when she learned that he was a policeman *and* a veteran, it was as though she was dying of thirst and he was an endless supply of water. Beyond that, he did not want this to be just another one-and-done fling that ended before it really began. He had accumulated enough of those already.

"Corinne, I've made enough mistakes in life for two people. And while doing... *this* on a first date may be frowned upon, I don't think this was one of those mistakes. We connected tonight, in more ways than one, and I'd like us to... build on that, you know? See where it leads." He thought that was a well-reasoned response, but she was not having it.

"Yeah, but I-I... can't do that. I'm not the 'girlfriend' type, and I won't be; not for a long time." She paused, then went on, "There are things about you I *really* like. And if you want to do this again—" she motioned with her hand over the bed "—just give me a call. But it won't go farther than that. It *can't* go any farther."

Knight had gone through a dry spell at the academy, and when Corinne accepted his offer of a dinner engagement, he felt like a blind man having his sight restored. She was a fun lady to be around: twenty-three years old, a Spurs fan, very attractive. He did not care for the blue streak in her hair, but she had other physical qualities that distracted him from this.

"I understand. And I do want to keep seeing you, but it can't be just about the boudoir."

"The boo-what?"

Damn it.

"Not important. The point is that I want us to get to know each other on a deeper level, one that involves something more than just crawling into bed after dinner. There has to be more to it than that. It may sound great, but that kind of life is emptier than a politician's promises." Though just shy of twenty-seven, his words bore credibility.

"That's too bad, Rick." She reached over and took his hand as she pursed her lips, and followed with, "I suppose we should get dressed, then..." He really did not want her to go, but it would be quite hypocritical for her not to follow up on what he had just said. At the very least, she stuck to her guns.

"Yeah... I, uh, suppose we should. I'll wait here while you slowly walk backwards into the hall," he said, hoping she would appreciate the joke. If she did not, then it would only make things more uncomfortable.

Her laugh said it all. "Maybe next time. Perhaps on *that* date, you'll get to see my place," she added, with an optimistic tone at the end. But he knew there would be no next time. For Knight, most relationships had not lasted long enough to see the other's residence, and it would appear that his tryst with Corinne would be added to that sad list. She walked to the hallway, gathered her clothes, and dressed in the living room, away from him. He also reverted to a mostly clothed state before joining her.

"Do you need a ride? I don't mind taking you back to the restaurant." He may have just slept with a woman on the first date, but he remained a gentleman at heart.

"No, but thanks. I just called a cab. It'll be here soon." The silence that followed was both awkward and long, even though it only lasted about ten seconds. "Will you be stopping by tomorrow?"

"Always. Without my coffee, I'm just not my usual sunny self." They made small talk, but the urge to know her as more than just another woman he had bedded was killing him. Mercifully, her ride arrived a few moments later.

"The cab's here. I gotta go. Please... call me." She leaned forward and kissed him on the lips. Then she picked up her purse and walked out the door.

He headed over to the window to make sure she safely entered the cab and watched as she disappeared from view. He lingered at the window after she was gone, wondering what would happen next, and angry with himself that he would spend another night alone.

MONDAY, 19 MAY 2008

"All units in the vicinity of Mission and Isabel, 10-92 in progress, please respond." The call came over the radio, and Knight mentally annotated the street names, taking the receiver and awaiting the green light from his supervisor to respond.

"Go for it," he said, glancing over and tilting his head to the right. He was never one to avoid a call.

"Dispatch, this is Two-William-Three-One, we are en route to the scene." The call ended, and the driver hit the gas, launching the police cruiser down Chavez Boulevard toward the suspicious activity, though it likely was not much more than an overactive neighborhood watch member who thought he had witnessed a crime in progress.

"Any idea what it is?" Knight asked. Counting his time at the academy, he had lived in San Antonio for around one year and was still learning the ins and outs of the area, along with the hot spots for suspected criminal acts.

"Probably nothing, as usual, but we should still check it out."

"Copy that."

Knight's trainer, Corporal Ryan Gagner, took his job as an officer quite seriously, but he was realistic about the prospect of a crime happening every time the radio lit up. Knight respected him immensely and was thankful that he had been assigned to him. The two were around the same age and their rapport was solid, even after only a few months of working together.

Gagner had been on the force for close to twelve years and had seen his share of drama on the streets of San Antonio. The man had a sturdy, medium build that was often betrayed by the presence of his vest, and his light-blue eyes were typically shielded by black-rimmed glasses. His round face and slight gut, accrued from years of long nights and frequent takeout meals, were not the most flattering of features, but he had other gifts. Gagner held the precinct record for the fastest mile for officers in his age bracket. When asked how he ran at such high speed, he always answered that his shaved head made him more aerodynamic than others. His prowess could also be because he was on his high school track team and focused on sprinting whenever he trained.

"You need a haircut," he tossed over at Knight while keeping his eyes on the road. This was more a statement of fact than an admonition, though it was easy for Gagner to make such a remark, considering that he took the clippers to his own scalp every week before his first shift started. Still, he was the boss.

"Like yours? I can't pull that look off."

"Just a trim off the ears. The lieutenant has a certain expectation for us, and it would be better to stay on his good side for as long as possible. Besides, it's just hair. It'll grow back."

"Maybe. Didn't for my uncle. He was a mechanic in the Air Force, and one day, he went to get a haircut, and he didn't have to go back. Not as regularly, anyway. Must've killed the roots or something." Privately, Knight was concerned the same would happen to him one day, but he was not so vain as to fret over that aspect of his personal appearance.

"Just make sure you get it done before tomorrow's shift. And don't forget the power of the image."

Knight had endured countless group lectures about appearance from his seniors in the Army, and he was on board with those standards. But he had never heard it described quite like that before: "the power of the image."

"Care to expand on that?"

"Think about some of the most famous photographs from history—like that one from Vietnam. The one guy shoots the handcuffed guy right in the head on the street. How different would it look if he wasn't wearing the cuffs? It's still a guy getting his head blown off, but he at least would *appear* able to defend himself. Or, what about that one with Stalin, Churchill, and Roosevelt? The other two were sitting down because FDR was in a wheelchair. Imagine them standing while he couldn't, and think about the difference in power it would project, especially in the middle of World War II." For a street cop, this was a level of insight that Knight had not expected.

"I hadn't thought about it like that."

"Not many do. It may seem small, but things like haircuts, polished boots, pressed uniforms—they go a long way, and people take note." He was right again.

"I'll be sure to remember that." Knight had polished his boots at the academy, as all cadets did, but he had not given them the same attention that his trainer was describing. His take on it had always been one of practicality: why polish something that will be ruined by day's end? But looking at it from Gagner's perspective, it could be worth it to break out the shoeshine kit now and then. At the very least, he would have met his superior's demands, and that goes a long way for the new guy on the job. "We're coming up on Flores."

Gagner looked around the area and radioed back to the station that he and Knight had arrived on the scene. Both men departed the vehicle and drew their flashlights, scanning the grounds for signs of anything suspicious. They located a small group of young teens walking around harmlessly enough, though a few did look on edge when the officers arrived. "How do we handle this, rook?" Part of learning a job is doing it yourself, and Knight needed as much experience as he could acquire.

"They're not doing anything illegal. But it is late on a school night, so maybe all they need is a reminder of the time. The fact that someone called us might hammer home the point."

"Let's give that a try, see how it goes."

Knight cleared his throat before announcing, "Gentlemen... good evening. Ya mind talking to us for a sec?" The officers approached the group, mindful that though they were young, it was still dark, and neither wanted this watch to be their last. The youths exchanged glances with each other before one stepped forward.

"What's the problem?" His voice was deeper than expected, but still that of a child. "We breakin' the law or somethin'?"

This kid's seen too many movies.

"Actually, no. But we did get a call about something suspicious near here. You guys know anything about that?" Knight was trained to handle scenarios like this with adults, but children were a different story, especially when they acted as though they had law degrees in addition to acne.

"We didn't do nothin'. We just walkin' around." The others with him nodded in agreement.

"Fine, but does anyone here think it's a good idea to be out this late on a Monday? What about school?"

"Fuck school, man." The kid's response caused both Knight and

Gagner a moment of involuntary surprise, but Knight had a hint of respect for the bravery the young man was exhibiting. At that age, few would speak to an officer of the law in such a blunt manner.

"You know... I never cared much for school either," he admitted, offering common ground. "But like it or not, everybody's gotta do it, and best of all, the school year ends in a week. You'll have three months to hang out whenever you want." This prompted some unenthusiastic mumbling from several of the teenagers.

Knight still had the upper hand, though. "We're not going to arrest you or tell your parents, but someone around here felt the need to call us, even while real criminals are out doing their thing. How would you feel if someone else around here needed help, but we couldn't do anything because we had to deal with you?" The group became very quiet when he posed the question, and even the ringleader outwardly admitted a subtle defeat.

"Yeah, whatever, man. We just out 'cause we wanna be. We ain't hurtin' nobody."

"I can see that, and I want to make sure no one hurts *you*. So, why doesn't everyone just call it a night? You can meet back here after school tomorrow, and it won't be any different."

"Jimmy..." One of the kids in the back finally spoke out loud, "I don't wanna get grounded again. My dad said the next time would be for the whole summer."

Gagner chimed in, "Listen to your friend, Jimmy. Summer's just around the corner. It would suck to spend it in your bedroom."

The boys silently coordinated with each other before Jimmy shook his head in mild frustration. Knight caught a glimpse of the stitches above the boy's left eyebrow, and the deep gash they had sealed in his brown skin. Had he been in a recent fight at school? "Fuck this, man. I'll see you bitches tomorrow. Fuckin' pigs..." He walked up the road and turned into the third driveway, disappearing into the front door of the house.

"Can I assume that the rest of you live around here as well?" Knight's question elicited a series of nodding heads. "Does anyone need a lift? Because we can put the cuffs on you and bring you back home in the squad car," he said, gesturing toward the vehicle. Their eyes expanded to the size of footballs as they all shook heads frantically.

Knight smiled in response. "Good call. Go home, guys. In the future, choose a better time to hang out. Have a nice night." Both men lingered near the cruiser as the gathering dispersed, with some of the young men heading in one direction, while the others walked in the opposite, but all returned home without incident.

"Impressive. But you know we can't actually cuff them until they do something stupid, right?"

"Yeah, I know that. They don't," he said with a sly grin.

"Well said. Call it in."

TUESDAY, 26 AUGUST 2008

The tires came to a halt as Knight parked the cruiser outside the Tower Life Building, with the men stepping out into a light rain as they responded to the call from the building's director of security. An employee had climbed onto a window ledge and threatened to jump. Though outside their district, they were the closest unit in the area, so Knight and his mentor were first on the scene. The officers took a moment to survey the building height and get a sense of the situation. A crowd of onlookers had formed, and a news van had just arrived. Gagner was not pleased that the press were already setting up shop. "Jesus Christ, *we* just got the call. I swear, these people have ESP or something."

"More like a top-of-the-line radio scanner and a complete lack of scruples. Are you trained to deal with a jumper?" Knight's inquiry was not an effort to avoid taking responsibility, but rather out of concern that he would say the wrong thing at this most grave of moments. Being tactful was not one of his better qualities, even as a public servant.

"Basic negotiation, establishing a connection, that sort of thing. I'll try to stall him until the guy gets here, but that could take a while. The best thing to do is just go up there, talk to him, and see where his head's at, ya know? Get a feel for whether or not he's serious." Knight was partial to Gagner's no-nonsense approach to police work. He always went right to the heart of the matter, regardless of the situation.

"Understood. How many times have you done this?"

"Counting this guy... one. Huh." At least he knew what to do in theory. "Take notes, rook. Both of us might learn something."

Knight radioed back to the precinct that he and Gagner were heading to the upper levels. They confirmed a few personal details about the subject with the head of security before taking the elevator to the twenty-second floor. The ride was silent, as Knight kept his mind focused on how to handle what would happen in the next few minutes, wondering if he would witness a man plummet to his death. Gagner appeared rightly preoccupied with the whole situation, nervously tapping his fingers on his leg. The doors parted, and the officers entered the hallway, stopping outside the door.

The corporal removed the weapon from his utility belt and handed it to Knight, who tucked it into the back of his shirt. It may not have been the smartest move to disarm, but Gagner wanted to show the disturbed man that he was not a threat to him, and that he was there to help.

"Good luck." It was all Knight could think to say.

His mentor moved through the office door and toward the windowsill, the air of the ventilation system hitting the cold sweat forming on his brow. Gagner strode toward the man-sized open window. The subject stood outside with his back to the building's siding, weaving a bit, on a tiny faux balcony that was just for show. Knight hung back, but remained close enough to hear the conversation without drawing attention to himself.

"Hey, there. How's it going?" The jumper, a middle-aged man in a gray suit, did not acknowledge Gagner's efforts to establish contact. He already had the man's name, but he sought to get to know him through direct conversation. "You wanna talk about anything?" He leaned out the window, and the employee turned to see who was speaking to him, only to become overtly hostile when he saw someone approach.

"Get the hell away from me! Just stay back!"

"Whoa!" Gagner held his hands up to show he was unarmed. "I'm not gonna hurt you, man. Not gonna hurt you, I just wanna talk—that's all. Is it okay if I come out there?" There was just enough space on the short ledge for both of them, but the 400-foot drop to the pavement could accommodate anybody.

"No, it's not okay! Now get back, or I swear to God, I'll do it! Just go away! Please!" The man was inching closer to the edge, so Gagner had little choice but to comply with his demand.

"Alright, alright. I'm backing away. Just don't do anything you'll regret, please." He slowly retreated in reverse, never taking his eyes off the suited individual as Knight held the door open for him. He made his way back to the hall before quietly saying to his colleague, "I don't know if it's the uniform or maybe I wronged him in a past life. Any word on the negotiator? Is he on the way?" he asked, wiping his forehead.

"Yeah, but no word on ETA. What do you think? Is he gonna do it?"

"Can't tell. I didn't get a good look at his face, but his voice, his body language... that said it all." Gagner anxiously checked his watch, paused to think for a moment, and continued, "You go talk to him. He had to know we'd be up here eventually. There's a crowd of people down there plus our car, so maybe it's something else—I don't know. What I do know is that we gotta stall him until our man shows up. So, your turn. Get out there and see if you can get through to him. Here, give me your pistol."

"Are you shitting me? I'm not trained for that! They gave us a two-hour lesson at the academy. If he jumps, it'll be my fault!" It sounded selfish when he said it, but Knight was ultimately correct.

"And if we wait here and he jumps, it'll still be your fault because you failed to act."

Gagner was also right. The catch-22 of it was infuriating: risk doing nothing, and the man may jump. Send an untrained rookie to talk to him, and the man may jump. But officers are trained to be men of action, so the veteran had little choice but to send his inexperienced partner into the fray.

"We may not be prepared for everything, but sometimes, we gotta roll with it and do what we can. Now, hand me your gun and go talk to this guy!" Knight took a massive breath and relinquished his and Gagner's pistols before walking into the office. He took a moment to familiarize himself with his surroundings, idly thanking his lucky stars that he patrolled in the field. A few desktop computers were still running, casting an eerie glow throughout the room. In the distance, he could hear a phone ringing, even this long after the workday had ended. The cubicles seemed less like office space and more like a makeshift prison for the white collared.

Shit. I'd jump, too, if I worked here.

He approached the window. "Good evening, sir. My name's Rick. Ya mind if we have a little talk?" He hoped a slightly different angle would work, and it appeared to make a difference as the man glanced back at Knight and did not instantly dismiss him.

"Wh-where's the other guy?"

"Back in the hallway. You won't see him again if you don't want to. I'm Rick Knight—I'm with the San Antonio PD. You've got some people worried out there. You wanna tell me what's going on?"

"Well... *Rick*... I'm, uh,... Ben. I work in the... downstairs on the, uh... seventeenth floor." His voice was weak, and his breathing labored as he fought to speak the words. "What do you want?"

"Well, like I said, I just wanna talk. I get the feeling that not a lot of people are listening to you, so that's what I'm gonna do. What made you come out here?"

"Right, yeah, I really don't wanna get into that with a stranger. So, if you'll excuse me, I think I'd rather be alone now."

Knight could sense the desperation in his voice, and it sounded all too familiar. "It's about a woman, isn't it?"

The man did not respond, but Knight sensed agreement.

"I know that feeling, Ben. Better than most."

The man turned to look at Knight briefly before locking his eyes on the horizon again.

"You feel like there's this... hole in your heart, like the pain is never going away." Knight slowly inched his way toward the sill, determined to make as little noise as possible with his movements.

"She left me. She... just told me today that she's leaving. And she left me for some guy who looks just like your friend in there—" his voice went hard "—so he needs to stay the hell away!"

Knight leaned toward the man and saw the wedding band around his finger. "Ben, I'm really sorry about all of this—I am. For me, it wasn't a wife that I lost—it was a chance at one. I think. I, uh, don't really know."

Ben scoffed. "Your *girlfriend*? That's not even close to... My wife... Talia... I gave her everything!" Tears formed in his eyes as he fought to maintain his composure.

Knight had to think quickly before this escalated. "No, Ben. She wasn't even that. There was this girl—an incredible woman. Smart, kind, beautiful—everything. I finally had my chance with her, and it was *everything* I wanted it to be. Then I went to Kuwait and found out that she was pregnant." That got his attention. "She told me in an email that she had... taken care of it. No warning, no nothing."

Ben slowly turned his head back toward Knight. "And? Did you love this woman? Did you buy her a house, get up early to make her breakfast, share all your hopes and dreams?"

"No. I didn't get to do any of that because the chance was taken from me. After she told me about it... she wanted nothing to do with me. She told me to stay away from her when I got back. She was... the first woman I had ever... loved? I don't really know... but now, she doesn't even know that I'm alive." His voice dropped, and he said, as if to himself, "I would've done anything she needed... for her, for the baby, for anything. That could've been my life. And it would've been a damn good one. But now... it's gone. And I'd give anything to have that chance again." Knight was also fighting to keep it together as he remembered why he was there. "You're not alone, Ben."

"Rick... I appreciate the honesty, I really do, but this is..." The man's voice cracked. "I love her more than anything, and she took everything I gave her and threw it all away!" He clenched his fists together.

"I know—I can see that. And Ben... I can't even imagine how any of that feels. But this won't help the ones who still love you right now. The pain you're feeling will go away with time, but what your loved ones will carry... it will never fade. I promise you that. You need to do right by them." Knight was silently begging and pleading with every divine force for Ben to back away from the ledge. Slowly and quietly, he placed his hands on the sill, unseen by the distraught man, who appeared to have reached some sort of threshold.

Ben inhaled and exhaled deeply through his mouth. He looked up at the setting sun, and then down at the mass of people, news vans, and other officers assembled below. His whole body rocked back and forth. Finally, he shook his head, tears running down his bearded face. "I *can't*. I can't do it."

What does that mean?

"Ben? Are—are you alright? Is everything okay?"

Carefully, he turned around to face Knight. "No… but it will be." And with that, he took a deep breath, closed his eyes and stepped back from the ledge.

Knight lunged forward, wrapping one arm around Ben and clutching at the window frame with his other hand. This caused Ben to struggle, and Knight had to let go of the window and lock the other arm around Ben's chest. Their combined weight pulled him over the sill and out onto the ledge.

People in the crowd below gasped as both men teetered precariously on the ledge, at the mercy of gravity alone, twenty-two floors up. Knight jerked backward against the side of the building and braced his legs, fighting to keep both himself and Ben upright, but he knew that he could not do this alone.

"Gagner! Get in here now!" Knight screamed the words as loud as he possibly could, praying his partner would get there in time to assist. But Gagner had been covertly observing the whole time. Within seconds, he had a death-grip on Knight's utility belt and was helping pull the men back into the safety of the office, through the open window and across the accompanying sill. Once inside, Knight remained on the floor with a tight lock around Ben.

Gagner secured the window and radioed downstairs that the now-former jumper had been brought inside unharmed. The two men rose from the floor, and Knight wrapped his arms around Ben again, silently weeping with this near-total stranger as the situation came to a close. Gagner looked on, dumbstruck, as Knight escorted Ben back inside the hall, and the three were soon riding the elevator to the first floor.

"It's gonna be okay, Ben." Knight kept a comforting hand on his shoulder until the doors opened and they exited into the lobby, meeting Lieutenant Daniels and the building manager.

"Lieutenant, this is Ben. He's the gentleman from upstairs," said Gagner.

The look in Ben's eyes was that of sorrow and regret, but also of gratitude to be alive.

"Mr. Harper, I'm glad to see you're still with us," Daniels said, his tone serious, but warm and understanding. "There's some people outside who would like to speak with you, if you don't mind."

Ben stammered, "Sure... I-I can do that, I think..."

"Okay. Please follow these men." Two plain-clothes detectives escorted Ben through a side door, and the lieutenant turned his attention back to Gagner and Knight. "Great work, guys. This could've been a shit-show, but you handled it. I'm putting both of you up for commendations."

"Sir, if I may... Knight is the only one deserving of anything. The guy didn't wanna talk to me, so I had him go out. I didn't hear everything they said, but he saved that guy. He's alive because of him."

Knight could only remain silent as Gagner sang his praises to their superior, merely grateful that he had any role to play in the saving of Ben Harper's life.

Daniels nodded in reply. "Knight, I want a full debrief in my office by the end of your shift. Go ahead and start the paperwork when you get back to the station. Gagner, help him out as needed."

Both men answered together, "Yes, sir."

Daniels turned toward the door to speak with the press, but not before looking back at the men once more, saying, "Guys... I mean it. Great job tonight." He smiled as he turned and headed outside.

Gagner placed a well-deserved pat on his protégé's back.

"Let's get something to eat. I'm buying."

TUESDAY, 26 OCTOBER 2010

> Rabbi,
>
> Hey, it's Knight. I haven't heard from you in a while, so I figured I'd see if anything is new. How is Rebecca? Where are you working? I'm down in San Antonio with their police department and it's going pretty well. It's kind of like our work at Lewis, but with more action. Hope to hear from you soon.

He clicked Send and the email was whisked away to the digital playground of the Internet, off to its destination in the greater Chicago area. Knight had not seen any of his friends from the Army in years, so he tried to keep up with them when possible. His work as an officer often made this difficult due to the sheer mental and physical exhaustion he felt upon returning home from a shift, but that was the life he had chosen. The hour was late and he had already written to Rabinowitz, DeVaughn, Ritter, and Bailey. Then a sudden urge came over him, one that he had not felt in months.

He ventured down to a nameless folder and opened the only email stored there: the one from Amy, sent in the spring of 2003. Reading through it again, he closed his eyes for a moment before quietly saying, "No matter where you are, I hope everything worked out for you." He returned to the inbox and prepared to close the laptop when a familiar tone sounded. He forgot that he was still logged into Skype from an earlier conversation with his parents, and when he looked at who was ringing him at this hour, he was surprised to see that the username was "acpeterson."

Pete?

Knight accepted the call and was internally shocked to see the image before him. A mere four years had passed since they were last in the same room, but Peterson's appearance was drastically different. The man with the perfect haircut, perpetual barbershop shave, and impeccable military image had been replaced by someone with shoulder-length hair, a beard that rivaled those of ZZ Top, and a white undershirt that had seen better days. Somehow, he was even paler than he used to be.

"Pete! Man, you look a bit... different." He hoped that did not sound insulting. He only meant it as a statement of fact. "What have you been up to?"

"Well..." Peterson looked around the room he was in and then back at the camera before continuing, "Not much."

The curtness of his response was certainly out of character, considering how they had remained friendly for the duration of their time at Rucker, though Peterson was not the same when their unit returned from deployment. Knight had offered to take him out to LZ Charlie for a celebratory drink, but he refused. When he turned down another offer to go out the next night, it became clear that there would be no "welcome home" festivities for him, and while their time together as roommates was largely unaffected, the drive in him to enjoy life had been diminished. Clearly, that trend had persisted.

"After I got out of the Army, I sort of went... nowhere. Had to move back in with my parents while I got myself straightened out."

Peterson was an intelligent and resilient character. He was eyeing a career with the FBI.

What happened to him? Oh. The grenade.

"Are you seeing anyone about it? Like a VA doctor, or anybody?" Knight did not want to sound like a third parent, but he was worried about his friend. The attack itself had been limited to a single hand grenade that exploded in Peterson's vicinity, and he had been struck by only a few fragments in nonlethal areas on his body. But the damage was done, and he struggled daily to recover from the psychological effects. He was the only soldier Knight knew personally who had earned a Purple Heart.

"I go to a psychiatrist every week. She's helping, but it's..." He trailed off for a second before resuming, "a process. I think about quitting my job and going back in as a contractor every day, but I doubt they take crazies like me."

Knight hated hearing these words, even though they came directly from the source. Peterson would know better than anyone what his mental state was. "What are you doing for work these days?"

"Security guard. I work the graveyard shift at this warehouse outside Milwaukee. They pay pretty well, and they don't care that I won't shave or get a haircut, so it works out for everyone." He could barely keep his eyes focused on the camera, looking around the room, and even behind him a few times, as the call continued. "And you? You still like being a cop?"

"Yeah, so far. It's not the same as Rucker, but it's kinda close. I joined the color guard a few weeks ago and I'll be marching in the Veterans Day parade next month. Should be interesting." He knew that Peterson did not want to hear this kind of generic detail, so he racked his brain for something else to discuss. "Would you like to come visit? I have some time off coming up in January, and I was just gonna stay here, but if you're free—"

"Sure." He looked directly into the camera at this point, and Knight could see a glimmer of the old Peterson for just a second. "Yeah, I'd really like that."

"Good to hear. I'm off the second week that month, Monday through Friday. Anything you want to do, we'll do it. Just say the word."

"Thanks, Rick. I really appreciate that. I'll get the plane tickets and... I'll... I'll let you know." With that one conversation, his whole demeanor had changed. A partial grin had appeared, and his voice bore flashes of his old self.

"Pete... I'm not a therapist or whatever, but if you ever need to talk to someone other than your doctor, I'm here for you, man. You helped me through the roughest part of my life. I owe you that. Call me on Skype, over the phone, email, text, whatever, whenever—it doesn't matter. I *will* answer."

"I'll think about it. For now, let's just start with a basic trip to Texas. What can we do while I'm there?"

MONDAY, 14 MAY 2012

Walking into the station thirty minutes early for his second of five consecutive night shifts, Knight was beyond ready to get things started. His one day off last week saw him return to work for half a shift when another officer called in sick. This time, the schedule lined up to where he would be off Saturday and Sunday, and there was a barbecue at a friend's house that he was anxious to attend. Between then and now, another forty-eight duty hours remained, and clocking out on Friday morning could not come soon enough.

He greeted the desk sergeant before turning toward the hallway, where he spotted his old mentor on his way into the locker room. Knight ventured over to chat. Gagner, recently promoted to sergeant, was buttoning his uniform shirt over his vest as Knight approached. They shared a firm handshake.

"The stripes look good on you, boss." If anyone deserved a promotion, it was him.

"Not as good as the ones on you, Corporal. How ya been?"

"Working my ass off, it feels like. I was in the parade last month, then escorting for that string of funerals... oh, and Memorial Day's in two weeks, so we'll all be maxing out hours on that one." Knight was not complaining. Though he felt overworked most of the time, he loved his role as an officer, even when it left him with minimal personal time and not enough sleep. The fact that he donned his uniform for almost every major American holiday was a point of pride with him.

"Well," Gagner said, "tonight should be sort of a break from that... in a manner of speaking." The grin on his face could not have been more obvious.

"Aw, shit. The rookies are here, aren't they? Son of a bitch..." Knight smiled slightly, thinking back to his days as a new officer on the job, and how Gagner had shepherded him through the minefield of his first year. The combination of his leader's tutelage and his own personal performance had seen him promoted to corporal in a short span of time, and his record as a trainer of academy graduates was known throughout the department. Knight was partly responsible for a 12 percent drop in complaints against rookie officers, and this had, no doubt, aided in his rapid advancement.

"Yep. And from what I've seen, they look like a tight group. One of 'em's already off to a bad start, though."

"What do you mean?"

"You'll see. Come on."

He led Knight out of the locker room and down the hall toward the briefing room, where only one new officer was seated. Gagner motioned further down the hall to the officer standing by the vending machine, and Knight immediately noticed the glaring lack of handcuffs on his belt. All he could do was look at his friend, grin, and shake his head.

Gagner nodded wryly. "Captain's gonna rip him a new one for that."

"Let's hope not too much." Knight hated seeing people get yelled at, even when they were in the wrong. Maybe it wouldn't be that bad.

The men returned down the hall to the main cubicle area and quickly brushed up on existing cases, threats, and the roster of new personnel. Knight read aloud, "Benitez, Davis, Hernandez, Jones, Kowalski, Mitchell, Ward—sounds like a fun bunch."

"Let's just hope they can handle the first night. Remember how yours went?" It seemed as though all thirty-two of Gagner's teeth were visible when he smiled at Knight.

"Yeah, it was... *grand*," he said, the comment dripping with sarcasm. He took a big sip of his coffee and tried to forget that whole experience. The two waited around a few more minutes before meeting the other officers and heading to the briefing room, which was now occupied by San Antonio's newest keepers of the peace.

Gagner led the way as Knight tailed back, preferring to remain unseen as he observed the crop of rookies. He was the fifth to enter the room, and he stealthily made his way around and behind the desks to the front, pulling a clipboard off the podium and taking a position in the corner. Though the clipboard held no paper, he positioned it just below his eyes as he scanned the front row of new officers, each one as fresh-faced and eager to begin as he was all those years ago, and yet it had not been that long at all. He saw the one who had forgotten his handcuffs, another with a slight gap between her teeth, and another who would need a haircut in two days. And that was when he saw *her*.

Seated to his two o'clock at the far edge of the front row, with her dark brown hair pulled back in a perfect bun, was a woman whose beauty defied all reason and logic. She was chatting with the rookie to her right and had a notebook open on her desk, with several hand-written notes in the margin.

Her entire look ensnared Knight in a mere moment. Her face was absolutely captivating, without the slightest blemish or hint of imperfection, and the color in her hazel eyes was visible even at this distance. The angle of her nose came into view as she turned her head toward her associate again, and she looked just as incredible even in profile. Her lips were full and vibrant as she laughed at a humorous remark. And that smile nearly made him drop his coffee.

Whoever this vision was, Knight was instantly jealous of whomever she was dating. But he had little time to process that feeling; he saw Captain Daniels coming down the hallway toward the room. Placing his coffee mug and clipboard on a nearby desk, Knight greeted the captain as the senior officer briskly strode inside.

The other officers took note and sat up straight immediately, their academy training kicking in. The captain went through his personal introduction and, as Gagner had predicted, called out Officer Mitchell for lacking his cuffs. Knight exploded with internal laughter when he learned that his mentor was tasked with training this rookie.

Don't worry, kid. He'll get you through this.

When Knight learned of his pairing, he took note of the officer's name, as its Polish heritage stood out to him. The captain wished the new troops good luck on their first night and went to leave the room, with Knight bidding the captain a good shift. Seconds later, the veteran officers were talking to their new trainees while he remained in the corner, and that was when it hit him: that new officer, who could easily appear on billboards and grace the covers of magazines, was Kowalski. She was assigned to him.

Would he be able to remain professional? Was she as sharp an officer as she was physically bewitching? Knight had seen plenty of lovely ladies in his day, but there was something different about this one. She had been eyeing the corporals and sergeants a few moments prior, likely trying to deduce which one was her trainer. She sat back down at her desk to write something in her notebook.

Now's as good a time as any.

He walked over, taking a moment before stating, "Officer Kowalski?"

"Yes?" She looked up, both annoyed and curious.

"Corporal Knight," he said, extending his hand. "It's good to meet you."

CHAPTER 9

MONDAY, 14 MAY 2012

"IT'S good to finally meet you as well, Corporal."

Kowalski was trying to be respectful of her new trainer, but she still did not understand why he waited to approach her. Was she giving off a bad vibe? Their handshake lasted for about three seconds, but she noticed that he did not appear ready to let go when she was. His brown eyes were fixed on hers and hid something behind them, a kind of untreated aching. His dark brown hair was neatly parted on the left side of his head, and tapered off just above his ears. His cheeks had signs of light scarring, likely from some adolescent bout with acne. When he smiled, his lips curled up toward the right corner of his mouth, though his full smile also hid some measure of pain. His jawline was strong, but it was also the only aspect of his face that really stood out to her, and the rest of his build was what she expected—neither impressive, nor mediocre.

"Have you taken care of the pre-shift paperwork?" Knight asked Kowalski. "Do you need to sign anything before we get started?" All officers must clock in to register as on duty and to get paid, an important matter to those earning such meager salaries.

"Yes, Corporal. I did that about forty-five minutes ago, and I'm good on the paperwork." Her answers were delivered with poise and confidence, which she felt would make the best impression on her trainer.

"Excellent. In that case, you still have a few minutes to use the restroom or get some coffee if you need," he said, raising his cup slightly. "Have you ever worked nights before?"

"Yes, in the Navy. I was on shift the whole time I was in, so coffee and I are good friends. I think I'll take you up on that offer." She stood up straight and smiled politely at his inquiry, though she wondered if he had asked because she seemed that inexperienced.

I've probably seen more shit than you can fathom.

"Ah, a sailor. Well, it's good to have another vet in the department. I did my time in the Army, but we'll compare stories later, I'm sure. There's coffee in the breakroom if you'd like to grab a cup before we head out."

She nodded, and he led her down the hall to the lounge to obtain the caffeinated elixir that she would need to start her evening. With java in hand, both officers made their way outdoors and to a squad car parked near a light pole.

Knight commented on how nice the weather was. Kowalski was not as enthusiastic. "I'm from the Midwest, so this is a bit warm for me."

"Then I'm sure you'll just *love* the summers here," he responded, with moderate sarcasm included. "Where in the Midwest?"

"Illinois. Joliet, specifically."

"Joliet... *Joliet*... Oh, right. The *Blues Brothers* movie was shot there!" He seemed proud of himself for knowing that.

"Among other things, yes. You like movies?" Perhaps finding some common ground would help her overcome the irritation she had felt earlier in the evening.

"I do consider myself a film buff of sorts, but some are better than others."

Everyone thinks they know films, she thought.

They entered the vehicle, and Knight turned the key, the dashboard coming to life as the engine roared.

"Alright. Before we begin, tell me about what you hope to accomplish as an officer."

She could not help but wonder, again, if this was normal for him, or if it was connected to something else, some quality about her.

Knight put those fears to rest. "It's something I ask everyone the first night." He backed the car out of the parking spot, navigated around the other vehicles, and turned left, heading east on Mayfield Boulevard and into the wild.

"To be honest, Corporal, I just hope to help people and not get killed in the process. I could give some grand answer about service and community, but that'd only be half true, and I'd rather keep it real." She hoped that answer would go over better than the one she used during her interview with Dr. Reddy.

"Good answer, Kowalski. And while we're in the car, you can mostly drop the formalities. No need to add my rank so often, just remember to lock it up if the brass are around."

So, he liked to keep a casual atmosphere behind closed doors. She pondered whether her predecessors felt as odd about that as she did.

"Understood."

"At this point, I'm just glad you remembered everything on your belt. Poor Mitchell's already on the captain's shit list, and he's been on the job for less than an hour."

Kowalski did see the humor in the observation, but she also spotted an error in what he said. "Um, that was Davis, not Mitchell," she said, as respectfully as possible. She did not like to correct her superiors, but he did indicate a preference for a more relaxed setting.

"Wait... are you sure?" He glanced over and raised his right eyebrow as he asked.

"Yes, Cor—er, yes, I'm sure. Davis and I sat next to each other during the final six weeks of the academy, and I helped him in study group. He'd always forget to bring a pen to class, so him forgetting his cuffs didn't surprise me."

"Huh. Well, I guess I was wrong on that one. Could've sworn he said 'Mitchell'..."

Kowalski slid her eyes at him.

How? The two sound nothing alike...

"Anyway, you're an academy grad and a vet, so I'll spare you the usual speech. Generally speaking, the job can be broken down like this: 99 percent of the time, it's fairly boring, and 1 percent of the time, it's pure terror. The city is quiet for hours on end, and then everything gets dialed up to eleven because of a robbery, or a drunk driver, or what have you. The emotional highs and lows are also something we contend with, so get ready for that. Sometimes you get to save a life, sometimes you watch someone die of a drug overdose right in front of you." He went quiet for a moment, perhaps to let her absorb his remarks, before continuing. "Speaking of being a vet, what did you do in the Navy?"

"My rate was called master-at-arms. It's our version of—"

"Military police. That's what I did in the Army. Aren't we a couple of clichés?" He was not totally off. The number of former MPs and MAs walking the beat nationwide was high.

"I'm surprised you've heard of us. Most people I've met don't even know the Navy has cops."

"I like knowing things. Knowledge is power."

Coming from anyone else, that would have sounded incredibly arrogant, but Kowalski detected a kind of verbal modesty that she did not anticipate.

He knows some stuff, and he's not an asshole. Off to a good start.

"Did you join right after high school?" he asked.

"I went to school for two years in Pennsylvania. Arcadia University," she added, anticipating his next question. "I was studying acting and theater, but it didn't go well, so I joined up." It had been more than six years since she dropped out, and yet discussing her failed venture at higher education was still a sore subject.

"Never heard of Arcadia."

"It's a private school, but you'd fit right in."

"Why is that?"

"The mascot... is a knight."

He chuckled as he glanced her way. Before anything else could be said, a call came over the radio: "All units in the vicinity of Clovis and Burton, accident with no injuries, please respond." Knight apparently saw this as a good opportunity to test this rookie.

"What were the streets on that call?"

That was too easy. "Clovis and Burton."

"And are we close enough to get there within a reasonable amount of time?"

"We..."

Damn it. Where are we?

"I don't know. I don't really know where that is from here." Honesty was the best way to go. It was the first night.

"I'll buy that. The short answer is 'probably,' but we already have units on that side who can handle it. There were no injuries, so in all likelihood, one officer can handle the scene." Within seconds, another car had responded, and taken responsibility for the accident. "We won't be able to get all of them. It took me forever to accept that when I was in training—"

I know something about that.

"—so we get the ones we can, and hope we get there in time. For now, we're going to work on as much as you can handle every night. Just pay attention to the radio, learn the city as much as you can, ask questions, and don't hesitate to speak up if you see something. It's a high-stress job. All of us make mistakes, and an extra set of eyes is invaluable."

Kowalski listened intently, grateful that her earlier annoyance with Knight had vanished. Whatever that was, he compensated with a clear vision of what it meant to be an officer, and that was what she needed.

The next several hours saw them going through a series of memory drills and quizzing on city traffic laws, with Kowalski answering nearly all of them correctly, though Knight did manage to stump her on a few of the more obscure policies. He also asked about her time in the Navy, and she gave him a rudimentary rundown of her years at Coronado and Camp Victory. But she never mentioned Hawkins, or her subsequent struggles to keep herself in check. It seemed like the wrong time to bring all of that to light.

Then he asked one question that she did not want to answer: "Did you see any action over there?"

She did not think the query came from a place of jealousy or one-upmanship, but she still hesitated to respond.

He may have sensed why. "I ask because I was in Kuwait when the war started, but I never got to go to Iraq. *That's* a different story altogether."

I'll bet there was more to it than that.

"My base was hit once while I was there, not counting indirect fire. I did what I had to." She kept her gaze on the road the whole time as she spoke, unaware that he had turned and noticed the glassy-eyed look on her face, the one that she rarely allowed anyone to see.

Please don't ask anything else.

The Humvee continued to stampede through the sandy streets toward the perimeter wall, and Knight's next statement was the only thing to bring her back to the safety of the squad car.

"I understand. Look, we don't have to discuss that any further. I was just curious if your experience was anything like mine. That's all."

"Thank you. Perhaps another day." She did not want to follow up on that, but figured it would appease his curiosity for now.

"Gotcha." Knight took the next right turn and maneuvered the car onto the highway, merging with what traffic was on the road. As he drove, the duo made small talk about academy life, and whether Sergeant Domingo was still the lead instructor for the traffic enforcement block. As it turned out, he was.

They were headed along Interstate 35 when a sports car blazed past, seemingly unaware of their presence. Knight ordered Kowalski to activate the lights and siren, and they pursued the speed demon. She took the radio and called in the details: "Dispatch, this is Two-William-Four-Five, in pursuit of speeding vehicle, westbound on Interstate 35."

"Good work. Thank you."

The other car was built for speed, but the modern police cruiser had an engine designed to rival just such a vehicle. Within minutes, the car was off on the shoulder, and both officers exited the cruiser.

"I'll take the lead on this one," Knight said. "You stay vigilant and head over to the driver's side." She shot him a look of partial confusion. "Keep an eye on the passenger from the opposite window. It gives you a better view of their hands."

Huh. I never thought of it that way.

"Copy that." She could feel the adrenaline build as she followed her leader, mindful that this would likely end up being a simple speeding ticket, but also recalling the violent dashboard camera footage she viewed at the academy. That would *not* be her.

Knight walked over to the passenger window, which was already down, and said, "Good evening, ma'am. May I see your license and registration, please?" He had her dead to rights for speeding, but

Kowalski noted that his courtesy toward her remained intact, another sign of diligent training. The driver handed over the requested items without a word as Knight thanked her, and the officers returned to the car. He passed them to Kowalski and asked her to run the info through the vehicle's computer, which she did easily. The driver, a twenty-year-old woman who lived in Kingsborough Ridge, had a clean record, but it would not remain that way for long. Knight prepared a ticket before leaving the car.

"What was the speed when she passed?" he asked Kowalski. "Ninety-five?"

"Ninety-seven. The posted limit is seventy-five." The car was equipped with an onboard radar gun, yet another taxpayer-funded gift that no patrolman ever took for granted.

"Got it... ninety-seven." He completed the ticket but did not tear it off just yet, motioning for Kowalski to follow him back to the vehicle.

They both approached their respective windows again, and he resumed his discussion with the driver, with Kowalski observing his calm demeanor and ever-present professionalism. "Ma'am, I'm issuing you a citation for driving ninety-seven miles per hour in a seventy-five mile per hour zone." He ripped the ticket off in one smooth motion. "If you wish to contest this citation, you'll have the chance to do so in approximately three to five weeks in city court. Here's your license and registration, along with the citation itself. Do you have any questions for me?"

Her tiny voice was barely audible over the ambient noise of the highway. "No, sir."

"In that case, my partner and I will remain behind you until you get back on the highway. Please drive safely."

Shortly thereafter, they entered the squad car again, and the newly-ticketed vehicle was out of visual range moments later. The whole encounter had lasted about fifteen minutes from start to finish. Knight looked over at Kowalski and congratulated her on her first traffic stop.

Yeah... big deal.

WITH DARKNESS all around and sunrise over an hour away, the shift began to wind down around 0530, with Knight driving them back to the substation and returning the car to its original spot. He and Kowalski headed inside to close out their paperwork, and debrief the incoming officers. It was a taxing process, but a necessary one, as many court cases had been overturned or tossed out entirely because the arresting officers forgot to fill out a form or properly document evidence at a crime scene. This was harped on at the academy, and Knight made sure to stress its importance to Kowalski even more, closely observing as she completed all of them without so much as a comma in the wrong place.

"The Navy was big on this as well, so I get it," she said.

"That you do." He looked over the forms once more before filing them in an inbox by the captain's office. "Good work tonight, Kowalski. With any luck, all of our future shifts will end like this one." He meant it, but she knew it would not pan out that way. She had been fairly optimistic in her younger years, but her time in Iraq had destroyed her hope for a bright future for humanity.

"One can only hope, Corporal."

"On that note, I'll see you back here tonight. Go home, get some rest —we do it all again at six."

"Got it. Have a good day."

Is he always this upbeat about this job? He said he hated working nights, but he seems like he could do another shift right now.

She turned toward the parking lot and, at last, her first shift had ended. She did not die, she was in no danger, the world had not ended. Cranking her car's engine, she sat for a moment and considered how far she had come in just under a year, grateful to be gainfully employed and performing a crucial function, but still unsure if she had made the right call. Her mind wandered to other topics as she made her way back home.

Slowly walking up the stairs to her apartment, Kowalski fished out her keys, opened the door, and barely had the presence of mind to remember to lock the deadbolt after it closed. She hung her belt on the hat rack, fought to get her boots off, and plopped down on her couch. She had barely managed to take half of her morning meds when her computer rang for a Skype call. She nearly reached for her Taser.

It was her father. She had not seen him since she was released from the academy for Christmas break, so she had little choice but to answer. She accepted the call and saw him manifest on the monitor before her. "Hi, Dad! How are you?" She hoped her exhausted appearance would be a hint that this needed to be a quick chat.

"I'm good, Jenny. I just wanted to check in and see how everything went." Mike was not a helicopter parent, but he did care deeply about his daughter's well-being, given her profession.

"Not bad, all things considered. We did a traffic stop and a lot of training while we made the rounds. It was pretty uneventful. Oh, and they assigned me to this trainer who is... just... I don't know, Dad. He's a character." She had no other way to describe Knight at this point.

"How so? Did he yell at you or something?" He sounded as though he was willing to fly to San Antonio to defend her honor if called upon.

"Not like that. He's... well, he's Knight, that's about all I can say."

"What does that mean? 'Knight' like the armored guy on a horse, or 'night' like when it's dark?"

"The first one. He's kind of a joker, but he knows the job like no one I met at the academy. He was bringing up laws and stuff that I couldn't even find in my training manual, and a few people in our area seemed to know him. Like, we were out on a foot patrol, and they came up and spoke to him, and he asked about their families. It was *weird*."

"Sounds like you've struck gold as far as trainers go." He paused for a moment, looking pensive. "Do I need to worry about this guy?"

"Oh, no, Dad. He's really... no. Not really my type, and it's the first night on the job, and he's my direct superior. Just... no. And he's another officer. I said I wouldn't do that... wait... crap!" She just remembered something.

"What's wrong?"

"I forgot to get some milk on the way home."

"Well, you did work all night. You're bound to forget something."

She hated it when simple logic prevailed.

"I wouldn't have forgotten if Knight hadn't made that stupid pun about—"

"So you were thinking about your trainer and you got distracted?"

She grimaced at her father's insinuation. "Dad... I was really tired when I left the station, his joke came to mind, and I laughed. That's it." She was flying on excessive caffeine and minimal sleep, so she did not want to deal with this kind of paternal interrogation.

"Whatever you say, Jenny. Did everything else go alright?"

"It did, yeah. The work isn't quite the same as the Navy, but for now, I think it'll be okay. I have a year on probation, so I have to keep my nose clean because they can fire me for pretty much any reason."

"Keeping your nose clean is tough for some people. It's a job that you really don't want to blow." She could practically hear the slide whistle as he awaited her reaction to this most "dad" of dad jokes.

"Oh, my God... Knight makes puns like that."

"I like him already!"

"Good night, Dad. I'll talk to you later."

"I love you, Jenny."

"Love you, too."

And with that, the call ended. A shedding of the uniform and a shower followed, with Kowalski finally crashing into bed about thirty minutes after arriving home. Others in the family had asked for updates on her new job, but they would have to settle for a Facebook post when she woke up. The lady from Joliet needed to rest.

WEDNESDAY, 24 OCTOBER 2012

"You have the wheel now. I'm gonna observe and assist if you need help, but you're driving and calling the shots," Knight said, handing her the keys as they approached the cruiser after a late dinner from a food truck. The streets were fairly quiet apart from the usual near-midnight traffic.

Kowalski had been performing quite well as a peacekeeper. She completed the first phase of new officer training with ease and was adapting to the nightly grind of being a street cop, with Knight providing only minimal input most of the time. The professional relationship between them had grown exponentially, with him getting her to open up about her time at Arcadia and some of her military career. Still, she did not discuss the Memorial Day attack, or losing her friend. The subject was still raw, though she found herself breaking down over it less frequently. Concerning Knight, she found his time in the Army to be quite bland, but he did have an edge over her in the education column, which only reignited her sense of collegiate achievement. Even if it was not from a fine arts department, she would have a degree at some point.

Kowalski engaged the engine, and a call came across the radio almost immediately. "...in the vicinity of Pleasanton and Southcross, 10-56, subject is a Caucasian male, late twenties, wearing blue jeans, white T-shirt, red baseball cap. Approach with caution."

She looked up at the street signs and realized that they were within walking distance of the call. "We can take care of this one," she said to Knight, hoping he would agree.

"Absolutely. Call it in." Kowalski replied back to the substation that she and Knight would deal with it, and he resumed training her. "How do we handle it?"

Her mind raced.

Code 10-56, intoxicated pedestrian, approach with caution, ask if he needs help getting home, if he's too drunk, we may have to take him back to HQ, it may just be somebody who had one too many and another person felt unsafe, no need to go ballistic...

"We approach him and assess his state visually at a safe distance, and ask if he needs help getting home. If he's too drunk, we can take him back to the station for the night, or assist him in going to a treatment center. He's possibly looking at a Class C misdemeanor and a fine if it's the first offense." She was impressed with her recollection and quick evaluation of the scenario, with it sounding more instinctual than rote memorization.

"Excellent. Let's find this guy and help him out, but first, pop the trunk."

She pulled the lever as they exited the vehicle, and Knight walked to the rear of the car, emerging a moment later and placing something in his pocket. She threw him a quizzical look.

"You'll see," he said with confidence. "Lead the way."

Their route took them north on Pleasanton Road a few blocks, toward the intersection, with both officers keeping their heads on a swivel. San Antonio is a city known for its nightlife and drinking, so for someone to request police assistance, the potential for a problem was real, especially this far from downtown.

"You see that? Over there by the Dumpster." Kowalski spotted a man in jeans and a red hat walking slowly toward a Chinese restaurant, though he did not seem to be a threat from this distance. "Call it in... um, please." She had the lead, but Knight was still in charge. It was a delicate balance.

Knight could only chuckle at her directive. "Dispatch, this is Two-William-Four-Five, we have the 10-56 in sight and are approaching with caution, over." The call was acknowledged, and they made their way toward the suspect, who was still walking ahead of them and oblivious to their presence. Knight glanced at Kowalski. "It's all you, rook."

She took a deep breath and hailed the man. "Excuse me, sir. Do you mind if we have a word with you?"

He stopped in his tracks and turned around, off balance, eventually facing them with his San Francisco Giants cap pulled slightly to one side of his head and his belt unbuckled.

"Hi, sir," she repeated. "Are you alright?"

He blinked a few times and slowly put both hands in the air, seemingly on impulse.

"Sir, you're not under arrest. We just want to talk to you. What's your name?"

"J-... Jason." It was a start.

"Alright, Jason, I'm Officer Kowalski, and this is Corporal Knight. We just need to know if you're doing okay and if you need help with anything. It seems like you may have had a little too much to drink tonight." She was following procedure to the letter, but sometimes, not everything goes to plan.

Jason suddenly gripped his stomach, dropped to one knee, and vomited all over the sidewalk, with some of it splashing onto Kowalski's boots. Though she was ready to take her nightstick to him for doing that, she understood that the problem had likely resolved itself.

"Jason... are you feeling alright?"

"Never better," he said, rolling over on his back and away from the fetid evidence of his misadventure. "Sorry... 'bout that. Friends... left me at the bar. Giants game... Woooooorld Serieeeeees," he slurred, pointing to his hat.

Kowalski continued, "Can you call them and get a ride home? Do you need a cab?" He already had the phone out and fumbled to dial the number.

"Hey, asshole... what the fuck, man? Yeah... where am I?" He looked around briefly. "Great Wall... that... China place on... Southcross. Uh-huh... there's two cops here... I just... puked on one of 'em, so hurry." He ended the call and tried to get back on his feet, but that was a bridge too far for Jason.

"Easy, sir, just take it easy." Knight stepped in to assist. "We're going to wait with you here until your ride shows up. In the meantime, drink this." He produced a small bottle of water from his pocket and handed it to Jason, helping him to a seated position.

The inebriate began sipping it almost immediately, and Kowalski took note of how her partner had planned for that contingency. She shot him a look that said she got it. He really was good at this job, and she never felt like he was trying to assume control from her.

Fifteen minutes went by before a blue sedan pulled up by the curb, and a young man stepped out onto the street. His face was a combination of genuine concern and restrained laughter at realizing what his friend had done.

"Yeah, laugh it up, Frank," Jason said, as Knight helped him to his feet. "I hope I throw up... on the way back."

"Sorry, man, we thought you called a cab. The game was over, you went to the bathroom, and then half an hour went by. What were we supposed to do?"

Kowalski had an idea about that. "Next time, do a roll call before you head out. You'd be amazed at how much easier it is than getting us involved."

Frank looked a bit panicked at hearing that last part. "Is he facing charges or anything?"

Knight looked over at his partner, as if to indicate that she would make the call.

"We could bring him in on public intoxication, but he wasn't making a scene or acting violent. To be honest, I don't know why we got the call." Upon hearing this, the relief that washed over Jason and Frank was both visible and authentic.

"Thank you, Officer, for all the help. We'll be on our way now." Frank helped Jason into the front seat, and Knight handed him the half-empty water bottle, advising them to drive safely before they headed off.

The two officers lingered on the sidewalk for a moment.

"Kowalski, that was textbook. Very well done."

She could tell that Knight was impressed, but it seemed like he meant more than just a congratulatory word. "Thanks."

She called in the results of the encounter to the substation, and they began making their way back to the squad car. On the way, Kowalski stopped at a gas station restroom to give her boots a mild cleaning. It was hardly perfect, but it would have to do until she could get home.

She emerged from the lavatory and met Knight, but as they walked through the parking lot, she stopped dead in her tracks. Her eyes locked on a man resting his back against a wall between buildings. She had seen men like him before, with the ratty hair, unkempt beards, filthy clothing, and "homeless vet" signs, but his missing right leg caused her breathing to accelerate, and she could not move from her current spot. Even Knight coming over to speak to her had little effect, as she remained motionless, her face showing signs of distress.

"Kowalski?" Nothing. "Hey, Kowalski." He waved his hand in front of her face, finally getting her to blink and breathe, and she came back to the world.

"Yeah, Corporal... I'm... I'm okay." Even she did not believe her own words.

"Let's get back to the car." His tone was firm, but also indicated an awareness of something she had not shared with him, and she wondered what he was thinking as they took their seats inside the cruiser.

She waited a few moments before putting the keys in the ignition and starting the car, but he was not ready to leave. "Do you wanna talk about what just happened?"

She had hoped that he would not ask, but Knight was naturally inquisitive about certain things, and his coworker's wellness was high among them. "He just... he reminds me of someone I met... in Iraq."

"Officer Kowalski, I think it's time we had that discussion... the one you've been putting off since we started working together." He typically did not address her as "Officer" unless she was on the brink of a public mistake, and since they were in the squad car, she was doubly confused.

"I really don't think it's a good idea—"

"If I may, please. You're under no obligation to talk to me about anything personal, and unless you've broken some kind of law or you're a danger to yourself or others, I won't say anything to anyone. You have my word."

She could tell that he was really trying to reach her, and not for personal gain, it seemed. What was the catch? What was his angle? He had to have some ulterior motive.

"Corporal... another time, please. I'll try to talk to you about it, but... not tonight. I'd rather just focus on training if that's alright with you." The strain as she endeavored to remain professional and emotionally neutral was great, but she held it together, as she had done countless times before.

Knight decided to honor her request. "As you wish."

"*The Princess Bride.*" Privately, she prayed that he was not referring to the dual implication of that line.

"Hey! Nicely done!"

They headed back into the night, patrolling the streets, answering calls on the radio, running scenarios, and covering an array of topics, none of which pertained to Kowalski's time in the Middle East. Eventually, the sun began to set on their shift even as the moon was in full view, and they drove back to the station. The car was clean, the paperwork was signed, and the metaphorical bell had rung. The only thing left to do was go home.

They returned to the parking lot, and he called her over to his car. He opened the door and retrieved something from the center console, handing it to his pupil. "Here." He held a square box, not much wider or thicker than a silver dollar, and added, "It's nothing, really, but everyone needs to get something on their birthday." He flashed that half smile.

"How did you know?" She had not told him that today was the day, nor had they even mentioned birthdays since they started working together.

"I'm a corporal with the San Antonio PD. I have connections." She raised an eyebrow upon hearing this. "And I saw your personnel file. I needed it to finalize your first phase of training, and there was your birthday. Don't worry—I won't tell anyone."

His look reassured her, but she still did not know what to make of this. He was her trainer, her supervisor, her superior in many respects— why did he get her a present? More importantly, what was it?

"I just ask that you open it at home, please."

"Okay." She placed the gift in her pocket and kept thinking about what it meant, if anything, and this came through externally.

"Relax. It's nothing—just a trinket."

"If you say so, but I gotta be honest... I don't know what to make of this. You're my boss."

Her concern was not groundless. Another officer had been severely reprimanded for a similar offense over the summer, but that also involved an extramarital affair and a $300 cocktail dress. Knight was not inclined to spend that kind of money on someone who was not even his girlfriend, and a student, to boot.

"Well, hopefully, you'll be sure by the time you get home. Drive safely. I'll see you back here tonight."

Even after expressing her concern over the appearance of potential impropriety, his timid smile never left his face, and she found herself grinning after he left, not completely sure why, but somehow happy that someone had given her a gift. She entered her car and made the brief trek to her apartment, remembering that she had promised to contact Alex before going to bed. She did so not long after walking in the door.

Her friend answered as she was unbuttoning her shirt and removing her Kevlar vest. "Well, hello, Officer! Is this a video chat or am I getting a little show?" Alex asked, semi-flirtatiously. As her college roommate, Alex had seen more of Kowalski than most anyone else, so this banter was common.

"Play your cards right and you might get both," Kowalski said, releasing her hair from its confines and letting it fall over her shoulders. Instantly, Officer Kowalski was back to being Jen, though fewer than twelve hours remained until she would make the transformation again. "How is everything with you? You still liking the job?" Alex had recently been hired as a biologist at a medical research company in Virginia.

"Eh. It keeps the lights on and my car running, so I suppose I'll stick with it a bit longer." She paused briefly and smirked. "So... tell me about work. Are you still getting along with your trainer?"

Kowalski rolled her eyes, saying, "I knew you were going to ask about him." She shook her head slightly, irked with herself for mentioning Knight in their previous calls.

"Well, you did spend most of last week talking about him."

"Yeah, because his jokes are awful and he's a great officer. Both can coexist in the same universe." She, too, could employ logic when needed.

"Uh-huh. Did you get the card I sent?"

"Um, no. Sorry, I haven't been to the mailbox since... Thursday, I think. My days are starting to run together." That was when she placed her hands in her lap and remembered Knight's offering in her pocket.

"Damn it..."

"What's wrong?"

"Nothing, it's just... Knight got me a present." Now, just saying the words bothered her. "I don't know what it is," she said, pulling out the black case.

"Ooh! Show me! Open it!" Alex was more excited than Kowalski was annoyed.

"Alright... hang on." She found the seam in the case and opened it, revealing a coin inside. It was embossed with a picture of Kuwait on the obverse, with a star next to the capital, and on the reverse, the words "United States Army" and "Camp Udairi" encircled an insignia of crossed flintlock pistols and a fleur-de-lis. "It's a challenge coin."

"A what?"

"Remember that thing I got from the Secretary of Defense when he visited Iraq? It's like that, but this one is from his unit in Kuwait." She looked at it again. "Why did he give me this?"

"It's your birthday. He obviously can't give you a normal present, so maybe he wanted to do something different? Hold it up, so I can see."

She moved it close enough to the lens and rotated it around, showing both sides.

"That may not be from someone important, but you can't just get it in town." She looked right into the lens, saying, "He's into you, Jen." Alex's eyes were bright with the hope that Kowalski would experience what she did with Dominic some years ago.

Kowalski's face dropped slightly as she frowned, looking down at the keyboard. "It's a nice gesture, but I-I can't keep this," she said, placing the coin back in the case and clamping it down. "He's... just... no."

"Jen. Don't write him off yet. There is clearly something going on over there," she said, making her case. "You work together night after night and see each other a lot, but, I mean, it's not like you have to marry him or—"

"Let's not even go there."

"Sorry. Too soon."

"To say the least."

CHAPTER 10

WHILE THEY WERE ONLY a few hours removed from the holiday itself, Christmas came and went for Knight and Kowalski as they settled into their shift, with the heater working hard in their squad car. The temperature had dropped into the thirties, but there was no snow anywhere to be found, which saddened her, though he was overjoyed. Knight was unaccustomed to snowfall, despite having lived near Tacoma, and he was virtually incapable of driving in those conditions. She, on the other hand, could cruise over pure ice and never once have the tires skid. The vehicular contrast was sharp.

Knight's stomach grumbled. "There's a diner just off the highway if you're hungry. They're open all year, and they'll give us a discount for working a holiday. So, that's an option."

He hoped she would agree. Kowalski's training had progressed so well that she likely could have taken less than a year to complete all four phases, but no department would relax that policy, even for a combination as effective as these two. In the seven months since she joined the force, she had issued parking tickets, assisted with numerous arrests, taken part in the execution of search warrants, responded to domestic disputes, and saved one woman by performing CPR on her.

Knight continued to monitor her progress in his training reports, and the department had already notified both of them that she would be with a new trainer after the first of the year, so that she could gain exposure to a different officer. This was fairly standard for rookies, but he hated the idea of not seeing Kowalski each shift.

"Let's do that. We've worked eight hours on Christmas, and I doubt we'll see anything major for the rest of the night. Why not?"

Pleased, Knight imparted the exit number, adding his hope that the blueberry pie was still as good as it was last year. He was also planning to use this as an opportunity to speak to her once more about everything he had seen in her over the last few months, such as her aversion to discussing her deployment, and the incident with the homeless man back in October, but that was entirely dependent upon her being willing to talk.

She did say she'd go into it at some point. Might as well try for tonight.

"Make a right at the intersection. It'll be on the left after the Dollar General."

"Copy. Is this place any good, or is it the usual truck stop kind of joint?"

"It's a diner, so you won't find escargot or pinot noir on the menu. But it's open, I'm hungry… and we're about to drive past it."

"Shit!" She hit the blinker and turned the wheel in just enough time to nearly mount the curb, but no one else was on the road, so there was no real danger.

Knight was just glad to be headed toward a semi-quiet place to talk. It was hardly an ideal setting for a heart-to-heart, but the history here was rich. The Yellow Rose Diner had been in business since 1963, and he was counting on it being mostly devoid of other patrons. Kowalski pulled forward into a parking spot marked as reserved for uniformed personnel, and seemed surprised to see such a feature, though Knight had come to expect such amenities in the Lone Star State.

The building façade was fashioned in the style of a speeding semi-trailer, a nod to its roots as a truck stop in the early days of the interstate highway system. Old road signs decorated the walls. The handle on the double doors was a cutout of Texas with a yellow rose in the center, and the interior was completely modernized, which Knight felt was a nice contrast to the throwback aesthetic seen from outside. They escaped the mild cold and opted for a corner booth, away from everyone, as both placed immediate orders for coffee. The waitress, a fifty-ish woman with graying hair and wearing a light-blue uniform, greeted Knight by his first name.

"Hey, Betty. It's great to see you again."

She escorted them to their seats, passed out menus, and returned with their coffee in under a minute.

She turned to Kowalski, saying, "Hi, I haven't seen you here before. Are you new to the force?" Betty was always polite to her customers, but she especially cottoned to officers of the law, owing to her brother who spent twenty-seven years wearing a badge. The owner already offered discounts to everyone in uniform, including first responders, but it was Betty who took it a step further by adding an extra five percent off on holidays.

"Yes, ma'am. I'm Jennifer, and I've been an officer since May."

"Well, you've got quite a partner, Jennifer. He did the Heimlich on a guy here last Thanksgiving. Saved his life." Betty recounted the event enthusiastically, and it was all Knight could do to downplay his role. In truth, it was far simpler than she described.

"Thanks, but it really wasn't anything. He did most of the work. I just held him up straight."

"Sure, Rick. Whatever you say." She flashed a "yeah, right" look at Kowalski as she drew a pencil wedged behind her ear. "What can I get for you two?"

Knight motioned to his protégé. She ordered a garden salad and a grilled chicken sandwich, and then he followed with his own request for a bowl of chili and the chicken-fried steak. Betty tore off the stub from her pad, and like her spiritual predecessors from comparable eateries across the country, she shouted the order to the cook through the slot between the counter and the kitchen.

"You know that stuff will kill you, right?" Kowalski was hardly a health nut, but she did prefer low-fat dishes whenever they stopped for a bite to eat.

"True, but so will a bullet," he said, pointing to her pistol. "And you said it yourself, we worked on Christmas, so this is sort of a present–to me, from me." It may have been his own reasoning, but to him, it sounded as though it was straight from the mouth of Socrates.

They each sipped their coffee and chatted for the next few minutes, discussing their respective plans for New Year's Eve and beyond. Normally, officers who worked one of the two major holidays at the end of year had the other one off, and that was the case this time, though Knight would have been fine with working both. "What are you doing next week? Do you stay up and watch the ball drop?"

"Ward invited me to this shindig at her apartment. The management is opening up the leasing office and converting one section into a party room with food, drinks, and a DJ." Kowalski mentioned her friend Ward frequently, almost as much as Alex, and it seemed like the three of them were inseparable, even though Ward and Alex had never met. "And you? You got anything planned?"

"Probably just staying up, having a few drinks, maybe a movie. Nothing too exciting, really. My circle of friends is fairly small here and the hours don't make for a real social life." Knight did have some colleagues with whom he would hang out on occasion. He even attended sporting events with them, but his real friends were in the military, and none of them lived in Texas. "I did have an Army buddy visit earlier this year, though. He once helped with something that was really bothering me, and I took it upon myself to try and help him." His eyes became intense and serious for a moment, which Kowalski was not expecting, and it seemed that her curiosity was growing.

"You seem really put together. What... was going on? Wait, no—never mind. Not my business." She waved both hands in front of her, palms toward Knight, as she uttered the words and then sipped her coffee, but it was clear that she wanted to know more.

"I don't mind. We've gotten to know each other over the past few months, and we're likely to the point where we can discuss certain things... if you catch my drift." His eyes were wide as he gave up trying to be subtle about his goal. If he was going to understand this new officer, then implications and hints would not suffice. "I said you didn't have to tell me anything you didn't want to, but now might be a good time. We're sort of alone, the odds of getting a call are low. My offer of silence still stands." He was doing everything he could think of to help her come out of her shell, and yet she still seemed unconvinced of his altruistic intent.

"What happened with you?"

He did not expect that. "What do you mean?"

"You said your friend helped you. What did he help you with?"

Is she using reverse psychology on me?

Knight smiled at her playfully. "Is that how we're doing it? I go first, then you?"

"Maybe." In reviewing her file, Knight had seen her military service record, and he spotted one key detail: she had been recognized by the Navy for being in combat, so her bravery was not in question. He knew that she would only speak if he did.

Here goes nothing...

"Alright. Are you ready to hear this? It... doesn't have a happy ending."

"They rarely do."

"Fair enough." He then went on to break down the tragedies of his time in the Army: Amy, Kuwait, Rucker—the whole shebang. He included how he had spent a lot of time in the bottle mourning the life he could have had with the barkeep from Callahan's, how he did not understand why she rejected him as she did, and how it was Peterson's intervention that set him back on course. Knight owed an incredible debt to the man from Milwaukee, and he sought to pay it back whenever possible.

"It sounds like he really helped you."

"Like you would not believe. Besides getting me to talk about all of that, he did what no one else could, and what I needed the most: he got me to move on from her. It took him slapping me upside the head with a cold, hard shot of the truth, but it eventually worked. I was so hung up on her and the thought of what could have been, that it derailed my life for years—I wasn't myself. Now... I'm a new man," he said with a smile.

"That's good to hear, and I'm really sorry about her. What was her name? Amy?"

"Yeah, Amy Barnes."

"Well... do you miss her? Do you still think about her?"

Hmm... why is she so interested?

"Not like that. I wonder what she's up to every so often, but I've resolved to put all of that behind me. I went through too much shit to linger on something that could never be." There. It had only taken nine years, but he had finally managed to say the words to someone other than Peterson, and they were to the most beautiful woman he had seen since the one who had captivated him so long ago.

"I imagine it was hard to tell me all of that." She had both hands around her coffee cup, with the right one looped through the handle.

"You could say that. It's gotten easier with time, but... you know." His eyes softened, and his expression indicated a level of vulnerability that even a blind man could see.

It was then that Betty brought their food over, and the moment was lost forever, though no one was to blame. They were in a restaurant and had ordered their meals from the waitress—what else was she supposed to do? They ate largely in silence, though they did inquire as to the quality of the other's entrees, as if that was somehow on par with the gravity of the overall subject matter. Their meals complete, silence overtook the booth, with it becoming even more clear that Kowalski was not keen on the idea of divulging such personal information.

Knight had resigned himself to learning nothing further about his partner's clouded past when she blurted out, "I lost my friend in Iraq."

There it is.

He closed his eyes and exhaled, somehow relieved at hearing this terrible revelation, and trying to calculate how to proceed from here. Thankfully, Betty had just returned with a full pot of coffee, which he asked her to leave on the table. She removed their plates and walked away.

He gave Kowalski a meaningful look. "You don't have to continue if you don't want—"

"It was Memorial Day in 2010. Hawkins and I had just had some coffee at the Green Beans on Victory, and I was walking back to my post. They hit us with... rockets... mortars... small arms. It was coordinated."

Her face was blank, neither frown nor smile present, as she stared down at the table. "I tried to help a guy who was pinned under some rubble... but ... I failed. He lost his leg. I nearly killed one of our own in my rage, but it wasn't his fault." She paused, letting the images wash over her, Knight supposed.

She went on, "Another guy had me go with him to a tower... but they had it zeroed before we even made it up the stairs..." Her breathing had quickened, and it was clear to him that she was barely hanging on at this point. "That soldier and I hit the deck when they opened up on us... nearly blew the tower to pieces... he-he called in a helo... saved us both. It was later on I found out Hawkins... never made it."

Her eyes had not moved since she started, but Knight knew the scene was playing out before them as she carried on. "She was heading to her post when it started... did what she was supposed to do. The official report said she went prone for a minute, then she got up and ran... ran toward a T-wall for cover when the next volley was fired. She had a fifty-fifty shot of picking the right side... never even saw it coming."

"My God..." His words failed him.

Her eyes finally rose to meet his. "God was taking that day off."

Her delivery sent a chill through his body. Asking for more details would be incredibly risky, but he decided to take the chance. "You said you nearly killed one of your own. What was that about?"

She audibly scoffed. "Major Higgins... was under some reinforced concrete, rubble from the building he was in... I called this guy over to help me. I wanted him to pull the slab up and hold it while I pulled the major out from underneath..."

Knight noticed that her right hand was clenched so tightly around the mug that the color was draining from her knuckles. But she continued, "He couldn't hold it up... I wasn't strong enough to pull him out, and the concrete just... took his leg off." Her voice cracked. She paused for a good minute, struggling to keep sharing. "If I had just... stopped and thought about it... all I had to do was help the guy lift the slab... and move it away. But I tried to do it all myself, and now... Major Higgins is out of the Army. And I probably traumatized the guy who helped me—did more damage to him than the attack itself."

Knight could only stare at this brave soul and be grateful that she finally did what she likely thought to be impossible. Talking it out would help her process the event, and that was the only way for her to heal. The silence took over again, as Kowalski remained in a trance, though she drifted back to reality when the waitress returned and asked if either of them wanted dessert.

Knight knew his partner was finished eating for the night. "I think we're good, Betty. Thank you."

The waitress placed the tab near the edge of the table. As she walked back to the register, Kowalski finally shed the tears that she had desperately fought to control. Knight peeled off a napkin from the dispenser and handed it to her, but she waved it off. He wanted to keep her engaged. "I remember hearing about that on the news," he said, letting her know she was not alone in the memory. Her eyes met his again, and her expression said that while he may have seen it play out on *CNN*, she had witnessed it firsthand.

Knight acknowledged that he had not known about the man trapped in the rubble. He pointed out that the fellow might have died right there had it not been for Kowalski's intercession. "It took a lot of courage to share all of that."

"Yeah, well, now you know."

"I'm so sorry about your friend."

She seemed to be regaining her equilibrium. "A few months after getting out," she said quietly, "I got a memorial tattoo. It's her name over my right shoulder blade. That way, she always has my back."

Knight could only offer a half-smile and nod. Though he had been in the military twice as long as Kowalski, hers was a world he knew nothing about. All he could do was quietly admire this seaborne warrior for what she had endured, and, simultaneously, chide himself for his reaction the first time he saw her. Yes, she was beautiful; yes, she made him forget about every other lady he had met before her; but she was far more than just a pretty face. She was a woman who had stared down the enemy and lived. She was a woman who deserved far more respect than he had given. Her physical allure was one thing, but this... history... was something else entirely.

Knight gave a light sigh. "Are you, uh, ready to go? There's a lot of crime not happening out there," he said.

"Yeah. Just let me run to the bathroom first." Kowalski left the booth and headed toward the back of the diner. Knight grabbed the check and quickly paid for it, tucking the receipt into his pocket before she could return.

Betty cashed him out. "Smooth, Rick. Are the two of you...? Hmm?"

"I'm her trainer, so, no."

"You won't be forever. She's really pretty, and I picked up on something between you. Not sure what, but keep at it. You look good together."

"I'll keep that in mind." Kowalski returned just in time to miss the exchange between customer and cashier, and appeared ready to depart the diner.

"I took care of dinner. Call it a Christmas present."

"Thanks, boss. Shall we?" she asked, returning her hat to her head.

"See ya next time, Betty. Thanks for all the coffee."

"Be safe, guys. Thanks for all you do!"

Stepping out into the near-empty lot, the officers returned to their squad car. Before they left, Knight turned to Kowalski to make sure she was alright.

"It got pretty real in there. You sure you're okay?"

"I've never told anyone what I've just told you, not even my mother. It's not something I ever want to repeat, okay?"

"I'll never bring it up again. I'm just... glad you trusted me enough to share." He put the car in gear and drove out of the parking lot, returning to the interstate, and awaiting the next call on the radio.

SUNDAY, 23 FEBRUARY 2013

Awakening in his king-sized bed, Knight was assaulted by the piercing alarm from his cell phone as it blared its afternoon alert, robbing him of rest and reminding him of one price he paid for his profession. He hit the snooze button to kill the noise, but dared not resume sleeping, as he might not wake up again anytime soon, and an important task awaited his attention. He sat up in bed and looked around the room, convinced that he had made the right call by moving to this house, and thankful to be away from his apartment. At nearly thirty-two years old, he felt that it was time for him to put down roots and invest in a property instead of wasting money on rent. Thus far, he was enjoying the freedom of owning his own home. It may not have been an extravagant manor with excess bedrooms and a four-car garage, but it was *his*, and he was able to purchase it through a VA loan. In only thirty short years, it would be totally paid off.

Too easy.

He finally mustered the will to leave the bed, procuring a clean shirt from his dresser, and made a much-needed trip to the restroom before walking into the kitchen and pouring himself a glass of water. Breakfast would have to wait, though, despite his stomach letting him know just how long it had been since he had last eaten. He staggered into the living room and took a seat at his desk, barely awake, and waited for the Skype call to go through on his laptop.

It was time for his weekly ritual to keep those at home informed of what was going on in his life. Since he'd returned from Kuwait, few weeks had gone by when he did not contact his parents through some means, a phone call at minimum, about work, the Army, the police academy, college, and so on. This time, though, the subject was something he had not yet touched upon with Thomas and Michelle, but he was at a loss for how to proceed into this new territory. He had previously shared his accounts of emotional anguish and professional embarrassment, but today's call would be different.

With the connection finally established, Michelle appeared on the screen and greeted her son. "Hi, Ricky, how are ya?" She called him

"Ricky" as though he was still that eight-year-old on the playground in their neighborhood. Some things never changed.

"Hi, Mom. I'm a little tired, but I just woke up, so..." He shrugged his shoulders. Being tired was nothing new for him, but it did get old after a decade or so.

"Really?" She checked her watch. "It's almost four-thirty over here. When did you go to bed?" Michelle was accustomed to long hours on her feet due to her years as a hairstylist, but she had not been subjected to working shifts.

"Close to nine. I had to get some groceries on the way home, and then I couldn't fall asleep because I was wired from all the coffee I drank last night. Had to break up a fight between a pimp and one of his... shall we say, 'employees,' and then I had to arrest him for taking a swing at me. It was not a pleasant morning," he said, deadpan, though not regretting his line of work.

"My goodness." She knew these problems existed, but it was different when your son was the one tasked with cleaning up the mess. A new topic was definitely in order. "So, what's new on your end?"

"Let's see. I had been training a new officer since May, and... I don't know. Something strange is going on."

"Is he not learning the job?"

"*She*... is learning it, and doing really well, but it's not her training that's getting to me. She's with a new trainer at this point, anyway." His gaze ventured over to the side for a moment before his eyes returned back to the screen, his hesitation evident as he fought to find the right words. Given the colored nature of his personal relationships with women, it was harder for him to discuss such a personal matter, especially with his mother. "This woman... there's something about her that I can't figure out. Well, for starters, she's drop-dead gorgeous, even in uniform, and you saw the women in my academy class—that outfit is not flattering." She laughed in agreement, nodding. He continued, "We met last year, and I've been drawn to her ever since."

"Oh, yeah? You seem pretty smitten."

"Yeah. I'm in deep smit. The more I've gotten to know her, the harder it's been to concentrate on training her sometimes. She's incredibly smart, she loves movies, maybe more than I do. She was in the Navy, and while it sounds really superficial... did I mention how hot she is?" It was a rhetorical question, of course.

"Yeah, that came up," Michelle said with a smile. "Is she aware of all this?"

"I have no idea. I was her trainer, and we're in the same chain of command, so I can't just ask her out. But I thought I picked up on something when we were talking a few months ago. Nothing much—just some things she's said. I got a feeling that there may be something on her end, but I can't just bring it up. If she says no, then I look like an idiot for presuming, and then things are awkward. If she says yes, I still can't do anything until she's off probation, and that won't happen until May."

"Okay... so what's your plan? What are you gonna do about this?" Michelle always tried to make her kids think about things for themselves instead of deciding for them. This had likely aided Knight as an officer.

"Right now... there is no plan. All I can do is wait and hope to God that she isn't already seeing someone. She's never mentioned anybody and I've never raised the topic—it didn't seem appropriate on the job. One thing I know for sure is that breathtaking women don't remain single for long." He spoke from experience.

His mother paused, gathering her thoughts for a moment before adding, "You really do like her, don't you?"

"That's an understatement. I've met plenty of women over the years, and you have an idea of how my dating life has gone," he said, vaguely hinting at an embarrassing incident from last year in which his father had discovered a bra under the couch when they visited him, likely an escaped undergarment from a dalliance that never made it to the bedroom. "Jen is... she's something else."

"At least she has a name. I was wondering when you were gonna say it."

"Good point. Jennifer Kowalski from Illinois. Joliet, specifically."

"She's a *Yankee*?" Michelle asked, expressing faux concern.

"Illinois is in the Midwest, so no. She's very particular about that. Family is third-generation Polish-Catholic. She went to college for a few years, it didn't work out, so she joined the Navy."

"Does she know you're Lutheran? That should make for quite the discussion." Her smile was ear to ear.

"She hasn't gone to mass in years, likely won't go back. Her faith has kind of been shaken due to life events, which I understand. It doesn't make me want her less." Saying all of this to someone other than himself was liberating. "Is Dad around? Is that him behind you?" He thought he saw his father at the desk behind Michelle.

"Yeah, Son, that's me." Thomas spun around in his chair and rolled it over by his beloved wife. "And yes, I've heard everything you said."

"And what do you think?" Knight valued the opinions of both his parents, but his father's take on things always seemed to provide more of a guiding force in his life. It was Thomas who suggested enlisting as an alternative to college, wisely pointing out that their farming town offered little in the form of employment after high school. He also suggested looking into the San Antonio Police Department after he left the military. His track record on parental advice was second to none.

"Son, I don't mean to dredge up old wounds, but it sounds like you're into this girl more than Amy." In addition to doling out sound advice, Thomas also did not like to beat around the bush.

"Honestly... yeah. It feels that way. It's been nine months since we met. We've never gone out or seen each other away from work, but I cannot stop thinking about her," Knight said, introspectively. It was this realization, achieved weeks earlier, that drove him to think of her as more than just a subject of desire.

"Then as long as you're not breaking some rule about fraternization, or whatever they call it on the force, I say go for it. Wait until you're not over her anymore, and then take the leap."

"You think that's the best way to go? Just take the leap?"

"If *I* hadn't, you wouldn't be here."

"Tom!" Michelle interjected, surprised at his candor.

"What?" He turned to Michelle. "If I hadn't hit on the pretty lady at the PX barbershop that one time, none of them would be here."

It was a valid point, but one that Knight did not want to hear. "On that note, I believe it's time for me to go," he said. He enjoyed the opportunity to speak with them, but there had to be a limit on his parents' romantic history for one afternoon. "I won't see her for a while because she's with another trainer, but I'll try to catch her before our shift starts, or—or in the break room or something. I don't know." He looked concerned, but all he could do was think about what to do next and how to go about it, how to tell Kowalski that she was at the forefront of his thoughts, and that he wanted to get to know the woman behind the badge.

"Alright, Son. I hope you get her."

"Thanks, Dad. Oh, and one more thing... happy birthday," he said, looking on with respect for this man, both his father and a veteran. Knight's job kept him inordinately busy, but he always made it a point to contact his parents on their birthdays, and the accompanying card arrived no later than the day of, even if it entailed overnight shipping.

"Well, thanks, Rick. I thought that turning sixty-two would somehow be easier than sixty-one, and it hasn't been that bad so far."

"Dad... you've been this age for sixteen hours."

"Eh. Have a good day, Son. Stay safe. Your mother and I love you."

"I love you, too, Dad." With that, the call ended.

Knight sat back from the desk, looking through the window into the distance, wondering how the next few months would play out, and whether Kowalski would accept his future offer of a social interaction. Did she see him as anything other than a trainer? Why was she curious about his feelings for Amy? Did their age difference matter to her? Six years would hardly qualify as a real gap by most standards, but some in the department might assume that there was something between them while he was training her. He may have harbored a physical attraction toward her for months, but this emotional yearning did not appear until recently, and his only wish was that she would one day reciprocate his desire to be with her. What was he feeling? Could it be something more?

TUESDAY, 21 MAY 2013

"Captain, I didn't know this was for a full week. I thought it was just a one- or two-day gig and I'd be back the next day. Can we afford to have me out for that long?" Knight had not realized what he was getting into when he had raised his hand back in March and volunteered to teach at a summer activity in Dallas. Now, he was worried that his willingness to help would hurt the department, and he was trying to see if he could be replaced by someone else.

"Sorry, but they've already finalized the roster. Everyone is locked in across the state for the boot camp. So, the only way you're getting out of it is if you come down with something the week of, and that'd look sketchy as hell. You're going, Knight. End of story."

"Yes, sir. I'll make sure the kids have a good time."

The "kids" in question were high school-aged students who had an interest in law enforcement, and who participated in what was essentially a scouting program for police departments across the country. They wore modified uniforms, trained with officers, learned about enforcement techniques, and, once per summer, they could take part in a week of training that was akin to what countless officers endured at the police academy, though it was not nearly as rigorous or intense. The point was to give them an idea of what real police training was like, not to create a junior cadet league with arresting powers and firearms.

"That's the better answer."

"Will that be all, sir?"

"Yeah, that's it. Be safe out there."

Knight rose from the chair and departed the captain's office, stopping by the lounge for some coffee and reading through some field reports as he prepared for his shift. His eyes trailed up from the paper for a moment, just in time to see Kowalski enter the room. Instantly, his day was that much brighter.

He had not seen her in some time, as she was training on day shift. It seemed that somehow, she had become even more beautiful than before.

What was that? Did she just smile at me? And is she walking over?

"Corporal. It's good to see you."

"Same here. How have you been? I heard you made it through the probationary phase—congratulations."

"Yeah, well... I had some great teachers," she said, her eyes showing something new, something he had never seen in them before.

What's going on?

She continued, "And day shift is certainly different. More traffic violations than I imagined. It's scary how many people are drinking at ten o'clock in the morning."

"Yeah, that happens," he said in a cavalier manner. All he could do was think of how much he wanted to be with her, and how he had to act for that to happen. "Listen... I know you're about to leave, but can you catch me by my car before you head out? I wanted to talk to you about something... privately."

"Um, sure. Can we talk now? I got a ton of paperwork to do, and who knows how long that'll take?"

"Yeah. Let's head out." He led her out the door and into the scorching Texas sun, both quickly realizing that inside the cruiser would be the better option. He waved her in and then turned the air on as soon as the engine was cranked.

The cool air helped both of them immensely, given the extra body heat generated by the vests. Knight had no idea how to proceed with her. Kowalski was not some random girl from the gym or anyone that he wanted to add to his list of bad decisions. She was the one who had captured his attention from the moment he first saw her, the one whose significance had grown markedly in the intervening months. Most of all, she was the one who trusted him with her pain. He had to know if there was anything more to this than just a unilateral attraction.

"Listen, Kowal—may I call you Jennifer?" He realized that he had not addressed her by her given name before, and he wondered how she would react to hearing it from him.

She smiled, warmly, he thought, saying, "I guess that'll be alright, Corporal."

Well, at least I can use hers.

"Good. I mean—thank you. Um... I wanted to see if, maybe... you would like to hang out with me some time. Off duty."

"Are you asking me out?"

"Yeah."

Trying, at least.

"Wow. I, uh… hmm. That was… unexpected."

That's not good.

"It's not a big deal. I didn't have anything planned, really. I figured we could meet up and just sort of… like I said, hang out, or whatever. I liked being around you, and… I miss it." He tried to offer a debonair look of confidence, but his heart was practically beating out of his chest, and he was probably sweating bullets as well, even with the air on full blast. She, on the other hand, seemed as calm and collected as ever. "I checked with HR, and they said since you're on a different shift with a new team and everything, we wouldn't be breaking any rules. Unless you're not interested, in which case—"

"I'd like that, actually. When are you off next?"

Holy… was that a yes?

"Uh… I—let me check." He drew his cell phone and scrolled through the calendar. She did the same, calling out several dates before they finally settled on one. "Sunday, the twenty-sixth," Knight echoed. "When is a good time for you?"

"I'm on a day schedule, so it's really more about when is good for you."

"How about eleven? That'll give me time to take a nap, and we can get some lunch or something. I'm sort of playing this by ear." His shy and slightly unsteady demeanor appeared to have an effect on her, as she could not stop smiling while they solidified their plans.

"That works for me, Corp—may I call you Rick?" Her eyes had never been brighter than when she asked this question.

"Yeah." He had to remember to breathe. "Well, your shift's over and mine's about to start. Thanks for speaking with me. And for saying yes."

She chuckled, adding, "Not a problem. I'll text you my address. Be safe out there." She placed her hand on his briefly before exiting his cruiser.

His heart was still working overtime while he crashed from the high of her affirmative answer. Somehow, he had secured a date with her, and it was incumbent upon him not to ruin things between now and Sunday morning. What would he wear? What would they do? He remembered how some of his first dates had gone in the past, and while those served as further evidence of a misspent young adulthood, he had already vowed that the same would not hold true for this one. Somehow, it had to be different, and best of all, Kowalski did not strike him as that kind of woman—the "one and done" type. He still had a few more days to think about it, though, as his shift had officially begun ten minutes earlier.

He took another sip of his coffee, along with a deep breath, and made the drive toward his usual patrol route. His phone chirped a few moments later. It was a text message from her:

4909 Sterlington Way :) Looking forward to it.

CHAPTER 11

"HE'LL BE HERE in a bit. I should be nervous, but I'm not." Kowalski sat on her couch, with her laptop on the ottoman, conversing with Alex about her pending date with Knight and doing her best to assure her friend that she was totally relaxed. "Is that a bad sign?"

"It could mean you're so comfortable that him coming over is just the next step." She was not sure how to process that, but her friend's next words were truly unsettling. "It could also be that you agreed out of sympathy, and not because you really *wanted* to go out with him."

"Damn, Alex. I'm not *that* shallow."

"Um, Jen? Didn't you say he was only average-looking? I mean, he is, but he's still sort of handsome, and you said yes!" It seemed that she also minored in philosophy.

"I was at Coronado. You couldn't throw a rock there without hitting a SEAL or a commando, and those guys were *men*. Knight is just... *not* one of them. That may not be fair to him, but it's just a fact, even if he is intelligent and kind and thoughtful... and other things." She went quiet, recalling the conversation at the diner, and that it was Knight—not anyone else—who had brought her to a point of being able to discuss her trauma. He may not have been what she wanted in the physical sense, but he was definitely what she needed in all other departments, though did this matter? Could she see past his perceived shortcomings to become something more than a colleague?

"See? You're doing it again. You did the same thing a few days ago. Jen... you clearly like him. Maybe it's just a crush. Maybe he's not the right guy and only time will tell—I don't know. But from where I sit, you're thinking about him as more than just another cop. And you've got about a minute before he gets there. By that point, it'll be too—"

Three firm knocks reverberated from the door. Knight was punctual to a fault.

Kowalski could only sit quietly for a moment, her eyes wide and looking to her right as Alex beamed, saying, "Good luck!"

Kowalski closed her computer, rose from the couch, checked her look in the reflection of the framed picture on the wall, and walked over to the door. One deep breath later, she unhooked the latch and opened her home, greeting her date with a warm and welcoming smile.

"Hi." His own smile toward her was beyond dashing.

She stood opposite Knight, dressed in form-fitting jeans and a semi-loose burgundy shirt. She wore her hair down and went barefoot. The effect was irresistible, but he did not let on. He stood with one hand behind his back.

"Hey, Rick. Please... come inside."

As he crossed the threshold, he produced a small vase with three purple lilies and some greens, and graciously handed them to her, his eyes never leaving hers. "I already cut the stems, so they should last an extra day or two."

She thanked him and placed the flowers by a windowsill. "How did you know those were my favorite?"

"You mentioned it on patrol once, back around... Halloween, I think."

"And you remembered? This whole time?" He could only shrug in response. "Wow... thank you."

"It was no trouble." He looked around the room, impressed with what he saw, and praised her decorative tastes. A brown sectional couch was positioned in the corner, pointed toward a TV stand with gaming consoles, DVD shelves, and surround-sound speakers—everything a gamer needs. The kitchen was small but modern, with a new refrigerator, an island with storage cabinets, and almost enough counter space.

"Your place is nice. When did you move in?"

"A few days after the academy. I really like the complex, even though it doesn't have a pool or a gym. The low rent makes up for that."

Knight ventured over to her DVD shelf for a closer look, and did a double-take at the sheer number of World War II-themed items in her collection. Everything from mainstream movies to documentaries was present, as were several video games depicting campaigns from the world's largest armed conflict, and this thoroughly charmed him.

"You, uh, seem to be a bit of a historian."

"Yeah, I've been obsessed with that era ever since I could remember. It sounds cheesy, but... I really do believe I was born in the wrong decade. I'd give anything to have lived back then and be part of it." He saw a twinkle in her eye, a genuine longing for a period of time that she had never experienced, and he only wanted her more. He once mentioned that history was one of the few academic subjects he excelled in throughout his schooling, so finding a beautiful woman who also enjoyed taking trips to the past seemed like quite a rare achievement. "Can I get you anything? Maybe some tea or coffee?"

"Coffee would be good, unless you happen to make your tea sweet." It was a long shot, but he had to ask.

"No, I can't do that. I've had southern tea before, and it was basically pure sugar."

"The best kind," he said, with a slight grin. If the tea did not have two cups of sugar, then it was not tea, according to Knight.

"How do you take your coffee?"

Kowalski could see that he was fighting tooth and nail with himself not to make a joke about "blonde and hot," but he won the battle. "Cream and sugar, please."

She had the machine going shortly thereafter, and both were standing by the island as she turned around to retrieve mugs from a cabinet. She poured two cups and added the requested augmentation, bringing both back to the island and sliding Knight his cup.

"Here you go."

He reached over to take the mug and made contact with her hand, but neither he nor she retracted upon doing so, and his fingers remained on the top of hers, warmed by the coffee, as their eyes met. "You, uh... gonna let me have that?" His nervous smile concealed the countless thoughts going through his head, but she could see through the mask. Still, though, she did not rush to move her hand from his.

"Oh, yeah. Sorry." With incredible grace and that smile still a fixture, she took a sip from her cup and waited for him to do the same, before moving things to the couch.

They talked for an hour about everything from friends and family to college and world events. They reminisced about some of the more humorous moments from Kowalski's training, like the time she nearly arrested a priest after mistaking him for a suspect who was dressed all in black. Knight kept his full attention on her, his thoughts easy to read in his rapt expression.

"Would you like another?" she asked, pointing to his coffee cup.

"Yeah. Let's reload and go again." Knight accompanied her on the short walk back to the kitchen. As she began to refill their cups, he reached over to grab the sugar canister by the microwave. She turned toward him, trying to reach the same canister, and their arms brushed against each other. Instead of apologizing for bumping into him, she gently grasped his forearm. He could only look into her eyes and then at her hand as both stood in the kitchen, each absorbing the electricity in the room and contemplating what to do next.

Whose move is it? Mine? His?

She waited to see what he would do next.

He placed the sugar back on the counter and brought his right hand to her cheek, cradling her head and gently stroking her face with his thumb. She closed her eyes in response, still holding his forearm with her left hand, and reaching out for his left hand with her right, squeezing his fingers. She opened her eyes in time to feel his lips on hers, and she responded by placing her arms around him, matching his fire with her own, as this first kiss became another, and another... and another.

He withdrew himself from the perfection of the moment, still holding her close to him, saying, "You have no idea just how long I have wanted to do that." He leaned in and planted a kiss on her forehead, wrapping both arms around her, and pulling her in closer.

"I'd say... about a year?" Her intuition was keen.

"Close to it," he said sheepishly. "Did you still want coffee?"

"No. I want this." She pulled his head down toward hers, resuming their passionate embrace, and directed him to remove his shoes and leave them by the door.

A moment later, she led him over to the couch. For the next few hours, time seemed to stand still, as her lips rarely left his, and neither of them left the couch.

"We, uh, never had lunch. Are you hungry?" he asked, between the long kisses.

"Yeah, but it can wait." And the passion between them resumed yet again, intense but restrained, as Knight was struggling to keep his base urges in check. Sensing a spike in the moment, he asked her to wait, and had her sit up with him on the sofa.

"Listen, I really want to keep this going... you have *no* idea how much... but we need to slow it down. I mean, we haven't even gone anywhere, and it's nearly four. I don't want to screw things up my moving too fast with you, Jenny."

"Jenny?" He had not called her that before.

"Yeah. Like the girl in the song?" He offered his best rendition of the chorus from "867-5309," but Knight was no singer.

"I know that one. It's one of my dad's favorites. He's never admitted it, but I have a feeling that's how I got my name."

"Good song. Anyway, I want to see you again. Tomorrow, the next day, and most likely, the day after that. Kissing you just now is like... kissing an angel."

Corny, but he means it. Aww.

"But let's take a breather."

No way.

Kowalski hated this, but appreciated his effort to ensure this would not be a mistake for both of them. "I don't know, Rick... I was getting real used to this," she said, pressing her lips to his once more, her tongue contacting his as she ran her hand down his chest. For someone with so little history with men, she felt that she was quite good at this. Maybe too good. "But you're right. Why don't we call it a day on this," she said, gesturing to the couch with her head, "and go get something to eat? You've got to be hungry, and I know if I try to make dinner, I'll burn it."

"You're afraid of overcooking?"

"No. Because if we stay here, it's going to move into there." She looked over at the bedroom door.

"Ah. Good call."

She walked over to the front door and retrieved his shoes, grabbing her own in the process. Soon, both were nearly ready to go, though Kowalski needed time to adjust the mess that her hair had become from their time on the sofa.

"Any place in particular that you'd like to go?" Knight asked.

"There's a Steak 'N Shake a few miles away. Oh, and that strip mall at the intersection has this amazing tapas bar."

"You want to go to a topless bar?" he asked, his eyes wide with intrigue.

"*Tapas*," she replied.

"Oh," he said, slightly embarrassed.

"Yesterday was your birthday, so this one's on me."

His face alighted. "How did you know—"

"I... *may* have looked in your file as well. Can't really say why, though." Her half-attempt at looking innocent was working.

"Nicely done."

"Thank you. Now, lunch. What are you thinking?"

"Both sound good, but there can be only one."

"Okay, *Highlander*..." She thought for a moment, then the solution came to her. "One sec." She walked over to the small table by the front door and retrieved her purse, unzipping a compartment and withdrawing a familiar item. "We'll flip for it."

Knight recognized his old unit's insignia right away, and the look on his face as his eyes met hers told her that she had far exceeded his expectations.

"Sounds like a plan."

"Call it in the air."

MONDAY, 27 MAY 2013

Kowalski held Knight's hand as she drove her car under the archway of the Bellevue Memorial Gardens cemetery, quietly taking deep breaths as she and her new beau prepared to exit the vehicle. They had been there earlier that morning, having worked security and traffic control at one of the many Memorial Day services at locations across the city. Knight had suggested returning later so they could privately honor those lost. She agreed, but was apprehensive about the prospect of breaking down in front of him; it had nearly happened while she was on duty. Now, it seemed, the odds were even greater, since they were alone and out of uniform. But she had to take that risk.

She parked in one of the designated spots by the mausoleum, with Knight squeezing her hand to get her attention. She looked over at him, tensely, and he said, "I'm right here. I won't leave your side."

He says that like he means it, and it's only our second day together. I shouldn't feel this way for him, but...

"I know. Thank you, Rick." He brought her hand up and kissed the top, assuring her that she now had a support network far greater than she realized. They left the car and began strolling through the grounds, stopping at the graves of veterans and paying respect to the fallen warriors interred there. Headstones decorated with little American flags dotted the landscape. But there was one area that Kowalski was drawn toward, and she knew that having Knight there meant she could venture over. She motioned toward the monument close to the main entrance road.

"Are you ready for this?" She knew his question was not a commentary on female frailty. A new memorial had been dedicated that morning, and it was of particular relevance to Kowalski.

"No. But I need to see it."

Her determination and courage were inspiring. They followed the curve to the sidewalk and strolled down the path to the newest war memorial, one that honored the fallen from Afghanistan and Iraq. It consisted of three granite panels with the insignia of the military branches, plus the Department of Defense seal and the Prisoner of War/Missing in Action symbol near the top of the center panel. Commemorative plaques honoring those who served in the post-9/11 era were affixed to the outer panels, with topographic maps engraved beneath them and sandblasted images of troops engaged in missions across the base of all three. At the apex of the center panel, on a perch with its wings spread, sat a bald eagle, ready to take flight. In the middle, at eye-level with Kowalski, was a quote:

The State of Texas Honors the Men and Women of the United States Military Who Answered Their Nation's Call. Here, On These Hallowed Grounds, the Memory of Those Lost is Preserved For All Time.

Reading these words, Kowalski reached out with her hand, placing it on the center wall, and then fell to one knee. Knight dropped down beside her. She could feel herself shaking as she fought the memories of that day, and the agony of losing her friend, with only one word escaping her lips: "Jailah."

Knight placed his left arm around her, providing whatever comfort he could in this time of grief. While she did not want to admit it to him just yet, she was incredibly grateful that he was there.

"She knows you miss her, Jenny. As long as you remember her, she's never really gone."

"I know. I just... it's hard to believe that sometimes. I still see her in my dreams." She seemed to be looking through the wall itself, seeing what lay beyond the granite paneling. Knight remained quiet, waiting for her to speak. It was his idea to return to the cemetery after regular hours, but the goal was for her to honor her friend.

After a few more minutes in front of the new memorial, Kowalski rose to her feet, fought back more tears, and handed her keys to him. She knew better than to get behind the wheel when she was feeling this unstable.

"Here. You drive."

"Are you sure?"

"Yeah. I have a full shift tomorrow, and you work tonight, so let's go."

"Alright." The couple walked back to her car beneath the Texas sun, his arm around her in a meaningful way on this most sacred of holidays. Again, he opened the door for his lady before she entered the vehicle, and made sure she was ready to depart. She nodded, mute, and he maneuvered the car around the curve and back under the archway, making the turn toward her apartment.

CHAPTER 12

WEDNESDAY, 26 JUNE 2013

KNIGHT'S PHONE BUZZED.

> I put your mail on the kitchen counter. If you want, I can go back on Friday in case it piles up. Just let me know.

He smiled seeing the text, replying that she could check his mail again if she felt so inclined but adding that he was not expecting anything. He had given Kowalski a key to his place before leaving—not entirely sure if it was too soon—with the convenient pretense of him teaching at the Police Explorers Junior Academy in Dallas. After four days, the end was in sight, but he was not ready to go home. He missed his lady severely, yet he found the classroom environment very rewarding. The cadets seemed to enjoy his instruction and were highly engaged, even during the boring blocks.

Still, after hours, he had found himself thinking of Kowalski more and more.

Their relationship may have been in its infancy, but it was flourishing. They saw each other before and after work, on their days off, and when opportunities presented themselves. Amazingly, Knight had demonstrated a high degree of self-discipline with her, as they had not yet taken things to the next level. But Kowalski also deserved credit for this exercise in restraint. The Friday night before he departed, she revealed something about herself that he never would have guessed: despite her years in college, her enlistment in the military, and her time at the police academy, she had been with only one man in her life.

He did not believe her at first, but when she explained how devoted she was to becoming an actress, coupled with the trauma of her deployment, it made sense. He was not complaining. If she had chosen him to become her lover, then it was an honor worth waiting for.

On this morning at the academy, Knight was tasked with imparting a fairly simple but complicated lesson: the role of the peace officer. He had studied the slides the night before and knew the material quite well. But he found it to be exceedingly bland, and he knew that if reading it wearied him, then teenagers would likely expire from boredom within the first ten minutes. Nevertheless, the organization had standards, and one of them was using the prepared subject matter without deviation. So, he made his way toward the classroom as the previous lesson was about to come to an end, and quietly slipped into the back of the room.

Sergeant Palmer, an eighteen-year veteran of the Austin Police Department, was wrapping up her lesson on the moral reasoning necessary for officers of the law. She did so by highlighting that the American public trusts its officers to be moral individuals, and that no one wearing a badge is above the law. The cadets listened intently, and Knight could tell that many were resolving right then and there to become more upright in their behavior, even if they did not one day become officers. Palmer was simply that good as an instructor.

She dismissed the class for a ten-minute break, and Knight coordinated with her on setting up the slides for his lesson, taking a moment to praise her for the work she had done over the week. "Thanks, but it's just part of the job. If I don't do it, who will?"

"Good point."

He accessed the shared folder on the classroom computer and opened his presentation, cringing when he saw that the slides numbered sixty-seven. How would he hold anyone's interest that long?

As the break came to an end, the students began trickling into their seats a few at a time, with some greeting Knight as they entered the room. The clock struck eleven, and he commenced the lesson right on time, taking the remote and clicking the button to reach the first slide... and that was when the computer crashed.

Several of the cadets chuckled, and Knight also found the humor in the situation. He held the power button down for a few seconds, hoping that would revive the system, but no dice. He turned to the cadets, and asked, "Does anyone know CPR?" Being Police Explorers, all of them raised their hands promptly, to which Knight could only reply, "Right. Maintain that qualification."

He fiddled with the computer for a few more minutes before deciding that he would have to improvise. "Old school it is. Who can tell me what the role of a peace officer really is?" A few hands went up, so he called on the first one. "Go ahead, Cadet Leddick."

"To keep the peace and uphold the law," she said with confidence.

"Okay, I'll buy that. Anyone else?" More hands. "Cadet Pham. Let's hear it."

"To... maintain law and order, and to protect people."

Two for two. "Also correct. But there's more. Now, bear with me on this."

He proceeded to take them back in time to the Middle Ages, to an era when warriors on horseback served king and country, and when a code of honor was a unifying trait among those dedicated to service. "It is easy to ascribe the role of a knight just to those in the military, but having been an officer and a soldier, I speak with some authority when I say that we are also their spiritual successors. Every man and woman in this country wearing the uniform is a protector and a defender."

He let this sink in, and then said, "Think about it in a different way. Nowadays, before we go out on a shift, we put on our armor in the form of a Kevlar vest. We keep a weapon at our sides, and we train to use it properly and safely. A shield accompanies us as we guard society," he said, pointing to his badge, "and our horses, thankfully, don't get nearly as tired as the ones from back then. And they smell a lot better, too."

The cadets smiled at his joke, so he went on. "This shield does little in terms of protecting us from harm. But it's what it symbolizes that matters most: a commitment to serving our communities and protecting the people who live in them." He looked around the room and saw recognition of his point. He continued, "It is this commitment, and the character necessary to uphold it, that make the police officer, the state patrolman, the detective, the sheriff's deputy, the air marshal, and even the game warden... the modern-day knights. The warriors of that era swore loyalty to their king. Today, we swear an oath that reminds us of who we are, and who we serve." There. That was what he had been trying to say. "It's not an easy life, but as someone I know once said, nothing worth having is easy." He glanced up at the clock and noticed that his time was nearly up. "Class leader, we're gonna wrap it up now and head to lunch a little early. Let's get 'em outside and in formation."

"Yes, Corporal!"

The students rose from their desks and filed out of the class by rows, and within thirty seconds, the room was empty, apart from Knight and one other person too old to be a cadet. He had not noticed, but the academy director had discreetly walked in through a separate door and sat in for the duration of his lesson. She was a retired major with over thirty-five years on the force, now serving as an adult leader in the Police Explorer community. She approached him after the last cadet had left the room, and he expected a mild reprimand for going off-book with his lesson.

"Corporal, how long have you worked in San Antonio?"

"Just over five years, ma'am."

"Well, in the time I've been involved in this organization, I must admit that yours was one of the better lessons I've heard, even if it wasn't in the handbook," she said with a wry smile.

"Yeah, the, uh, computer died, so I had to think on my feet. I just hope they didn't find it too boring."

"Oh, I can assure you, they *loved* it. And you didn't have slides, or videos, or anything. *That* is impressive, Corporal."

"Well, thank you, ma'am. I appreciate the kind words."

"You deserve them." She paused briefly. "Tell me, have you considered how your future as an officer looks?"

Um, shit, that sounds ominous as hell.

"What do you mean?"

"I know people in the right places, and in you, I see someone who could perhaps better serve in a different capacity. I can tell you're an outstanding officer. You probably have at least two or three commendations, plus whatever you picked up in the Army."

Where is she going with this?

"Have you ever given any thought to becoming a police academy instructor?"

SATURDAY, 29 JUNE 2013

The summer air was hot as Knight took the exit ramp toward home, turning the radio off in the process and calling Kowalski while the traffic light remained red. She answered after a few rings. "Hey, Rick. Are you back in town?"

Even over the phone, her voice was intoxicating. "I just got off the highway, I'm at the intersection by Whataburger. Should be back at my place in about ten minutes, then I'll head over." The plan was to go out to a movie later.

"I was thinking we could do something else tonight. The movie can wait."

"Is everything okay? You've talked about seeing this one for weeks."

He could hear her distinctive chortle in the background before she said, "Just head to your place, and we'll discuss it there. It's not safe to talk and drive, Officer."

"Fair point, Jenny. I'll call you in a few."

He made the left turn onto Robinson Avenue, turning the radio on again and singing along as the classic rock station blared out Blue Öyster Cult's "(Don't Fear) The Reaper." Knight's musical preferences consisted almost exclusively of tracks that were older than him, but when music is timeless, its age becomes immaterial. The song ended just as he made the turn into the Mercia Heights subdivision, and he idly wondered why Kowalski had suddenly changed her mind, but he had little time to think. Parked in his driveway was the unmistakable sight of a red Mustang, his girlfriend's chariot, coming into view after he crested the hill. His face lit up immediately.

We'll discuss it there. Well played, Jenny.

He parked his car in the grass by the driveway, grabbed his duffel bag, and walked up to the door to be greeted with a kiss from his lady before he could even reach for the handle. He had only been away for a week, and yet it felt like months had gone by since he last laid eyes on this insanely arresting woman. Her dress was floral, free-flowing, and knee-length, with thin straps over the shoulders. She had removed whichever shoes she had worn to the house, and her hair was tied back in a ponytail, which she usually reserved for while she was running or at the gym. He had seen her out of uniform many times in recent weeks, but this was somehow different.

"Rick... it is so good to see you." She hugged him with gusto after they both walked back into the house, and he noticed that she had her own overnight bag as he set his down on the floor. "I wanted to surprise you. I hope it worked," she said with a smile that could stop traffic. The look on her face was something he had not seen in her before.

"I'd say you nailed it, Jenny." He could not keep his hands off her, reaching out again to embrace her as he picked her up off the floor and looked into her hazel eyes. Placing her back on her feet, he said, "Wow, this whole outfit is just... you look absolutely stunning."

"Why, thank you, kind sir. I thought you'd like it." She mock-curtseyed as she said the words. Knight retreated to the restroom for a much-needed break, and then returned to find Kowalski patiently waiting in the living room.

"Now, if you will please come with me, I have a task for you, and I think it's one you'll enjoy." Her tone implied an air of mystery as she led him not to the bedroom, but to the kitchen. On the counter, she had neatly laid out multiple miniature bottles of various liqueurs and alcohols, saying, "I need you to help me get rid of these."

Knight's work with the Police Explorers had been burdensome at times and he had not been able to enjoy a drink since he left, so he had planned on having one anyway. But putting away that many? What was going on?

"Um, what? I don't really follow." He was telling the truth.

"Drink up. You had a long week, so I wanted to help you unwind a little. Here—have this one first." She twisted off the tiny cap on a bottle of Grand Marnier and handed it to him.

Knight smiled back at her, taking the drink. "Man, this is... unexpected. And I suppose this is why you wanted to skip the movie?"

"You'll be a detective in no time. Now drink up!"

He enjoyed a good belt of booze every so often, and now was a good time. While the junior academy had gone well, two cadets wound up getting homesick and asked to leave, while three others violated curfew and had to be disciplined. He licked his lips and finished off the first beverage in a few seconds, the combination of the orange flavor and its potency being a welcomed reward.

She passed him another. "One down, several more to go."

This is weird.

"If you insist, but aren't you having one?" He hated drinking alone, especially if she was with him.

"No. This is all about you."

He took the next bottle and emptied it in one go. Ready to stretch out, he motioned toward the living room. She picked up the rest of the drinks and accompanied him to the couch, placing them on an end table as he slipped off his black flip-flops. After fifteen years of combat boots, his feet needed as much of a break as they could get.

"How was the graduation? Did anyone pass out?"

"Not this year, but I was worried about one kid. She was sweating like crazy the whole time and I swear to God, her uniform and gear weighed more than she did."

He had eaten a light lunch before hitting the road, but these drinks were going straight to his head. It seemed right, so he placed one hand on her knee and his other arm around her, pulling her in for another kiss, and savoring the surprise of having her in his home. Somehow, despite his average looks, he had this knockout by his side. "You've never looked better, Jenny." He began to lightly squeeze her right leg as he felt a warm feeling overtaking him, the best side effect of alcohol. She seemed to enjoy the sensation, closing her eyes, and vocalizing her approval.

"Why don't you have another?"

Hard to say no at this point.

"You drive a hard bargain. Let's see... this one." He had already consumed cognac and vodka, so he picked the one labeled 99 APPLES and inhaled deeply as he twisted the cap off. "An apple a day," he said, and put away his fourth drink in just under half an hour, a feat he had not attempted in years. Knight had resolved not to drink like that anymore, but his guest was insistent, and he aimed to please.

Kowalski rose to her feet, took him by the hand, and softly said, "Follow me, Officer." Her face was brimming with something Knight had not witnessed before, and he let her lead them both to his bedroom, stopping in front of the bed, where she placed the deepest, wettest kiss on his lips. His hands firmly gripped her backside in response. The combination of the alcohol, the kiss, and the unexpectedness of the moment hit him all at once.

"What was that for?"

What a stupid question.

"Because this is something I've wanted to do for a while now, so just relax and let me take care of you."

The sun began to set, and the light came through the blinds, casting its beautiful glow on an already beautiful woman. She reached down and unbuckled his belt, unfastened and unzipped his jeans, and with her thumbs tucked into the waistband, lowered his pants and black boxers to the floor. She helped him maintain his balance as he stepped out of them, sliding them to the side, before she stood before him again and kissed him once more. This time, she gently grasped his cock and felt it expand as the kiss continued.

He may have been three sheets to the wind, but he was cognizant enough to obtain consent.

"Are you sure about all of this? Because you... I mean..."

She merely nodded in response. Her eyes locked on his, she walked him backwards to the bed and sat him down before climbing onto his lap, guiding him into a supine position. Silently, she slid his shirt out of the way, moved to his side, and wrapped her lips around his fully erect penis, practically French kissing it as she finally gave in to her base desire to please this man. Knight had not felt this sensation in a very long time, and her adaptation to it was immediate, with the sight of her taking almost every inch of him in her mouth only making him want her that much more.

The deep exhalations and groans coming from him meant she was on the right track, and she seemed to enjoy what she was doing for him, as she held the base of his shaft in her right hand and focused her attention on the head, gently running her tongue over his skin, and keeping him under her complete control. She remained committed to her task, never once yielding to the discomfort in her jaw, and making eye contact with Knight whenever he looked up at her.

Knight moved his hand over to Kowalski while she continued, running his hand beneath her dress and feeling the wetness underneath her panties. That was the only hint he needed. "Here. Get up." The direction to his lover was neither stern nor corrective. He got up off the bed as Kowalski moved toward him and he lifted her dress off over her head. He tossed it against the wall and pulled her body close to his, raining kisses down the side of her neck and squeezing her shapely ass, finally realizing that she had been wearing a thong the whole time.

"Jesus, you're full of surprises tonight."

"I knew you liked red." Her words were like that of a song. She unclipped her bra as Knight continued to focus his attention on her neck, but he quickly moved to her breasts now that they were unencumbered, with both nipples standing erect. He had seen her topless before when he stayed at her apartment, and she quickly flashed him one morning before work. But now, he had a full view of their glory, and he was awestruck by how they seemed to defy gravity.

Picking her up and laying her down on her back, he then moved his hands to her thong, quickly sliding it off. He took a moment to admire the now fully nude goddess before him, her porcelain skin seeming to radiate even as the room grew darker with the setting sun.

There has never been a more beautiful woman than her.

He opened the drawer on his nightstand and withdrew a condom, tearing it open and sliding it down, asking, "Are you ready to do this?"

She licked her lips and met his question with a very firm, "Yes," moving herself to the middle of the bed as he positioned himself. Kneeling between her legs and using his thumb, he gently rubbed her clit. She took a tense breath, her body seizing briefly as she gripped the blanket with both hands. Slowly, he continued this motion, and she closed her eyes and leaned her head further back into the pillow. He massaged her breast with his free hand, lightly pinching and twisting the nipple, and her body shuddered with ecstasy. Able to wait no more, she looked him in the eye and gasped, "Please fuck me!"

Knight had wanted to hear these words from her for over a year. He opened her legs slightly and moved his body directly over hers, kissing her deeply as he continued to massage her clit, then gently guided his cock into her quivering vagina. Her body seized like before, but this time, it was far more intense, with her moans replacing the sharp breaths, as she sank her nails into his back. He moved slowly at first, wisely giving her the time she needed to adjust to him. Then he cradled her head in his hand and planted a gentle kiss on her lips, thrusting his body forward and not once taking his eyes off hers.

The chemistry between them was palpable, with each movement akin to a choreographed dance routine. Kowalski wrapped her legs around Knight's waist as he drove even further into her, the heat from their bodies causing both to perspire. She matched his thrusts with her own movements toward him, something that he was not expecting from her. He could tell that she was nearing her climax, so he went to his knees and continued to thrust as he simultaneously rubbed her clit again, increasing the intensity. Her breasts kept time with their movements.

At long last, Kowalski found her release, arching her back and screaming out her lover's name as her orgasm tore through her body. The aftershocks of Knight's sustained thrusting kept her in suspended euphoria long after the initial waves had subsided. He kept going for as long as he could, but despite his desire to bring this woman endless physical pleasure, he was still a human being, and the will to maintain his erection gave way to his own climax. Kowalski looked on as his face twisted and he emitted low groans from his throat. Still kneeling before her, he slowly ran his hands up and down her body as both fought to catch their breath, spent from the vigor of their love making. She was still glowing from her turn, and though her eyes were closed, it was clear that she was in heaven.

After kissing her on the cheek, Knight staggered to the bathroom, returning moments later to lie down next to his girlfriend and share in her post-coital glow. "How are you feeling?" He slid his left arm under her neck and shoulders, then she rolled her leg over onto him. His hand caressed her body, still moist from the heat of their passion, as she struggled to form the words. Minutes had elapsed since the crescendo of their union, yet she still struggled to breathe as she came down from the high.

"Give me a minute," she said with a smile. "I'm still not all here..." Like a star in the night sky, her body glowed from the sheer joy he had brought her, and she planted kisses on his chest as he held her close, their bodies intertwining on his king-sized bed. They gazed into each other's eyes, both privately wishing for this brief moment to endure forever. While the sun had set on this day, the dawn had broken on a new phase in their relationship, one that Knight hoped would go on for years to come.

SUNDAY, 30 JUNE 2013

Awakening with a mild headache, Knight was grateful that Kowalski had brought him some water before he fell asleep. They had slipped under the covers before officially calling it a night, and the last thing he remembered was pulling her in close to his body with her back against his chest as they both drifted off.

Despite his prior encounters with women, all of the hook-ups and awkward mornings-after, and even the few relationships that lasted longer than seventy-two hours, making love to Jennifer Kowalski and awakening next to her felt like an act of redemption for his prior sins, a second chance to be the man he knew he could be. She was more than just a girlfriend, more than just another sexual conquest. She was his future, and that future was as bright as the morning sun rising in the sky.

As darkness gave way to the morning light, he finally laid eyes on her tattoo—a masterful work of art over her right shoulder blade that paid tribute to her fallen friend. It was a lone dog tag with the name "Jailah" emblazoned across, with the dates of her birth and death enshrined in scroll-like tabs above and below the tag itself. Seeing it, he further realized just how much she meant to Kowalski, and how heartbreaking it must have been to lose her.

She turned toward him and opened her eyes to the sight of her lover lightly stroking her hair and smiled, drinking in this simple act as she leaned up for a kiss. Her lips parted when they met his mouth, her tongue making soft contact with his. "Hey there. How did you sleep?"

My God... she just woke up and her hair is still perfect. How did she do that?

"Like a baby. Remind me to drink that much and then fuck a supermodel more often," he said with a smirk. He was not lying. He had not rested that well in years. He wondered how much of it was influenced by his lady alone and not the combination of her plus the stiff drinks. He was certain of one thing: he wanted her on more than just a physical level. "And you? Ya sleep well?"

She laughed briefly, closing her eyes. "I was out like a light. I didn't wake up at all until just now. Best sleep I've had in a long time." She pulled her arm from under the blanket to wipe the sleep from her eyes. As she did, Knight saw her breasts again and was still completely amazed at how perfect her body was. In all his years, he had never seen a woman quite like her, a lady whose physical beauty was so enthralling that even in her police uniform, she still had the look of an A-list movie star on the red carpet. But unlike the parade of plastic copycats and synthetic drones on his television, she was as real as could be, and she was in his bed after having engaged in the physical act of love the night before. He had to mentally slap himself to remember that this was no dream or fantasy—she really was with him. "Is everything okay? You haven't said anything in a minute or two."

"Oh, yeah. Sorry... you're just—it's hard not to stare sometimes.

There's something about you. You look like a Hollywood starlet, but you're someone I work with. It's still hard to believe."

He kissed her again and once more, looking deep into her eyes, and gently pressing his forehead to hers. She returned his kiss, and it began to intensify as the contact continued. "I couldn't help but notice that you're about three kinds of naked. You think you're up for another round?" he asked, his head tilted sideways. The corner of her mouth rose slowly as she simply nodded.

Once more, they discovered one another, and when they were finished, Knight whispered, "I wish we could start every day like that." He smiled as he closed his eyes.

"Who says we can't?"

He opened his eyes and propped himself up on one arm. "For starters, you'd have to move in. Or I'd have to move in with you, and I think it's safe to say we're not quite there yet. But we're on the path. I mean, I did see your 'oh-face' last night," he said with the most juvenile look imaginable.

"My what? Oh…" It finally hit her.

"Exactly. I'll talk to the captain about getting us on the same schedule to make it easier," he added, only half-serious. Even before the component of a sexual relationship was added to the mix, he truly wanted to be around her as much as possible. She enriched his life, and he wanted only to do the same for her.

She put up her hand as if to say, *whoa.* "We've both got to work tomorrow morning, so why don't we just play it by ear for now?" His face dropped a bit before she added, "Hey, it's not like that. This wasn't about fucking and running. I just… need time to process everything."

Fair, but the idea of not seeing her was hardly palatable. She caught his sense of frustration. "Rick. The last day has been a whirlwind that will keep me smiling no matter what kind of shit we see this week. So, you don't need to worry about anything. There will be an encore, I promise."

That was what he wanted to hear. Immediately, she had elevated his mood.

"I've been eating in an Army chow hall for the last week, and I'd like something edible for breakfast. What do you say we go to Denny's? My treat."

"I like the way you think, but I need a shower first."

"Same here. Care to join me?" He gestured toward the bathroom door as she glanced over.

"Lead the way." She placed her right hand on his cheek as they kissed intensely, almost forgoing the shower in favor of round three, but ultimately settling in for a much-needed cleansing. Whether it was the hot water or the heat from their bodies that fogged up the mirror could not be determined. But they did not need a mirror to see the connection that had been forged between them.

MONDAY, 8 JULY 2013

"Good morning, handsome." Kowalski groggily greeted Knight as he stood opposite the bathroom mirror, carefully guiding the razor upward along the contours of his face. Wearing the bathrobe he had bought for her, she approached from his right, wrapping her arms around his waist and resting her head against his back as he continued one step in his pre-work routine. In the side mirror, he saw that the expression on her face remained as joyous as it had been the night before when they returned home from the theater, and she initiated sex with him before he could get them inside. The trail of scattered clothing leading from the foyer to his bedroom testified to the physical bond between them, as did the marks on his body from her nails.

"Good morning, beautiful. You sleep alright?"

"Coming like that tends to put me out, so... yeah." Her second climax, attained as she rode him, was such that she could barely hold herself up in its wake. The first one was quite strong, but she could only describe the second one as "full throttle" when he asked if she was alright. "And you? How did you sleep?"

"Not too bad, but the company helps me sleep soundly any time she's here," he replied, reaching down to squeeze her hand with his own. It was true. His years on night shift in both the Army and on the force had affected his ability to sleep or fully gain restorative benefits, but with her by his side during his REM cycle, he was waking up refreshed, renewed, and ready to serve the people of San Antonio. He found her presence in his bed to be nothing short of soothing, and even when he did wake up in the middle of the night, he would wrap his arm around her again, desiring only for the night to be just a little longer.

It seemed he was having a similar effect on her. Since they began dating and spending so many nights together, Kowalski's nightmares had been on the decline, both in frequency and intensity. She had verbally attributed this to Knight and the positive influence that he brought to her life. Her health was better, her mood had improved, even after rough days at work. Each complimented the other in numerous ways, and everyone around them had taken notice.

"Keep tomorrow night open. We have a reservation at eight, so let's hope things don't get too crazy. I've wanted to take you to this place for months."

"Mmm... and where are we going?"

"It's a Japanese place just off the bypass. Hibachi. Nice, but not that fancy—I'll be wearing a button-up," he said with a grin, highlighting his disdain for most outfits that did not consist of a T-shirt and jeans, as he finished his morning shave.

"That sounds great! I have this black dress I've been dying to wear, and it sounds like just the time." She retracted her arms and gently ran her nails up and down his back, careful not to aggravate the marks she had left the night before, and fulfilling one of his most favorite requests. Few things were more simple or enjoyable to Knight than having his back scratched, and Kowalski was quite adept at pinpointing right where his itch was.

"You could show up in sweats and flip-flops and outdo any woman there," he said, completely serious, as he applied the aftershave lotion to his face. He had seen her in every state of dress—and undress—over the last few weeks, and she always looked camera-ready, no matter what. She was beyond gifted in the looks department, and as usual, she did not know how to take his kind words.

"Rick... you're really sweet for saying that, but you don't have to. I know you think I am, and I appreciate that, but I know how I look."

He shot her a look of utter bewilderment. "What are you talking about? Jenny, you're the hottest chick I've ever seen in any uniform. And out of uniform, well... I think I've made that point more than a few times now. You are... just... perfect. The way you are." He held both of her hands, running his thumbs over the knuckles and looking into her eyes, seeking only to assure her that he told the truth. While her beauty mystified him, he also recognized her as more than just a flawless physical specimen, though he had to come to terms with his own occasional failure to mention something other than her figure. If she did not echo his thoughts, then maybe she had her reasons. At least she understood that he meant well.

"I'll take your word for it, dear."

Sometimes, Knight realized, it was better not to press the matter, especially if the other party just woke up and would not likely agree.

Kowalski left the bathroom and headed for the kitchen, making coffee for both of them as he finished preparing himself for another twelve-hour shift, though he had long since realized that assigning a minimum number of hours to a workday was often wishful thinking. He had completed countless shifts at all hours of the day and night, only to be forced to stop a driver for speeding on his way home, or to intervene in an argument between customers at a gas station. This meant clocking an additional hour or two for which he would not be compensated, but to him, it was all part of the job.

Knight walked into the living room, put on his boots, and was met by his woman with a thermos full of hot coffee, made to his liking and far better than anything he could find in the substation lounge. They were both thankful that he successfully persuaded the captain to assign them to the same shift, even if their days off did not always coincide. Just a few hours together in the evening before bed could work wonders on their respective dispositions. Their lips met as she wished him a good day at work.

Knight made the drive and checked in with the desk sergeant before heading in for the morning briefing. There, he listened intently as the lieutenant discussed new and ongoing issues within their jurisdiction. During a pause, Knight sought clarification about one issue. "Sir, was last night's shooting tied to any sort of gang activity? Or maybe something organized?"

"Why? You got a theory already?" It was common to crack wise in this manner, as occasional levity often helped break the tension of these meetings, and it reminded the troops that their leaders also had a sense of humor.

"Not yet, but it did strike me as weird that there were no shell casings. The report said the victims were hit at close range, but whoever did it picked up their brass before they got away. Sounds like they knew what they were doing."

"We're on it. We'll get them eventually," said the lieutenant, not outright dismissing his statement, but also making it clear that Knight was still a beat cop, and not a detective or a crime scene investigator. For now, he would have to let others take the reins while he patrolled the city.

TUESDAY, 9 JULY 2013

Arriving at the restaurant twenty minutes prior to their reservation, Knight and Kowalski traversed the parking lot of Yokohama Ichiban, looking more like a pair of JC Penney catalog inserts than police officers. They took a temporary seat at the bar. As he would be driving later, Knight ordered a single beer for the night, while his lady requested a glass of bourbon on the rocks. She may have been but twenty-five, but she drank like the sailors of old. At eight o'clock on the dot, Knight's name was called, and the hostess escorted them plus six other patrons to a C-shaped table with an open grill in the center.

After a dinner of Americanized Japanese meals, Knight drove the two of them back to his place. Once inside, she motioned with an index finger for him to come to her. He locked the door and silently walked to her, smiling during the brief trip, and kissing her deeply, lifting her off the floor as he did. Without a word, she directed him to take a seat on the couch as she retreated out of sight, and he could only stare down the dark hallway, marveling at the wonder before him.

How is she with me?

He slipped off his shoes. Moments later, she emerged from the bedroom with her hair completely down, and her dress completely off, with a look on her face that he had seen many times before, though tonight, it was different. Her black bra matched the thong that encircled her hips, and the heels she was wearing made clear that he was in for something special this evening. What prompted all of this? Dinner was great, but hardly worthy of this gesture of thanks.

He rose to his feet, and she met him near the entrance to the living room. All he could do was quietly appreciate what his life had become since meeting her. The extra height from her pumps made her kiss that much easier to plant. As her hands began working on the buttons to his shirt, all he could think to do was inquire as to the occasion, as though she needed one to treat her man this way.

"What I feel for you is something I've never felt before," she said, "and I wouldn't do any of this for a man I didn't truly love."

Holy shit... she said it.

It was all he could do to remain standing as she leaned in close to his ear, whispering, "Rick... I love you." Then she moved her lips back down to his neck and continued unbuttoning his shirt. His mind raced. Kowalski, despite her inexperience with men, her postwar condition, and her previous assertion that she would never date another officer, had just declared her love for him, and even though he already felt this way about her, and had for some time, he had said nothing for fear of scaring her away. Now, *she* had said it first, and not in response to jewelry or a fancy weekend trip to a vacation destination—she simply said the three greatest words any man can ever hear from a woman.

"Jenny... I... uh, let's sit down for a minute." He placed a hand on the small of her back and led her over to the couch. He clasped her right hand in both of his, wet his lips, and prepared to speak, not totally certain of what to say. "You know about my... history. I wasn't sure if I was ever going to find what I have with you. Between what happened in Washington and everything else... I had sort of given up. Then you came along, and everything I thought I knew about myself, about..." He breathed deeply. "I was wrong."

He hoped that his rambling was not putting her off, but all she did was sit opposite him, holding his hand and listening as he continued, "This isn't the most poetic way of saying this, or anything, but Jenny... I love you as well. You are all I've thought about for months, even before I asked you out, and you will be all I think about for a while. And it's not just the sex or your body, it's... *everything* about you."

That must have been what she wanted to hear. "I-I've wanted to say it to you for a few days now," she admitted, "but I wanted to be sure it was real. When we went to work together last week and said 'goodbye' in the lot, I was dying to say something other than 'have a good shift' or whatever, but I didn't know what to do. That's when it hit me that something else was going on. I knew right then and there that you were... special to me. You saw the real me." She paused, closing her eyes before continuing, "I had never told anyone about Iraq, but you didn't judge me for what happened. You never saw me as anything other than someone who was over there. You also didn't laugh when I told you that I still wanted to be an actor, even though I'm probably too old to even think about that now."

In their discussions about the film industry, Kowalski explained that if she did not have an "in" with someone in the studio system by a certain age, then she would likely never achieve her dream. But Knight was unconvinced. "I could never mock you for that," he said. "I know if you set your mind to it, you—*you*, Jenny—can get there. You can live that dream. And I will do anything I can to help you because... well, because I love you." Saying it again made him feel like he could see Earth from space.

"It's really good to hear that."

"Which part?"

"All of it," she said, pulling him in by the shirt for another long kiss. "Now, if you don't mind, there are still several things I'd like to do with you this evening."

"Like... what?" he asked, coy as ever.

She slowly ran her other hand from his thigh further up his leg. "You'll see."

FRIDAY, 23 AUGUST 2013

After San Antonio had hit a peak of one hundred degrees, Knight felt as though he was back in Kuwait as he walked into the station near the end of his shift. He still had a mountain of paperwork to get through before he could officially be done for the day. Television cop dramas rarely depicted the administrative side of law enforcement, which typically consumed more time than dealing with actual criminals, and putting it off only made it harder. Knight resigned himself to spending a few more hours at his desk before he made it home, so he made sure to text Kowalski before settling in for an evening of signatures and police reports.

> Hey, got a stack of papers to get through, so I can't call unless you're up late. Just let me know. Be back around 10. I love you.

On the nights when they could not be together, they had an agreement to call each other. Even mundane discussions of work and the weather were something both craved.

He sat at a desk with a column of reports to his left and began going through them with a fine-toothed comb, ensuring that every space was filled out correctly before placing the papers in a separate column to his right, and moving on to the next one. It was then that Captain Daniels walked over to him, and Knight promptly stood up from the desk. "Knight, can you come with me for a minute? I need to discuss something with you—privately."

Immediately, Knight's talk with Palladino all those years ago came back to him, and he felt a sense of foreboding. "Yes, sir. Is everything okay?"

"Yeah, everything's fine, but I wanted you to hear this from me. Let's go."

These words offered no relief. He followed the captain down the hall and to his office, passing Mitchell and Baker as they plotted dinner that evening. After Daniels had closed the door, Knight took a seat, noticing that his own personnel folder was open on the captain's desk. Immediately, alarm bells went off. By his own estimation, he had been performing well as an officer—so well, in fact, that the state director of the Police Explorers had called Daniels directly to commend Knight for how well he did. He had not registered a single complaint against him in over two years. He had just completed his thirty-third ceremony as a color guard member, and his performance reports were stellar. Why had he been called into his superior's office?

"So how are things between you and Kowalski?"

Was that it? His *relationship?* "We're fine. Great, actually."

"And everything else?"

"Captain, I was in a situation like this before, and it didn't end well for me. If it's not too much trouble, might I ask what's going on?" Daniels was not one to mince words, so Knight hoped he would answer this direct question.

The captain nodded, replying, "You've been chosen to be an academy instructor. It seems that you impressed a lot of people back in June, and your name came up as one of three to fill a spot opening in January." He handed him a copy of the assignment notification before adding, "Take a moment and look it over."

Knight's excitement overtook him as he realized what this meant: the prospect of shaping a future generation of officers appealed to him, and completing a tour as an instructor often led to promotion. Although Kowalski had been joking when she predicted he would one day become a detective, he had given serious consideration to taking the exam. This would no doubt give him a leg up on that. Best of all, he would have a fixed schedule for the first time in his adult life! Whenever she had either Saturday or Sunday off, they could enjoy that time like a somewhat normal couple.

All of this flashed through his mind in the space of only a few seconds... and it took about that long for Daniels to destroy his hopes completely. "The position is in Amarillo. You'll have to move there to take the job."

"What?" Knight caught himself before continuing, "Sorry—it's where, sir?"

"The panhandle. Amarillo Police Academy."

Jesus! That's five hundred miles away. I just found a real reason to live —here.

"I won't bullshit you," the captain continued. "This is a real opportunity. You've been requested *by name* to teach at an academy you never attended. It's part of some exchange program. The bigwigs are testing this new proposal where they send officers who went to one academy to teach at another to see if it impacts the quality of instruction, and whether or not we need a universal training curriculum for the entire state. You wouldn't teach the city laws at first, but you would lead scenario-based classes and assist where needed. It's only for three years. It'll be over before you know it." He tried to make it sound as great as possible, and on paper, many officers would jump at this chance.

But how did this affect his lady? Could she potentially join him? Knight flailed inside, trying to make it right.

"What about Kowalski? Can she transfer there, and then come back once I'm done, or—"

"The request was for you. If you go, I'll be losing one of my best, and I can't afford to lose another. I'm sorry. It really isn't fair to either of you, and I'll understand if you want to decline, but I need to be clear that it will set you back career-wise if you do that. A lot of calls were made, a lot of strings were pulled to get this for you. If you turn it down, I don't really see you ranking up or doing anything other than patrolling for the rest of your career."

Damn... it.

"Why me? You said there were two others, what about them?" All he could think of was having to say goodbye to his great love. It seemed as though they had just found one another.

"You have a background that extends beyond regular policing. You were in the Army, you've been overseas, you taught at the junior academy... degree in criminal justice, immaculate record, not married, no kids—the list goes on. The other two are qualified, but don't measure up as well, and they'd be uprooting their families. You're the most logical choice."

Unbelievable. The combination of his efforts to improve himself through higher education, and the disaster that was his pre-Kowalski romantic life, had resulted in him being forced to choose between an unparalleled career move and the one woman who kept him anchored. They had been a couple for a grand total of three months, but in that brief span, he felt as though he had discovered the key to eternal life, and the thought of losing her made him physically ill.

"Captain... I... I need some time to think about this. It's a lot to process, and I'll need to talk it over with Jen—with Kowalski."

"They want an answer by Monday."

Of course they do.

"Understood. They'll have an answer by then. Was there anything else?"

"No, that was it." He closed the folder in front of him. "Rick... I'm gonna be real with you. I've known you for five years, and it should come as no surprise that I hold you in high regard. The only two reasons you're not a sergeant are time requirements and passing the promotion exam, which you'll easily do up there. An instructor tour will set you up to become anything you want: plain-clothes detective, maybe a lieutenant some point down the road... you name it. You haven't been with Kowalski that long, and it's definitely not my place to say so, but this is bigger than her. Bigger than you. I'm not saying it won't work between you, but I do ask that you look try and look at the big picture. Don't make this decision based solely on her."

You're lucky you're my boss.

Knight fought for control. "I get it—I do. And you're right that it's a good career move. But Captain... she is nothing short of incredible. I have never felt more alive than when I'm with her, and I can't imagine losing that."

"I know. Both of you seem... different, like you've changed." The captain rose to his feet, and Knight followed suit. "Monday. Take some time this weekend and talk to her. If it's meant to be, it'll work."

What the fuck kind of shit is that?

"I will, sir. Thanks again." He left the captain's office and trudged back to his desk; the life having drained out of him. Everything was moving so fast that he had to close his eyes to avoid screaming into the air. He had not felt this level of anger and uncertainty since that fateful day in Kuwait, and this time, he had a say in the matter. The beautiful future that he had privately envisioned for him and Kowalski stood on the cusp of imploding, and he was the one who would decide its future. The verdict was due within seventy-two hours. All Knight could do was glance down at the papers still awaiting his attention on the desk and sigh. If ever there was a time for procrastination followed by a huge drink, this was certainly it.

He stowed the forms in his desk drawer and walked out to his car. Before he began the drive home, he checked his phone. Kowalski had replied to his text that he was leaving the station, so he called her and spoke as soon as she answered. "Hey, Jenny... I need to see you. Right now. Can I come to your place?" His raw feelings were accentuated by his emotional exhaustion.

"Is everything okay? Did something happen at work?"

"You could say that."

KOWALSKI OPENED THE DOOR, and her friend, Officer Ward, hovered behind her, raising a hand in greeting, which Knight returned.

"Hey, beautiful," Knight said to Kowalski, making sure he was out of public view before leaning in to kiss his lady. Public displays of affection were to be avoided whenever possible, but he was not worried about Ward. He knew she had seen far more in her time. "Sorry for dropping by like this. I hope my call didn't freak you out." He held her hands in his as he gazed, lovingly, into her eyes.

Ward took that as her cue to hit the road. "And on that note, I'm outta here. I don't think this one's too keen on the idea of a three-way just yet," she joked, gesturing toward Kowalski, whose face colored at the quip.

Knight played along with Ward's remark, shrugging his shoulders and murmuring, "I mean..." as he turned his eyes toward Kowalski. This prompted her to smack him in the gut. She may have just discovered her own thirst for carnal activities, but a ménage à trois seemed like a longshot, much to his chagrin.

Ward laughed and left the apartment, and Knight resumed contact with his lover, hugging her close to his chest as she looped her arms around him, their eyes closed. They both needed this moment.

"Have a seat, dear," he said, kneeling to remove his boots. We need to talk about... something."

He joined her on the couch. Kowalski furrowed her brow. "What's going on? You sounded weird on the phone."

He did not know where to begin. This woman meant the world to him, and he was about to inform her of a dilemma that would force him to choose between love and career. But did it have to be that way? Could they not maintain a relationship while he was gone? Countless others had done it, so why were they any different? He drew a breath, then said, "Daniels just told me that I'm being transferred. And it's not to another precinct or even anywhere locally." He met her eyes, wincing at the concern he saw in them. "I want to be clear: I didn't ask for this. I never went to him or spoke to anyone. And it's pretty much an ultimatum. Do you believe me when I say that?"

"Of course I do." Her expression was troubled, but her soft tone gave him the encouragement that he needed.

"Alright." Kowalski listened while Knight laid out what the captain had told him, struggling to keep his rage against whomever had made the decision in check. It was an honor, certainly, but what he felt for Kowalski trumped everything else in his mind.

When he finished recounting the news, he waited for her reaction. It was not what he had expected.

She sat by him, looking down at her lap. She did not cry or wring her hands, and she did not appear upset—but neither was she outwardly happy or excited for him.

What was going on? When no response came, Knight prompted her, "What do you think? Should I—"

"Do it, Rick," she said decisively. "You have to."

That was quick.

"That's kind of where I was leaning, but then I thought about you, and how much I love you," he added, placing a hand on her left cheek. "I've waited my entire life to find you, and I'm not about to let you go, no matter what happens." He could only hope that she felt something similar.

She smiled at this, but behind her eyes lay another dimension. "I love you, too, Rick. And I want to be with you. But—"

His stomach tightened.

Here it comes.

"I don't know. I'm not sure long-distance is something I can do or even *want* to do."

Knight looked at her, incredulous.

She went on, "I'm twenty-five, and we've only been together for three months. I mean... waiting for three years, not knowing if this will last is... I just don't know. There has to be an end in sight for something like this, and... that's a really long time to be apart."

Knight could not speak. There was no sense in confirming that obvious fact, so he let her continue.

"One reason we work so well is that I get to see you—a lot. If you go up there, everything changes, and not for the better."

"But I'll come back to visit you. I'll pay for you to visit me. Money... it doesn't mean anything when you have what we have." He could only pray that she would see it through his eyes, but the more he spoke, the more he could feel her slipping away.

"Look. I need frequent, regular contact with you, and phone calls and occasional visits just wouldn't cut it."

"If it's just the logistics..." He sensed that there was something more —something that she was not saying. What had she and Ward been talking about before he had shown up?

"Rick... I don't want to be responsible for ending a relationship that we both cherish, and then end up crushing both our hearts. But I'm really not sure what to do."

At that point, neither was Knight. He was at an utter loss.

Kowalski could see that she had gone too far. "Hey... this isn't over. That's not what I meant. I'm just... conflicted, is all. All of this is new. You're tired, I'm tired... I just need some time to think."

Knight cleared his dry throat. "Do I need to leave?"

"No. In fact, I'd prefer you stay. There's still some pizza left, and I think I saw some of your running shorts in the dryer. Get out of that uniform and join me in the kitchen. Let's not talk about this anymore tonight. I just want to be with you right now." She planted a kiss on his mouth, which helped him forget how bad he felt.

Knight took this as a good sign. They still had much to discuss in the weeks and months ahead, but at the very least, he knew she was partially open to keeping things alive in his absence. It would be up to him to prove that he was the one for her—that their love was worth preserving, and that nothing could come between them, not even an assignment hundreds of miles away.

CHAPTER 13

SIPPING her soda from the last stop at the gas station, Kowalski was doing her best to appear as cool-headed as possible, but a sense of apprehension loomed in her mind, as she and Knight were on day two of a journey to Joliet. Since being notified of his pending reassignment, they had spent so much time together that they were practically living under the same roof, though she had not inwardly reciprocated his feelings toward her.

He reminded her almost daily of how attractive she was to him, how she had turned his life around, and how he would contact her as often as she needed to keep the relationship alive once he left San Antonio. But it had become a bit overbearing, and this, coupled with the guilt she felt for continuing to sleep with him in the shadow of his projected departure, had practically crippled her emotionally. She had to fight the urge to ask him to refrain from his adulation, even though she knew that he was merely attempting to elevate her mood, and remind her of how much she meant to him. Depression was setting in, and she knew that it would only become worse as January approached. She thought back to the night he had told her about the transfer—the same night that she and Ward had talked through her real feelings toward him.

Ward had sat watching and listening as Knight called to say he was coming over right away.

"That didn't sound good," Kowalski said to her friend as she placed her phone back on the couch. She had spent the latter part of that day off with Ward, who was still in her apartment enjoying a slice of pizza they brought home, and whose interest was immediately piqued by what she had heard on Kowalski's end of the call.

"What didn't sound good?" Ward asked, between bites of the pie.

"That was Rick. He said he needed to see me about something, and he was really... off. Like he was upset." Kowalski's expression changed to one of concern. "Do you think he's breaking up with me?"

Ward shook her head. "Not a chance. You said he's been so affectionate toward you, and so loving, and shit—he's probably just had a hard day, wants to get laid."

"We're already—never mind. I know he's happy on that front."

"But are *you* happy, Jen?"

Kowalski had not expected to be grilled over how she felt about her boyfriend of not even three months. "Of course. He's a great guy, and he really takes care of me. I love him."

"Yeah, I remember you saying that. I also remember you saying that he feels a lot stronger for you than you do for him. Is that still the case?"

Why is she doing this?

Kowalski considered the question. "I mean, I do love being with him. He makes me feel loved and special, and when we're in bed, he really lets me know I'm alive. He focuses on me so much that I wonder if I need to be doing anything else for him, but he says that he's fine with how it's going. Holy shit, there was this one time when I came home from the worst day ever, and all I wanted to do was just lay on the floor and cry, and he was there for me. He drew me a bubble bath, he went out to pick up dinner, he rubbed my feet after I finished eating... he really outdid himself." She trailed off, recalling how Knight had gone the extra mile for her. But then it dawned on her where her friend was going with the conversation.

Ward narrowed her eyes. "That sounds amazing, and all, but you haven't really said anything about *loving* him. You like it when he fucks you, you like it when he tells you how beautiful you are, you like it when he makes you forget about work. The question is, when you're with him, do you see a future beyond the next time you're at his place?"

"What do you mean?"

"I mean, do you think that far ahead?"

Kowalski recoiled in surprise. What was going on with her? Ward had never dated anyone longer than a few days; she admitted that she had slept with more men than Kowalski could count on multiple hands. So, why grill her over this? For that matter, why was she *not* thinking about Knight in that way? Was he just a consistent avenue for stress relief? He looked fine when he dressed nicely, and she loved the exhilaration each time they had sex, but was that the extent of her feelings?

"I *do* love him, and I *do* think about more than just our next day off together." Somehow, despite her supposed self-confidence and mental reassurances, this sounded less than convincing. Her friend could see it right away, and Kowalski knew it. The more she thought about it, the clearer it became to her as well that something was amiss in the relationship, something she had not seen before.

"Jen..." Ward said gently but firmly. "You need to think about that. Talk to him and get it all out in the open. It can't be lopsided... it just can't." Her words and eyes masked some deeper allusion, but her story would have to wait until another time. Knight had just knocked on the door.

Kowalski swallowed hard, knowing that Ward had been right.

Knight reached over and turned down the radio. "We still have a few hours to go. Do you need me to drive?" he asked, munching on some beef jerky.

Kowalski appreciated the courtesy, but she wanted to be in control—of something. "I'll be alright, but thanks." She had driven the entire way since they had left her apartment yesterday morning, and following a good night's sleep at a hotel in Springfield, she was wide awake.

"Is there anything else I should know about your family? Who can I expect to be there besides your mom and Ethan?"

"Let's see, I have an aunt and uncle visiting from Colorado, and I think there will be some family friends over as well. On Thanksgiving

Day, we're going to pick up Nana from the nursing home and bring her over for lunch."

"What about your dad? Did you decide if we're going to see him?" Knight had asked about this a few days ago, but she was not sure how good an idea that was at this point.

"I don't know. I'm going to see him that morning, but I don't know if bringing you is the right move."

"Did I do something wrong?"

What could she say? That she was so internally conflicted over being with him that it caused her endless guilt? That she was not totally convinced of his viability as a long-term partner? That they were just too different?

"No, not at all. I just... I don't want to stress you out by meeting so many new people at once. Mom already has a lot of stuff planned for us, and I don't want to complicate any of it by taking you over to meet my dad. He can be a loose cannon. Look, we'll be lucky if you just get along with Ethan."

"Why? Is he a bad stepdad? Or just an asshole?"

She remained silent for a moment. "He's just not my father." Knight seemed to understand what she meant, and she hoped that would work. "Anyway, we're going to a casino tomorrow, sightseeing in Chicago at some point, and there's a party tonight for us." At least that was true.

"Really? For us?" He sounded surprised and impressed.

"Yeah. They do this every so often. Dinner, drinks, ping-pong in the basement... the whole nine yards."

"I like the sound of that." He seemed to relish all of this and added, "In that case, I'll avoid discussing your dad, and I'll keep the focus on how awesome you are." He smiled and squeezed her right hand.

She hoped that her eye roll was not too obvious, as Ward's words about lopsided relationships returned for a cameo. "Thanks, Rick. I hope you have a good time."

"I'll admit... I'm nervous. Meeting the mom is kind of a big step. If you follow."

She did, not totally sure that she wanted to follow where he was going.

CHAPTER 14

PULLING into the driveway of Ethan and Evelyn's home, Knight was taken by the exterior beauty of the two-story abode, and the quaint, Midwestern appeal of the whole neighborhood. Had it not been so cold outside, he would have opted for a jaunt down the street before going in, but it was below freezing, and he was still from the Deep South. Retrieving his and Kowalski's suitcases from the trunk, he hurriedly moved to the front door, shivering as she locked the car and thankful that she had recommended a heavy coat for the trip.

Ethan waited by the door. After welcoming both of them, he directed Knight to his room and left him to settle in. At the very least, Kowalski's room was close to his, separated only by a bathroom. After dropping off the luggage, he walked back toward the foyer and was struck by the open design of the interior—there was a direct route from the living room to the kitchen, with no walls in between, and large windows revealed a surprisingly average-sized backyard through expensive blinds. Knight noticed the small bowls holding a dog's food and water near the back door, and remembered that Evelyn had purchased a pet while Kowalski was still in high school, though the pooch appeared to be elsewhere at the moment. Everything in the house, from the furniture to the high ceilings, evoked a sort of high society look, and it clicked why her mother did not have to work anymore. It was no mansion, but it was nicer than any home he had ever visited before.

He updated his family on his arrival from his phone, and he looked up to see Evelyn round the corner from her bedroom seconds later. Knight extended his hand to greet her just as Kowalski emerged from her own room.

"It's good to finally meet you," Evelyn said to Knight before brushing his hand away. "But I need to say hi to my daughter first. It's been too long." She scurried over to hug Kowalski, who was midway into the kitchen. She was not outright rude in her delivery, but the rebuff called into question the folksy mannerisms that his girlfriend had described as being ubiquitous in this region.

Nevertheless, at long last, he was seeing her mother in person. If Kowalski reigned as the most beautiful woman he had ever seen, then it was clear that Evelyn was the source of her comeliness. The woman was beautiful in her own right, even in her early fifties, with great skin, a shapely figure, and most of the blond in her hair remained original.

Releasing her daughter, Evelyn turned to Knight saying, "Now it's your turn." She gave him a big smile, foregoing a handshake for a firm hug that let him know how welcome he was in her home. "I'm so glad you're here, Rick. Jen's told me so much about you. It's great to meet the one who's helped her so much."

"She is quite the officer, Mrs. Miller, but all I did was—"

"Call me Evelyn, please."

His upbringing and military training compelled him to speak to her appropriately, but she had set the terms of address. "*Evelyn...* Jenny is a great officer, and I couldn't be happier than I am to be with her," he said, placing his arm around Kowalski and giving her a winning smile. He hoped he had made a good first impression.

Ethan strolled into the kitchen from the basement just in time to meet the small group and receive a firm handshake from Knight, followed by a half-hearted hug from his stepdaughter. "Hey, sorry about that," Ethan apologized. "I was on a call downstairs. Hi, Rick, how was the drive up?"

Knight had never seen a photo of Ethan before, but the man was exactly what he had envisioned: middle-aged with short hair, a trimmed, graying beard, brown eyes, and a moderate gut from being too many years removed from the Army. He had retired from the reserves as a captain, and was the owner of a small but clearly successful shipping business that he had taken over when he left the military. Due to his years in supply and logistics, not to mention his wartime service in Desert Storm, he had turned the company around and was now enjoying the fruits of his labor. It could also be said that Evelyn was enjoying them a tad more.

Knight gave the drive a quick review. "Not bad. Scenic, to say the least. I've never been through Oklahoma or Illinois before, so there were a lot of sights to take in. And I had quite an incredible driver at my side." He cocked his head at Kowalski, who squeezed him in response to the compliment.

"Well, we're certainly glad you're here." Ethan moved into the kitchen and started putting items on a tray. "And I hope you're hungry because we've got a lot of food for tonight, and Evelyn picked up some drinks for both of you as well. Jen mentioned that you like tequila, so we got you a bottle of the good stuff, and some bourbon for her. Here, grab that box and we'll take it downstairs for later." He pointed to a cardboard receptacle near the sink.

Knight picked it up and followed Kowalski through a nearby door, carefully descending the stairs into the chilly basement and placing the box on a mini bar in the corner. The spacious underground getaway featured a ping-pong table, television, stereo, and a work area that Kowalski said was where he ran his business. He not only cleared six figures annually, he did so from the comfort of home, and Knight could not help but feel both jealousy and respect.

On the desk was a framed black-and-white photo of Evelyn wearing an evening dress and a look on her face that screamed, "Take me now!" Kowalski noticed his interest; she reached for the photo and mouthed the word, "MILF" to Knight; he could only nod in agreement. They both suppressed grins as Ethan descended the stairs.

He unloaded some beers into the refrigerator behind the bar. "So, how do you like your steak, Rick? I'll be firing up the grill out back in a bit."

"Medium, please."

"And is ribeye alright?"

"Yes, sir." Knight preferred sirloin, but this was no restaurant, and he knew better than to make a fuss. He was glad that Ethan did not object to being addressed as "sir." He was a military officer, after all. "Do you need help with anything else?"

"I think we've got it covered, but thanks for asking. We're having a ping-pong tournament after dinner, so I hope you're ready for that," he said, flashing a look of Forrest Gump-level confidence before heading back upstairs.

Finally alone, Knight took this moment to plant a kiss on Kowalski and thank her for getting them there safely. "How are you feeling? Are you glad to be back?"

"Yeah, I really am. What do you think of the place?" she asked, looking around.

"It's fuckin' great! I mean, the house is huge, and it looks like something out of a magazine. What's not to love?"

"Give it time. Maybe Ethan will yell at my mom for something stupid."

"He does that? Doesn't strike me as the type."

"Trust me. I've heard my share of things living here. But I'm sure he'll be on his best behavior while we're visiting. Don't let the façade fool you. He puts on a good show."

Interesting. That would explain why she hates him so much. It wasn't just that he's not her dad—he could be verbally abusive.

"I'll keep an eye on him. We're out of our jurisdiction, but if you want, I can have the local authorities arrest him if you'd like," Knight joked, hoping it would help her.

"I'd slap the cuffs on him myself if I could."

"Let's hope it doesn't come to that. In the meantime, why don't we go back upstairs and join your mother? I think she said something about opening a bottle of wine before we came down here, and we've been on the road for two days. I think we've earned a little time to unwind."

"But you hate wine."

"For tonight, I don't," he said with a wink.

She hugged him in thanks for his understanding of her situation. Knight had experience with women, but he found that dating someone as complex as Kowalski entailed reading the room, picking up on her signals, listening intently to everything she said, and accepting that sometimes, she had already made up her mind. In this case, Ethan would always be an adversary to her, so Knight knew that there was no point in trying to facilitate a reconciliation. All he could do was hope that there would be no flare-ups between them, and that civility could be maintained.

They went back upstairs and returned to the kitchen. Evelyn invited them to take two bar stools at the counter and handed them each a full glass of Cabernet. The two of them caught up over everything, allowing Knight to join them in their discussion every now and then. Meanwhile, Ethan prepped the steaks and side items on the grill outside.

The doorbell rang as guests began trickling in for the festivities. Wanting to be as friendly as possible, Knight immediately sought to meet each one of them and learn their names. He had learned when interviewing suspects and witnesses that people responded much better when he recalled who they were by name and not merely by their appearance. All of these family members and friends were as cordial as he had expected. They matched his politeness with their own and asked the usual questions about how he had met Kowalski, what he had done in the Army, and what had happened to his accent. This was a common question. He usually responded that he once had a noticeable Southern drawl but that he had "gotten over it" after enlisting—which usually elicited a laugh. This group was no exception. The truth was that he had learned early in his career that his native accent was not the most intelligent sounding, and if he wanted to be taken seriously, he would have to work on neutralizing the way he spoke. Sure enough, after two tours and meeting a bevy of people from all around the country, he had largely succeeded in sounding as though he was from anywhere but the former Confederate states, and it paid off in dividends.

The conversations continued for another hour before dinner was finally ready. They were called to the formal dining table, and both officers received first crack at the bounty laid out, because, as Ethan explained, they had driven so far. The eight of them sat together, feasting upon Ethan's culinary handiwork. The steak was delicious, and cooked just right. It was clear to Knight that if Ethan's shipping business were to fail, he would have a backup career as a professional chef. The small talk over dinner went well, and overall, Knight felt as though he was meshing well with this group, and making a good impression as Kowalski's boyfriend, which he himself still had trouble believing was the case.

With dinner finished and the night still young, the party made its way downstairs to the basement. Folks took seats near the ping-pong table, opposite the work area, and it was just as Ethan had described: an actual tournament with a bracket and everyone's names listed on a dry-erase board. Knight was never one to back down from friendly competition, and despite the alcohol in his system and having spent two days on the road, he managed to defeat everyone in the house, with Evelyn falling last to his ping-pong prowess. It was not until after the match point that he realized he had just defeated his girlfriend's mother in front of her friends while in her own home. He briefly worried that he had committed some kind of social faux pas, but Kowalski reassured him that all was well.

The festivities continued for another hour or so. As the guests began to leave, Knight felt himself winding down and yet not wanting the evening to end, as he had come to enjoy the time he was having in this new city and state. Kowalski's mother was fun and energetic; her stepfather was engaging and entertaining; and their friends were likewise delightful. It felt as though they had accepted him on the first night, without the need for excessive efforts to fit in or be one of the crowd, and that was *the* outcome he had hoped to attain. After helping Evelyn and Ethan clean up around the kitchen, Knight wished his lady love a nice night and went to bed—but not before texting her about the wonderful time he had enjoyed. He added that he could not wait to experience everything else that lay in store for them in the coming week. Her reply, sent a few minutes later, was very simple:

Me, too. Love you.

CHAPTER 15

THURSDAY, 28 NOVEMBER 2013

A FEW NIGHTS LATER, seated next to Knight on an oversized sectional couch in her pajamas, Kowalski was updating Alex and Ward from her phone on how the week had progressed. She highlighted the trip to the casino and the Thanksgiving meal as the best parts, with eating at her favorite local restaurants as a close second. It was then that Alex asked if she had spoken to her mother about Knight, and the truth of the matter was that she simply had not been given a free moment away from him. Even now, as they both neared a food-induced coma, he remained with her, never leaving her side, though he appeared to be reaching the point of no return sleep-wise. Ethan had already retired for the evening, so as Evelyn and her daughter remained on the sofa and ready for bed, Knight bade them a pleasant evening and staggered toward the bedroom.

Finally.

Kowalski waited a few more minutes to be sure he had gone out of earshot and then moved closer to her mother, who sat dressed in her own pink pajamas and reading the latest spy thriller on her eBook. "Um, Mom?" she began.

"Yes? Do you need something?"

This was a conversation that she really did not want to have, but it had been weighing on her mind for weeks, and now was as good a time as any. "What do you think of Rick?" She thought she knew how Evelyn felt based on their interactions since Saturday, but she wanted to hear it from the source.

"Well, he's certainly a nice guy. He's polite, and he's obviously crazy about you, so that's a plus." The words were kind, but Kowalski knew better.

"Mom... for real. Tell me the truth."

Evelyn's expression changed slowly. She removed her reading glasses and placed them on the couch. She let her frown take over. "Jen... I just don't see it."

"See what?"

"*It*—you and him. He's... really clingy. And I know he loves you—I can see it every time he looks at you, but I don't see you looking back at him like that. Neither did Olivia or Gary." Kowalski's aunt and uncle had been around Knight for only a few hours that day, but it appeared to be all the time they needed.

"When did they tell you that?"

"Remember when you took Nana to the basement for ping-pong? Rick and Ethan were down there with your cousin and all of you were playing. I asked Olivia what she thought, and... she agrees with me. I mean, she even wondered aloud why you're with him because he isn't even that handsome."

"Mom! He might hear you!"

"Jen, you said so yourself when I asked about him, and when you put that picture on Facebook of the two of you at that restaurant, I wondered how long it would last because... well... he's just kind of average. And you're not." Kowalski had the usual self-esteem issues common to women, but Knight had helped her see just how beautiful she really was, and as a result, her confidence had soared. Gone were the casual outfits to which she had grown accustomed, as they had been replaced with form-fitting dresses and the regular application of makeup, even when the plan involved a simple stroll down San Antonio's River Walk.

"I never said I was with him for his looks. I *know* he's not a model, but he's done so much for me that I can't imagine what life will be like without him. I've been on antidepressants since before the academy. But now that I've been with him, I haven't needed them anymore."

"Are you serious?" That revelation snared her attention. "And you're sure it's because of him?"

Kowalski had not been taking anything too powerful, but she thought that reaching the point of not requiring them to function testified to the positive influence her man had on her. "I haven't refilled the prescription since July. Now... I just don't know anymore. I mean, I know he's the reason. But he's going away for three years and he wants to keep this up, and I don't know what to do. I love him, he loves me, we work so well together... but I was talking to Rachel a few months ago— do you remember her? From my academy class?"

"Uh-huh. Nice girl."

"She said exactly what you said earlier, about how I don't love him like he loves me, and it got me thinking... what if she's right?" Her own expression had changed from one of concern to one of deeper worry, as the cold reality began to overtake her mind again, setting up camp in the deep recesses where she tried in vain to bury her most depressing thoughts and fears. Here was a man who would lay down his life for her, and not just because of his profession, but out of genuine love. She could not be certain that she would do the same for him. Painful, but true.

"Jen... have you told him any of this?"

"It's not really a talk I've been dying to have. He's sensitive about this whole situation, and I don't want to hurt him. I just have this feeling that he's going to go away, and then I'm going to fall apart because he isn't around. Then what? I'll be back on the pills and maybe even pulled off patrol to work in the records department while I see the department shrink."

"That does sound less dangerous than what you do now. But what does that have to do with your feelings for him? Not wanting to feel bad is one thing, but I have to ask... do you feel the same way about him that he does about you?"

"Well... how could I? He has me up on this... pedestal... that I never wanted to be on, and now that I'm there, I don't know if he'll ever see me as a real person and not some sort of... goddess, or whatever. On the other hand, I like who I am now. He doesn't define me, but I am better than I was and it's because of him. There's no denying it."

"Jen… do you love him? And before you answer, what I mean is… do you love him enough to keep things going while you're apart?"

She took a deep breath, looking away as she pondered the enormity of her mother's inquiry and waiting too long for Evelyn's liking.

"The fact that you're taking so long kind of says it all. I mean, if we're being honest. I can tell there's something between you, but it just feels like maybe you're seeing him because he makes a fuss over you and then you feel better about yourself, or something. That's a good thing. But it's not love."

Fuck.

Kowalski grimaced. "I was hoping you wouldn't say that."

"I'm sorry, I really am. He's a great guy and I like him, but when I first met him and saw how he was around you… it was hard to believe you picked him as a partner." Harsh or not, she at least told the truth.

She's right, goddamn it.

All Kowalski could do was nod along. "It's going to be a long ride back home."

CHAPTER 16

AWAKENING in Kowalski's bed was an extremely common occurrence for Knight at this point, but he would have given anything to delay the morning's arrival just a little longer, for it was a day that he had long feared. His household goods and furniture were already in Amarillo waiting for him, and he had loaded his car to the gills with his uniforms and civilian clothing—only his physical departure remained. He found himself in his usual position in her bed, with his right arm draped over her body as she remained asleep. This time, he carefully moved himself even closer, taking in the lovely aroma of her hair. Their last night together had been marked by an exquisite dinner and the most passionate sex of their relationship. And yet, Knight remained conflicted as to whether he had made the right call.

Tomorrow, I'll wake up without her, and she'll wake up without me. I know this will help my career, but is it worth it if I lose her?

The thoughts barreled through his head like an army of steamrollers, but at this point, it did not matter.

"Good morning, handsome." He had not even noticed that she was awake. Had he woken her up by moving near her?

"Good morning, my dear," he answered, gently kissing her cheek. She reached up with her hand and placed it on his cheek, feeling the stubble of his beard beginning to form, and turning her head toward his for the first kiss of the day. "Did you sleep okay?"

"Not great, but we both know why." Her response, neither curt nor tinged with contempt, was merely a blunt assessment of the situation: this man, the one who had helped her healing process and who had shown her the world of functional relationships, stood on the cusp of embarking upon this new adventure without her. She was not handling it well. But for that matter, neither was he.

"Same here." That was all he could think to say. What else could he have added?

Come with me, Jenny. Quit the force, transfer, go AWOL—just come to Amarillo and be with me. I'll do whatever it takes to make that happen, and if you're not happy there, then we'll go somewhere else. Anywhere else. I just want to be with you... and you alone.

"I think once we eat and get some coffee, I'll feel a little better," he said, wrapping a leg around hers under the white comforter on her queen-sized bed. "And by that, I mean *we* will make breakfast together." He took her right hand and interlocked his fingers with hers, signaling that the time to rise was not yet upon them, but he knew that by remaining in bed, he was merely prolonging the inevitable.

Kowalski sighed. "I'm glad you put it that way. I want us to do as much as we can before you go."

Knight knew that she did not mean an early morning love-making session, but he was still compelled to make the joke anyway, and she still laughed.

She toyed with him. "Let's go, Corporal. I don't want you leaving without getting your fill."

"Well when you put it like that—"

"Of breakfast. Don't even try it," she said, playfully shutting him down.

"Yes, ma'am."

They left the warmth and safety of her bed and sauntered into the kitchen, gathering the materials needed for a hearty breakfast of pancakes, eggs, bacon, and sausage. She turned on the stove while he started brewing a fresh pot of coffee.

Within half an hour, they were sitting down at her dining room table, a rare occurrence for most younger people those days, and enjoying the morning meal. He savored each bite, but could not stop thinking about his immortal beloved sitting right across from him, and how for the next few years, he would see her through his phone during their nightly video calls, and on the odd weekend or vacation visit in person. Kowalski had been a fixture in his life for a mere seven months, yet to him, each of those days felt as though he had been given the chance to fall in love with her all over again, and he agonized over this fact as he sipped his coffee.

She is really something else. No matter what, I have to keep her with me.

"Something on your mind?" she asked, enjoying some bacon.

All he could do was look upon this living work of art and smile.

"Just you, babe. Just you."

She beamed.

They finished eating and brought their dishes to the sink. Knight downed another cup of coffee before hopping in the shower and completing what was, for all intents and purposes, the final step before heading for the panhandle. Kowalski followed his lead into the shower as he left the bathroom, and privately, he wished that she had joined him for one final time under the water, even if sex was not guaranteed. Seeing her undressed was like catching a glimpse of Heaven.

Knight paced back and forth mentally as he sat on the couch. The drive to Amarillo would take close to eight hours, not counting a break for gas and lunch, and he would require another brief stop to change into his uniform before reaching his destination. He had been in tense situations throughout his time as an officer, but the prospect of losing Kowalski had him more on edge than anything he had seen on the streets. He could only fight back the tears as he waited for her to emerge from her shower.

She eventually appeared, wearing jeans and the shirt from their first date. She walked over to him and sat on his lap, straddling him in a position they had often experienced in a different setting on that very sofa. He cupped her face with his hands, gazing deeply into her mesmerizing eyes before she gently kissed him on the lips and then pulled him in close, her arms encircling him. They held each other in silence. Each harbored their own feelings about the situation, but neither could find the courage to say anything, and the minutes turned into what felt like hours.

Finally, after too much time had passed, Knight knew what had to be done. "Jenny... I have to get going." He looked up at her with sadness in his eyes, taking in the sight of his woman for what he knew could be the final time... and that was when it finally hit him. The walls he had erected came crumbling down.

A single tear slowly moved south along his cheeks, yet he made no effort to wipe it away. If he were to have this kind of reaction, he wanted her to see it, to understand that she had transcended being a mere girlfriend or partner. The words became lodged in his throat. They came out only with effort. "I-I don't want to go. You know that better than anyone. But if I don't leave now... I probably never will."

She said nothing in return, only nodding her head as she fought back her own emotions.

Knight blew out a breath. "Alright, then. Will you see me off?"

"Of course," she croaked. "Here... I got you something for the drive." She walked over to the refrigerator and retrieved the largest canned beverage he had ever seen. The shred of a smile crossed her face. "I saw this a few days ago and thought of you. It should last you until you stop for lunch." It was a forty-eight–ounce can of a locally produced energy drink, labeled "The Defibrillator" due to its size and caffeine content.

He laughed upon taking it from her; it felt like a dumbbell in his hand. "Thanks, Jenny. That is—wow, I don't know what to say," he said, smiling through his pain and trying to keep it together. He was not raised with the "men don't cry" attitude, but he still maintained that keeping everything in check would prove a better course of action, especially in front of his lady. "I'll think of you each time I take a sip."

"I hope you think of me more often than that. You'll eventually finish this."

Hmm. Maybe she's not as torn up over this as I thought. Good sign.

"You know I will."

He grabbed his travel bag and they headed outside to his car. The morning was still chilly. Knight placed the bag in the only open space in the passenger's side floorboard. He walked back around to his side and took Kowalski by the hands, lightly squeezing them. He knew that he had to say something, but what could he say to her that he had not already said before? She knew of his devotion, of how he wanted them to go the distance, and she saw how his family had immediately welcomed her with open arms over Christmas. "There's a lot that I can't express in words. You are everything I want, inside and out. There is no one greater for me than you, Jenny."

I hope that wasn't too much.

"I love you, Rick. Call me when you can."

"I love you, too. I'll see you later." Kissing her on those full, vibrant lips one last time, he sat down in the driver's seat, put the car in gear, and ventured out toward Interstate 10, shattered. Amarillo would be a breeze after this.

TUESDAY, 15 APRIL 2014

"Get down! Take cover—move it!" The uniformed troops ran and took positions behind the squad cars as Knight barked out the orders. He knelt behind the left rear tire of one vehicle, an area that provided maximum protection from incoming fire. Posted opposite the bank, he had a decent view of the scene.

Suddenly, the silence was broken by the shattering of the glass door in the middle of the edifice. The ringleader had slammed the butt of his rifle into the pane, aimed through it, and opened fire on the gathering of vehicles. The personnel outside promptly returned fire, hitting the gunman's associate in the far-left window. The rounds contacted his chest in spectacular fashion and stained his shirt red as he disappeared from view. The exchange of gunfire continued with neither side yielding an inch and both inflicting casualties. The battle raged on, with Knight directing the others to hold the line and evacuate the wounded.

"What's the play, Ortega?" Knight prompted one officer. "What do we do?" The sustained volume of automatic weapons nearly drowned out his questions.

Without hesitation, Ortega yelled back, "I'll take a group around the back, and lock down the area!"

"Alright! Let's go with that!" Knight leaned up from behind the car and fired another volley toward a gunman aiming in his direction, hitting him in the shoulder before signaling two others to follow Ortega. The trio reloaded their weapons and waited as Knight directed the remaining personnel to provide covering fire while their colleagues hastily ran to flank the shooters and secure the perimeter. "Keep the pressure up! They'll run out of ammo soon enough!"

The shooting continued for another twenty minutes, with the those on the scene maintaining control of the situation as best they could, until a new development unfolded. The surviving gunmen ceased firing their weapons and announced their intent to surrender. A few moments later, they exited through the main door, unarmed and with their hands raised. Their blood-spattered clothing showed evidence that their comrades inside had been hit. The shooters, four in total, listened to their rights as the uniforms present cuffed them with aggression. They had turned their backs toward the bank as they began escorting the robbers off the scene. It was then that a fifth assailant—unseen by all—appeared at the door and opened fire with an automatic rifle. His rounds contacted the officer nearest to him—Corporal Knight.

He fell backwards, dropping his pistol to the ground a second before he hit the pavement. His teammates drew their weapons and returned fire ferociously, eliminating the new threat for good.

"Goddamn it!" The young man nearest Knight growled into his radio, "Code Ten-Zero-Zero! Officer down! Need an ambulance at our location ASAP!"

Ortega ran over to Knight's side to assess his wounds, but with that many rounds striking him in such rapid succession, an ambulance might be entirely superfluous. Thankfully, there was no need for legitimate medical attention.

"Cease fire! End of training scenario! Safety and holster all weapons. I say again: safety and holster all weapons!"

The instructions boomed over the loudspeaker as the academy staff members inside the makeshift bank rose to their feet. They gathered their weapons, unloading the magazines packed with paint-tipped rounds, and dabbed at their stained clothes with wet wipes while the cadets outside did the same. Knight sat up on the ground and took note of his uniform, peppered with red blotches across his chest and abdomen. He wondered if this crop of recruits would understand the magnitude of what had transpired. It was only a drill, but here the knowledge acquired in the classroom and on the shooting range could be applied in a real-world setting. If today indicated anything, this class still had much to learn.

"You alright, Corporal? Looks like they got you pretty good there." Sergeant Jerome Douglas, another instructor, was on hand to provide oversight and grade the cadets on their response to the threat. He had also become a good friend to Knight in the three months that they had known each other, and was helping him complete the process of becoming a certified instructor.

"I've been better," Knight grumbled, gesturing to his paint-stained torso, and rising to his feet with his friend's help. "Up until I was shot to pieces, it was going pretty well."

As the new guy, Knight had drawn the shortest straw, providing the students with on-site guidance during the simulated shootout. In the heat of the moment, the students had forgotten to verify if the last assailant to surrender was indeed the last one in the building. Seeing their instructor taken out was a lesson that none would forget.

"They'll get it right next time—trust me on that," he said, handing Knight a handkerchief. Douglas had been at the academy for two years, and before that he had worked in vice and the Amarillo anti-gang unit for close to twelve years. While he was solid in the classroom, he was better as a trainer of new instructors. "You did well out there. But you need to give them a chance to take the lead and figure out what to do. They won't always have a seasoned officer calling the shots."

Knight took this criticism in stride. Douglas was correct: he had a tendency to commandeer the scenario, and his shirt bore the evidence. Perhaps they would have figured it out if he had not said anything. "Hard to argue with that," he admitted, removing the magazine from his pistol and unloading the special rounds into a pouch. "For the next one, I'll hang back and wait until they're about to be overrun, if it comes to that."

"That'd be even worse."

"That's what they did to us one time at the San Antonio academy. The cadre opened up on us from three sides—"

"That's not how we do it here, Knight. We need to give them every chance to assess the situation before we pull the plug, and if it's clear that they can't handle it, then we failed as instructors." He eyed Knight. "We owe it to them *not* to fail."

It was even harder to argue with that. "Understood. I'll make sure not to crush them too badly during the debrief. We do need to highlight Ortega and his team for handling perimeter security—they nailed it."

"Yeah, we'll make sure they get a gold star or something." What Douglas lacked in student-teacher interpersonal relations, he made up for in dry humor. "How's your girl doing? You two still making it work?"

"Yeah, we're keeping it alive. I write to her before bed so that she wakes up to an email from me. You know, we text, have video chats almost every night. It isn't easy, but we're trying, at least." He was as committed to Kowalski as he was to being a policeman, and with their one-year anniversary on the horizon, it was a good time to subtly remind her just how much she meant to him. He did not have enough time off saved to visit her, so she had planned to make the trip to Amarillo to see him in late May. He intended to gift her with a bracelet he had seen at the mall.

"That's good to hear." Douglas looked forward to meeting Kowalski, especially after he saw her picture on Knight's Facebook page. He looked down at his watch before adding, "Thirty minutes 'til the debrief. You've got some time to get changed before we head back. The staging area has a bathroom by the main office."

Jenny would freak if she saw me like this.

"Thanks, man. I'll catch up in a few."

Knight hitched a ride back to the staging area and found the restroom. He went in to change, taking in the sight of how many times he had been hit, thankful that the rounds were simulated. He pushed thoughts of danger out of his mind and focused only on how much he wanted to see his lady later that evening.

CHAPTER 17

TUESDAY, 15 APRIL 2014

KOWALSKI'S HEAVY, plodding steps echoed as she ascended the stairs to her apartment, ready to find comfort in the bottle of high-end bourbon in the cabinet above the refrigerator. She had not even bothered to remove her boots upon entering the residence, as was customary, though they were off after she poured the first drink of the evening and took a seat on her couch. The memories of the day flashed through her mind: an arrest, changing an elderly woman's tire, six hours on patrol, and endless paperwork.

Taking a sizable swig from her glass, she placed it on the end table and began the process of removing her uniform shirt and vest, with the pants coming off next. Her knee-high black socks remained on the job while she transferred the accouterments from today's shirt to the one she would wear tomorrow. Before long, she returned to the couch and resumed nursing the rest of her beverage, though she felt the rising unease over what was to come. Like clockwork, her phone lit up with the familiar sound of Knight's custom ringtone, and she could only sigh in response to seeing his face on the screen as she waffled briefly over answering.

She swiped the icon to the right, and Knight appeared on the screen seated at his dining room table. Time to perform. "Hey, honey. How are you?" The concentration necessary to remain genuinely excited to see him rivaled that needed to perform surgery.

"Holy shit, Jenny… I've had a day," Knight said with a grin. He proceeded to give her a rundown of the training exercise that saw him "shot" numerous times, but she found it hard to focus, even through a story of such high drama.

Jesus, does he ever shut up?

"Sounds like quite a time, Rick. Quite a time…" She could only hope that the boredom in her voice was not as obvious to him as it was to herself.

"Yeah, it was something." He waited a few seconds, perhaps thinking she would ask for more information, but she stayed quiet, so he continued, "How was your day? Did Ward do alright testifying in that case?"

"Oh… yeah, she did okay. Guilty verdict." Another sip from her glass followed, as did more awkward silence between the displaced couple. It became clear that she should not have answered the call.

"I knew she would." She offered no further details. "So… Jenny… uh… how is everything else? I didn't hear from you at all today." She normally texted him right before her shift started or during lunch, and she would often respond to his daily email. But lately, her written correspondence had been inconsistent at best, and she could not place the blame on an uptick in crime or other nefarious activity.

"Everything else is… pretty much the same. Not a whole lot going on these days," she said, shaking her head and wishing for a quick end to the conversation.

"Are you sure you're alright? You seem really… distracted. Like, more than the last time we talked. I'm getting worried about you, babe."

"It's… the usual shit, I promise. Missing you, work sucks, thinking too much about things. You know."

"I miss you, too. But when it gets me down, I remember that what I'm doing up here is temporary. And then I remember that you are visiting pretty soon. In no time, you'll be up here, and then we are going to live it up."

How is he so fucking optimistic about this?

She flashed a fake smile back at him. "It sounds wonderful—it really does. That's definitely something I need right now... more than you know."

"Well, get ready, because I'm about to send you a link with airfare options, and I'm covering half the cost—no arguing this time." His own smile was both adorable and agonizing for her.

She had so much to tell him, but it would have to wait. "If you insist. But I do plan on making it up to you somehow."

"Considering that we haven't fucked since New Year's Day, I have a few ideas on how you can make that happen."

Well, that's something.

"Oh? Do tell."

"THAT WENT WELL," Kowalski said to no one in particular as she sank into the cushions. Finally able to enjoy the silence of the room, she rested her head against the back of the couch, but not before downing the rest of the drink she had poured before Knight had called. His consistency and persistence, once charming and endearing, were now part of her daily grind, and she did not know how much longer it could continue.

As the minutes dragged on, she found it harder and harder to force herself into the kitchen. The drink had hit her quite hard, and she had eaten lunch hours ago, yet another round was calling her name. Slowly, bracing against the coffee table, she pushed off the couch and wandered toward the refrigerator, grabbing the dish of enchiladas she had cooked over the weekend.

He can't even make this. *It's so easy—how can he eat so much takeout?*

She poured a smaller portion this time, wisely limiting herself as she reheated the evening meal, and took stock of her predicament. More than three months had passed since she had last seen her man, and her condition had slowly begun to deteriorate, starting with work. She was behind on administrative tasks, and nearly snapped at the dayshift desk sergeant when he asked about her patrol car. Kowalski was a mentally resilient combat veteran of the Iraq War, but even with that on her résumé, she remained human. While she loved Knight for what he had done for her well-being, she hated herself for not returning his feelings for her. Right on cue, her phone beeped with an email—from him, of course.

The message at the top read, "*Take a look at these departure dates and let me know what you think. Love you, Jenny.*" She closed her eyes for a moment, imagining him grinning ear-to-ear as he sent the message to her, and regretting that she had dragged it out this far. Kowalski sighed deeply, retrieving a medicine bottle hidden behind the breadbox. She had put this off for far too long. She popped the lid open and broke one pill in half, marveling at the power this miniscule dose contained, then washed it down with the remnants of her glass. If the combination of hard alcohol and medication had yet to take effect, the realization of what she had to do next certainly did.

She grabbed the phone and returned to the couch. As a tear began to form in her eye, she opened the email app on her phone, highlighted the message from the one who meant the most to her, and stared intently at two buttons: Reply and Delete.

God forgive me.

CHAPTER 18

COMMUNICATIONS HAD BROKEN down over the past month. Badly. Knight wondered if their last video chat was as ominous and foreboding as he had feared. Things had been going fine, but Kowalski had sort of lowered the boom when they last spoke. He paced nervously around the townhouse, desperately needing to hear that she had relented but bound by his own stubbornness to remain in the dark a bit longer.

Now what?

It seemed that the distance between them was no longer the driving force behind Kowalski's apprehension over sustaining their relationship, but merely a catalyst to exposing other factors that had not been fully discussed until that week—like what she described as his lack of maturity, his lack of ambition, how he could not cook for himself, and how their life goals diverged so starkly. While he was content with retiring as a police officer, she still entertained the idea of becoming an actress.

Why was this never brought up? And who cares if I get takeout a few times a week? She didn't seem to care back when we were basically living together.

Deciding that he had to know, he picked up his phone and initiated a video call, hoping to get answers, but also willing to settle for her not picking up just yet. His emotional readings were all over the map.

After a few rings, she finally answered. "Hey, Rick."

No term of endearment. No inquiry about his day. Merely his name. Something was definitely wrong.

"Hey, beautiful." He steeled himself for the line of questioning he had chosen. "Do you mind if we talk for a bit?"

"Um, sure. What's on your mind?"

"You. Us. We left things in a not-so-good place the other day. It kind of freaked me out." His juvenile manner of speech was the least of his concerns at this point. Compared to being on the rocks with the only woman he had ever really loved, sounding as though he had lost a few IQ points was a price he was willing to pay if it meant shoring up things between them.

"Well, I can talk for a bit, but I do have some things—"

"Did I call at a bad time?" His look of concern, with his eyebrows raised, bore a certain innocence brimming below the surface.

"No, it's not bad, I'm just... I need to see you—like, *see* you, see you, and I can't because you're way the hell up there." Kowalski glanced to the side and took a quick, deep breath, exhaling rapidly before she finished the rest of whatever she was drinking.

"Jenny... we knew this wasn't gonna be easy. We talked about it— about keeping us together when it was impossible to think about anything else but being apart. And we both said we'd do whatever it takes. Am I not doing enough on my end?"

The exasperation in her voice matched that on her face. "Yes, Rick, you're doing more than enough, but you're not listening. We worked best when I stayed at your place for the night, or when we went for a walk together after dinner... or when we were in bed. You made me feel things about you—and myself—that I just... don't feel anymore, and it makes me think about things."

"What things?"

"Things that... are hard for me to talk about right now."

"Try. Please."

She took another deep breath, much deeper than usual, with her eyes closed. "You and I are very different, Rick. I thought it wasn't a big deal when we first got together, and I didn't listen to my gut because I was having such a great time, and I didn't want to hurt you. But as time went by and you were tagged for the academy, everything changed... in the worst way."

Did she rehearse this?

When he said nothing, she continued. "The more I thought about everything that I was feeling, the more I realized just how incompatible we are, and that really... just..." It seemed as though a sob had formed, but she powered through. "You're needy, Rick. You're overdependent on me. You're emotionally immature, and I can't keep pretending that I'm okay with all of this—with you being up there, with me dreading each time the phone rings because it might be you... I just can't do this anymore."

"What do you mean... *this*?"

She sighed hard. "*All* of this."

Knight cringed. They both sat there, staring blankly at their respective cameras.

A flame of anger leapt into Knight's chest. "So, that's it? You're calling it quits over the *phone*?" He could hear his own heartbeat pounding as he awaited her reply and a sickening feeling in his gut began to manifest as he refused to believe what he heard. The fury coursing through him tightened his grip on the phone.

Now Kowalski's pent-up frustration came out. "What the fuck was I supposed to do? Fly up there, break it off the next day, and hang around your place for a week?" Her decisive look said it all. She seemed to appeal for some understanding that was not his to give. "This isn't easy, you know. I didn't plan for this to happen. I'd rather be there to tell you, but... here we are."

Again, they stared at one another through layers of technology. He could not deny the finality of the moment. The camera did not lie.

"Jenny, listen to me for just a second." He fought to keep his voice from breaking.

"I'm sorry... I'm so sorry, Rick. Really, I am."

"Look, wait, Jenny, we haven't even talked about—"

"I love you."

Knight both recoiled from and softened at this admission.

Then she vanished from his phone, and the home screen appeared. Behind the mosaic of apps was a photo of them from a beach trip that he had gazed at for longer than he could remember, an image of someone who had been a constant in his life, and who reminded him of things to come. Now, she had become the woman who had taken everything he gave her and had thrown it away. Why?

Needy? Overdependent? Immature? Incompatible? What the fuck happened? She was supposed to visit next month.

It was too much. Knight blindly gazed away before the phone fell from his hand, breaking the screen. He took note of the damage, the crack running between them on the home screen, but he was unfazed. Processing everything that had just transpired, he quickly grabbed the phone and tried to connect to her again, but she rejected his call within seconds.

His mind was a tempest of emotions, never once shutting down as he replayed the scene again, recalling each word and sensation, and begging anyone listening for help... but no one was there. His worst fear had been realized. No matter what angle he approached from or how he analyzed what she said, one thing was clear: he was alone.

MONDAY, 26 MAY 2014

Returning home from the Memorial Day ceremony, as he had done the year before with the love of his life by his side, Knight could only stare in silence at the framed picture of Kowalski and him on the mantel, the one from their date at Yokohama Ichiban. The woman in that photograph had turned his life around, and now, because she had never bothered to tell him that his efforts to be everything she needed were more than she could handle, he had lost her. He took the picture in his hands, gently touching the glass as his eyes fixed upon the one in the black dress, wishing only to be in her arms again.

Could it have gone differently? Why didn't she tell me?

She had messaged him over the weekend about how drunk she was out of guilt for ending things, and of how sorry she felt for hurting him, but it made no difference. She had made her choice and, apparently, he was simply a casualty of that decision, their demise a byproduct of the risk of human relations. The callous nature with which she had ended things weighed heavily upon him. He had opted to cope with copious amounts of alcohol, a regression to his time overseas. He walked to the ceremony that morning hungover, and the return home only made him long for something with a kick.

If ever there was a time...

He trudged into the kitchen and withdrew an unopened bottle of whiskey from the cabinet. Pouring a generous amount into a glass, he stopped just before he brought it to his lips. "To... better days," he said, his voice struggling to function. The memories of drinking with Kowalski on their nights off came flooding back, like how she could not handle more than two rounds without eating first, how scotch brought out a side of her personality that he enjoyed endlessly, and how they would never share another drink together. That realization him hard—harder than he was anticipating. He bowed his head, the pain inside never once relenting.

"She's gone."

It was a truth that he fought to ignore, but it was a losing battle. The contents of the glass disappeared in seconds, and he refilled it without hesitation as more memories surged through his mind. Then the glass was empty again.

Grabbing the bottle, he brought the empty tumbler into the living room and sat on the couch, still in uniform, and at the lowest point he had ever been. He poured another batch of poison and gulped it down, wiping his mouth with the back of his free hand. What happened with Amy was torturous, but losing Kowalski—the love of his life, the one he had truly wanted to marry—was excruciating, and proving to be too much for him to bear. All was lost. The vivid memories of their time together simply would not stop, as they competed with the revelation that he himself had ruined the relationship through his apparent neediness and immaturity.

It's my fault... all of it. Amy... Jenny ... What the hell is wrong with me?

The glass had served its purpose. Knight grabbed the bottle by the neck this time, drinking as much as he could in one go and nearly depleting the container.

I wish that Humvee had hit me... I wish I had fallen off that building... God help me... I just want... her.

Consumed by mounting depression and strong drink, time stood still in the quiet of his home. As evening approached, his vision began to blur, yet he continued to stare blindly at the picture. He knew the agony would not stop, no matter how much he continued to punish his liver. He then thought of something else, but he had never even remotely imagined entertaining going through with it... until now.

Focusing as hard as he could, his eyes slowly shifted to his right, as his pistol came into view, resting in the holster. Unsteadily, he rose from his seat and made his way toward the dining room table, each step heavier than the last. He took a moment to steel himself before reaching down... and grasping his phone. It took three attempts, but he finally inputted the security code before clumsily thumbing through the exhaustive list of names and numbers. At long last, he found the one that he needed, and dreaded what would happen. The phone continued to ring as his heart raced, his mind awash with trepidation. How would this call pan out? His breathing was quick but heavy, and the brief pause between each passing ring felt like an eternity as he struggled to concentrate.

At long last, the cycle was broken by the sound of a woman's voice, one he had not heard in over a decade, one he knew he would never hear again. "Hello...?" The inflection was just as he recalled, and hearing her caused him to exhale deeply. What would he say? Why did he call *her*, of all people?

"Hey... Amy... it's, uh, Rick... Knight. You got a minute?"

EPILOGUE

"SIT DOWN," the detective said with a hollow tone, as the officer took a seat. The air thickened and the atmosphere tensed, with three plain-clothes detectives in the room. All four had been here countless times before, but now, one of them sat on the wrong side of the table. An officer called his wife to tell her he would be home late while the second sipped yet another cup of coffee. The third, a seasoned investigator of far too many homicides, plopped a folder on the table. She leafed through the accompanying documents and preliminary reports, including some crime scene photos, before finally addressing the elephant in the room.

"How are you holding up?"

The silence was matched only by the tension. The multiyear veteran of the force sat, unmoving and glass-eyed, as the events of the last few hours unfolded once more.

"Well... I just, uh... killed somebody—"

"*Two* somebodies. The second one made sense, and the initial report seems plausible, but the other one... what happened?"

How does one respond to such a question? "I-I don't know... I... never... I've never shot... anyone before..." The collective distress was palpable, and sweat poured down the officer's face as the questioning continued.

"First time for everything, it seems." She took another glance through the folder and continued, "Do you understand the optics here?"

No response, other than intense breathing.

"I need you to answer me. Do you get what just happened?"

Again, no response, and the breathing intensified.

The detective was losing her cool. "Jesus Christ, go get him," she said, turning and gesturing to the detective on her right. The young man nodded and exited the room before returning with a familiar face.

"Captain, you may want to handle this. We're not getting anywhere." The concern on Daniels' face matched the intensity of his gaze as he took the detective's seat opposite his subordinate. They had worked together for years, but he had never seen the patrolman quite like this. For that matter, few had.

He slid a paper cup over, saying, "Here. Drink some water." Even directed by a superior officer, there was no reaction. Daniels could already see that this was not going to end well. "I can't help you if you don't talk to us. Two people are dead, one of whom you knew pretty well. I think you can figure out how it looks." Still nothing. Now, even the captain was growing impatient. "Hey! Do you hear me? Corporal—"

"I think I need to speak with a lawyer."

ABOUT THE AUTHOR

Robert Charleston is a former military linguist, veteran of the Afghanistan War, and author. While in uniform, he worked as an intelligence analyst and also taught at the Defense Language Institute in Monterey, California, where he earned distinction as a Master Military Language Instructor during his years on staff. Despite a 20-year career in the Air Force, his assignments saw him embedded at Army installations, and following his retirement, he commenced writing what would become his freshman foray into the world of the written word. *Knight Rising* is the initial entry in a two-part story that will conclude with its sequel, tentatively titled *Fallen Knight*, in the near future.

An avid fan of cinema and music, Robert can often be found enjoying films across multiple genres, and has completed numerous distance runs, including the Air Force Marathon. Born in Alabama, he was raised in Georgia, and enlisted in the military upon graduating from high school. Currently, he resides in Augusta, Georgia and continues to serve Fort Eisenhower and the military at large as a counselor for service members preparing to separate from the armed forces.

ABOUT THE AUTHOR

Tactical 16 Publishing is an unconventional publisher that understands the therapeutic value inherent in writing. We help veterans, first responders, and their families and friends to tell their stories using their words.

We are on a mission to capture the history of America's heroes: stories about sacrifices during chaos, humor amid tragedy, and victories learned from experiences not readily recreated — real stories from real people.

Tactical 16 has published books in leadership, business, fiction, and children's genres. We produce all types of works, from self-help to memoirs that preserve unique stories not yet told.

You don't have to be a polished author to join our ranks. If you can write with passion and be unapologetic, we want to talk. Go to Tactical16.com to contact us and to learn more.

All of Tactical 16's books are available on our online bookstore, T16Books.com. Visit it today to see more books from our selection of authors and to find a new adventure to read!